THE LODGE

JEREMY EADS

WICKED
HOUSE
PUBLISHING

The Lodge
By Jeremy Eads

Wicked House Publishing

This novel is a work of fiction. Names, descriptions, entities, and incidents included in the story are products of the author's imagination. Any resemblance to actual persons, events, and entities is entirely coincidental.

Cover design by Christian Bentulan
Interior Formatting by Joshua Marsella

Contents

CHAPTER ONE
A JUDGMENT CALL

Detective Weaver waited at end of the stack watching the line of armed and armored men in front of him. SWAT would clear each section before he entered it. Too old to be part of a raid, Weaver prayed his last action would become the capstone for a moderately successful career as a law enforcement officer.

Above the houses sat the Mill Mountain Star, which christened Roanoke, Virginia with its nickname: the Star City. Fall was slipping into winter. Crunchy little corpses of leaves piled brown and dead against the houses, blown there by the wind as if seeking the warmth within. Wind probed at Weaver's coat and his Kevlar vest underneath, finding no entry. SWAT lined up by the front door. Weaver, at the back, watched as Wilson moved into position with his "universal key." Impatience made Weaver want to scream, *Hurry up*!

Officer Wilson, battering ram ready, checked over his shoulder for a visual go-ahead. SWAT was ready for entry. Directly behind him on the shield, Gomez nodded. Wilson swung thirty inches of steel at the strike plate underneath the doorknob. *Knock, Knock* had been painted on the universal key's sides. Forty-five pounds delivering forty thousand pounds of force should have shattered the frame.

The door shuddered but didn't move. Detective Weaver flinched at the impact noise. *Never get used to that*, Weaver thought. Time was critical. Wilson swung again. With a loud crack, the frame began breaking. A third swing knocked the door inward. Wilson stepped back, making room for the team behind him to enter. Less than six seconds were necessary to make infiltration. Weaver was afraid it had taken too long.

The team moved as one, Gomez leading the way behind the shield. Officer Hill, behind Gomez, threw a flash-bang through the open doorway. Behind Officer Hill, Officer Carter threw one sting grenade filled with hard rubber pellets. A quick two count and he threw another. The team paused, tucking their heads to protect their eyesight from the explosions.

The team moved after the third explosion.

"Police! Get on the ground!"

Detective Weaver counted ten long seconds after Officer Wolfe, last man in line, made entry. Then he followed the team into a child-killer's home. Inside, the officers worked quickly to secure the house. Shouts of "Clear!" sounded from farther away. Room by room, Weaver hurried, looking for the kid. Hopefully they weren't too late. God willing, they would bring one child home to his mother before—

Best not to think about it. Do the job.

The house was unremarkable except for the rubber pellets rolling underfoot from spent sting grenades. From the splintered front entrance, the entryway opened to two rooms divided by a hallway. An oak dining table sat in one; a chair, lamp, and table sat in the other. Clean modern furniture had been perfectly placed on polished hardwood floors. The hallway led to a living space with a dark leather couch and recliner in front of a fifty-inch flat-screen television.

An open kitchen shared space with the living area. The kitchen was clean and orderly. Pots hung from a rack mounted on the ceiling. Knives gleamed from magnetic strips on the wall. It didn't appear the kitchen got much use. The place screamed *bachelor*. Nice but not too nice.

The house, while a bit sterile, could have belonged in any other suburban family neighborhood. Everything was clean. No paintings or decorations of any kind adorned the walls or anywhere else. No family photos. A model home. The type of home realtors used to fire the imaginations of prospective home buyers.

Every section had been cleared. SWAT stood debating if they had received bad intel. They had the correct address, so the department didn't have to worry about being embarrassed by kicking in the wrong door. They knew he had come home dragging the kid. The reported SUV matched the one in the attached garage. Where the hell was he?

Weaver did a slow three-sixty in the middle of the living room. He interrupted the SWAT team, not that it mattered now. Entry to the premises had been gained. His skills as a detective were needed. He forced himself to be still, empty, to keep his mind open, the way he'd been taught. *Calm down*, he thought, *breathe. Where is he? We know he's home. Where did he go? Breathe.*

Inhale… exhale… inhale… exhale. Open your eyes. Find him.

Weaver stopped turning. Opening his eyes, he faced the kitchen. He walked over, searching for a fresh anything to make itself known. Then he saw it. Small scratches on kitchen tile. Against the white, they were barely visible. Dirt had collected in shallow grooves. Scrapes from a large piece of furniture being dragged on the floor. A piece of furniture…

"The fridge!" Weaver pointed, moving closer to the appliance. The Samsung sat at a slight angle. In such an orderly space, the appliance might as well have been in the middle of the floor. "Help me move the damn fridge! He's behind it, in the wall!"

SWAT reacted instantly. Hill and Wilson pushed the large two-door unit to the side. They had worked with Weaver enough to respect his peculiar ability to notice the things others missed. If he said their boy was behind the fridge, they believed him. The other officers stacked in the kitchen, preparing to make another entry. Years of training told them exactly what needed doing.

Behind the refrigerator, a hole had been dug into the wall. Crude stairs had been cut through the foundation, leading into the earth below the house. Their boy had heard them coming. A panel installed on the back of the Samsung contained a bolt lock securing the unit into the wall. If it were engaged, moving the Samsung would have been all but impossible. Breaking through would have cost hours. But he had run for the secret compartment and forgotten or hadn't had time to set the lock behind him before SWAT came knocking.

The stink from the hole was tremendous—all rot, pain, and despair. *Please God*, Wilson thought, *let the child be alive. Let us be here in time.* The door had been slightly open. The killer hurried, hadn't locked up behind himself. Those thoughts kept tickling at the back of Weaver's mind. He felt events spiraling out of control. Something very wrong was happening. They weren't moving fast enough.

Weaver had hunted him for three years. A degenerate of the worst kind: a child-killer. Worse, the murderer was a ghost haunting southwest Virginia. Never crossing state lines, he had effectively kept the Federal Bureau of Investigation officially uninvolved. He kidnapped children between the ages of two and nine. He liked them young. He assaulted, tortured, and killed babies, leaving broken mauled bodies in his wake.

Over three years, Weaver had assigned twelve deaths, with another four possibilities, when the kidnapping matched their mystery man's modus operandi. The newspapers called the guy Ol' Snapper based on the condition of the remains. The lack of respect shown for the victims disgusted Weaver.

Snapper broke into homes where there were at least three children and always took the youngest. But finally, he'd made a mistake. He had broken into a home with private surveillance on the rich northeast side of Roanoke. Somehow, he'd missed the cameras all around the property. The security company had notified the police as he was taking four-year-old Jaren Banks from the home. The cameras had even provided a picture of the make and model of the car. Through the miracle of high-definition photography, they had a license plate.

An Amber Alert was issued before their perp had pulled away from the house. An alert patrol officer had spotted the perp's car heading south on Williamson Drive and followed discreetly. He sat on the address in the well-to-do Woodcliff neighborhood while Weaver was notified. Warrants were fast-tracked. SWAT was mobilized, the raid planned less than two hours after the kidnapping. A miracle of circumstance, timing, and good police work.

Running the plates had returned a name: Ben Stockmore. Stockmore was as vanilla as they come. Years after Stockmore's rampage began, Weaver had a name, a face, to put to the killings. Finally, a suspect—no, more than a suspect. They had their guy. No priors, no arrests, no parking tickets; nothing from his history indicated Stockmore was a vicious child-killer. Surprisingly, the guy used his own car in the commission of a crime. Weaver never knew if it was arrogance or stupidity on Stockmore's part.

Time was ticking, ticking. Weaver broke protocol, moving ahead of the stack. SWAT wasn't happy with Weaver endangering himself. They'd take the blame if any team member got hurt. But complaints would come later; the team sensed they were losing time. No one there wished to be responsible for another death. Weaver rushed into the black, where the darkness was broken by a single bulb hanging in the middle of a claustrophobic hallway. Four doors, two on each side, stood closed, with a fifth open at the end of the hallway.

The awful stink came from the rooms lining the hall. Earthen walls and ceilings supported by wooden beams that leaned precariously. The doors hung from crude frames bolted into the surrounding earth to make cells that wouldn't hold an adult captive but would keep children imprisoned just fine. There was a narrow window in the middle of each door, presumably so Stockmore could watch the suffering on the other side.

Weaver took a quick look as he passed the first cell on the right. He wished he hadn't. At a glance, he saw several small bodies in various states of decay. This was so much worse than Weaver had thought. How many children had died here? As he passed the window, weapon drawn and ready, he thought he'd seen bite marks on a tiny arm, a little hand missing two fingers, reaching for help that never arrived. *Don't think about it. Focus. Find this fucker.* Sounds of struggling came from the darkness beyond the end of the hall.

Weaver hurried ahead as SWAT cleared the cells behind him. "Jesus, he's been chewing on the bodies." Weaver didn't recognize the voice.

He burst through into the killer's den. Stockmore knelt holding baby Jaren by the jaw with one hand, his other holding a large hunting knife. Jaren cried, one eye swollen almost completely shut. Weaver leveled his weapon at Stockmore's head. The coward was using the little boy as a shield.

"Careful, Officer. Don't hit the boy." The knife moved closer to Jaren's tender throat. Blood—presumably from the children outside—dripped from Stockmore's face and dribbled down Jaren's chest.

"Let him go. You're done here."

"Oh, I have something else that needs doing before I go." The knife pressed hard enough to dimple the boy's flesh, but he hadn't drawn blood yet.

"That's not going to happen."

SWAT burst into the room, filling the doorway and fanning out behind Weaver. Stockmore found himself surrounded by angry police, a dirt wall at his back.

"Detective, we have two more recently deceased." Hill

nodded toward the hallway, never moving his gunsight from Stockmore's forehead. "Appears he ran through and slashed their throats on the way here. They're all dead, Detective."

"Very good. You should be the detective." Stockmore's voice was calm and even, though his eyes betrayed panic, flicking between all the hard faces holding semiautomatic weapons on him. Weaver stepped forward a few inches, regaining Stockmore's focus. Jaren was brave, trying not to cry, his bottom lip quivering with the effort.

"Speaking of detectives, how did you find me?" Stockmore jerked Jaren against him hard enough to let the knife bite, just enough.

"I'm a detective; you're a moron. That's how I found you. You got stupid. You're caught. Let Jaren go. Let him go, and I'll do you this one favor: I won't let SWAT turn you into a fine pink mist. Life in prison with no parole is the best you're going to get."

* * *

"No need for snark, Detective. I was merely curious as to how you found me. After all, I've got police in my sanctuary after two years of nothing."

Stockmore lowered the knife some—let them see the blood running so they'd know he was serious. He might leverage his way to his car. Maybe even escape, build a new sanctuary. He'd change his name of course; he'd done it before. New identities were easy if you wanted one. He was forty-two. Ben had been killing, moving, evolving for twenty-seven years. This was the closest they'd ever come. He was genuinely curious what had happened.

"Detective, take these men and leave my house. I'll follow you with sweet pumpkin here. We'll get in my car. I'll drop him off on a corner when I feel safe. I'll call to tell you where. Otherwise, I'll open him up. One last hurrah!"

"No. We aren't going to do that. We aren't leaving. You aren't hurting anyone else."

"You're wrong, Detective. I am leaving. Even if you manage to arrest me—which I will not allow—this child's blood will be on your hands. I'll cut his throat, and then you'll put the cuffs on me. I'll go to a mental hospital because I must be crazy. Then I'll escape. You'll never find me, and I'll kill everyone who's ever heard of you. Or you do what I say, I disappear, and all your people sleep soundly. That's the best deal you're going to get." Stockmore raised the knife, smiling at Weaver.

* * *

Ol Snapper's head was covered in green dots. Lasers from SWAT's weapon sights were ready to guide rounds into Stockmore's skull from every possible angle.

"Sir, you give the word, we'll remove his head from his shoulders. I'll personally take Jaren for ice cream."

Weaver held a steadying hand to Officer Hill without removing his gaze from Stockmore. Hill was barely controlled fury. Death was in the room, watching, hovering, waiting. The entire team had eyes filled with murder.

Jaren screamed as Stockmore ran the knife down his arm, drawing blood. Men's hard breathing and the boy's sobbing echoed against damp earth. Jaren's legs kicked uselessly against the dirty floor. Weaver's heart broke watching Jaren struggle to escape the monster hurting him, crying for help, for Mama.

It was enough. Detective Weaver centered his sights above Stockmore's right eye. The shot was eight feet away tops, easy peasy. Stockmore's days of terrorizing families ended here, today, in the stinking hole he'd dug under his house. Not in court or a padded cell blissfully unaware of his confinement thanks to five hundred milligrams of Thorazine every six hours. No, the game ended here.

Weaver looked at Jaren—crying for his mother, one eye

swollen shut, blood running off tiny fingers and dripping onto the dirt floor. He was so small.

Jaren was going home. Period. And this scumfuck was going to hell. Stockmore's face had twisted into a mask of hatred, veins in his forehead pulsing, cheeks red, spittle flying from his mouth.

"I said get the fuck out my way! I'll gut him right now!"

"No, Ben, you won't." Weaver pulled the trigger.

Chapter Two
A Most Fortunate New Hire

S hirley Duritz McGreggor walked casually toward her Volvo. Stupid police were on their way. Questions, they'd said. Be right over, they'd said. Don't go anywhere! They had a few questions about Warren. Of course, dear, she'd told them, I'll be right here. Where would I go? Ha. Ha. Ha.

She hadn't done much wrong. All her late husbands were better for her love. Her special attention. Every man loved some special attention. Nobody took care of a man better than Shirley did. Her mother had taught her. And all those men had made sure she was taken care of too. A man should provide for his woman.

Shirley carried her suitcase to the car. She smashed her phone on the curb before kicking the remains into a storm drain. Shirley took a final look at her home of the last three years. She'd miss the place—such a lovely garden she'd made! Shame, but the growing season was almost over anyway. Compulsively, she double-checked that the house was all locked up before leaving. No sense in leaving the place wide open for prowlers.

No need to make things any easier for the police.

Rude. There was no other word for it. It was plain rude the way the police were making her leave her home. They had come sniffing around before with their questions, their stares. She saw them, all of them wanting, staring with their lustful eyes. Dogs in heat.

She wasn't the beauty she had been at twenty-one, although the years had given her a dignity and charm that made up for the parts that maybe weren't so pert and perky anymore. Her hair remained the fiery red it had been all her life, with only a touch of gray. Some women thought her color paid for, but those women were jealous busybodies who wished their mid-fifties looked this good.

Shirley checked her reflection, making sure she didn't need any touching up. Vanity was her sin. It wouldn't do to be in public without her face. Her eyes flicked toward the backyard, toward the garage. *Why should I take this when Warren's car is right there?*

Warren had spent a fortune restoring a 1957 Corvette. It was his pride and joy. He'd droned on about the silly thing: three-speed manual transmission, V8, red-and-white exterior with red leather interior and a purring engine. A "finely engineered dream." Warren had installed a retractable hardtop. On one of their early dates, he'd hit a button, causing the roof to slide into the trunk. Shirley hadn't let on that the night air was ruining her hair, which she had spent three hours on to get perfect. Instead, she'd smiled while she told him what a lovely automobile he had.

Shirley stared at the garage, toying with her key. Warren never knew she had a spare dangling on her key ring. She placed her luggage into the space behind the seats, moved the Volvo out of the way, and shivered at the way the Corvette's cockpit wrapped around her. Roaring away from her home of the last few years in Warren's dream car gave her a euphoric sense of freedom. Good things were on the way.

Warren wouldn't be driving it ever again. Warren was planted beneath her beautiful vegetable garden. His eternity entailed helping her tomatoes grow, with the help of the crazy cat lady from across the street and that rude butcher from the supermarket. There might've been a teenage boy who cut through her backyard after school as well. Sometimes it was hard to remember. Getting old wasn't for the faint of heart.

* * *

Rolling down Interstate 81, Shirley decided to pull off for gas. Taking the exit for a microscopic town named Summit Valley at seventy miles an hour, she sped into the wild nowhere of southwest Virginia. Middle America and its dreary winters lay far to the west. The radio, tuned to southern gospel, provided inspirational hymns as an oddly appropriate sound-track to the mountainous country around her. Her enjoyment of the music switched to mild annoyance as a commercial for some Maple Lodge, a local area bed-and-breakfast, interrupted Andy Griffith's version of "Precious Memories."

The DJ should be fired! Imagine interrupting such a beautiful piece for a commercial?

The Corvette had wonderful power, leaping to obey her slightest touch; however, it was thirsty. She passed everything on the road except a gas station. Shirley giggled at the thought as she drove down what must have passed for Main Street.

This was pretty country, if a bit rural for her tastes. Even with the trees having dropped most of their leaves, splashes of color—reds, yellows, and the occasional fiery orange—dotted the hills crowding the interstate. She preferred not to pump her own gas, either. Excluding Oregon, where she'd grown up, that kind of filling station was getting harder to find.

Nobody believed in good customer service anymore.

She drove down the main street past McDonald's, Pizza Hut, Hardee's, and a Wendy's. These fast-food restaurants spread worse than disease. Apparently, they were the only places to eat in this town. Why didn't people appreciate a home-cooked meal anymore? People were so lazy. No one wanted to make the effort. A home-cooked meal was always preferable. Good food, good times, and especially good sex, should be a bit inconvenient.

There, next to the Wendy's, was a Wilco. Across the street, a CITGO. She turned into the Wilco so she could make a right turn when she was done here. She always avoided lefts across traffic—such a bother.

Shirley walked into the store after filling the tank. She always made sure to pay with cash as she'd read somewhere that credit cards could be tracked. A bored-looking clerk, missing no fewer than four front teeth, watched a news report. About her. Ignoring the news, Shirley put on her most dazzling smile, leaning forward on the counter and thrusting her ample cleavage toward the clerk. Her nipples had stiffened in the crisp fall air. *Better give the simpleton something to watch other than my face.*

It worked. The clerk never once made eye contact. The entire exchange took place with his eyes on her breasts. The news report changed stories. Some druggie had shot a druggie. *Hardly news,* she thought, straightening up. The disappointment on the clerk's face was comical. *Too bad, dummy. Show's over.* She spun on her heel and headed back to the Corvette. Men were too simple. They needed a good woman to direct them. Shirley had been thinking it'd been too many years since she'd seen the ocean. Florida might be a nice place to shop for a new husband.

The Corvette purred amiably as she turned into the light flow of traffic. A deputy sheriff pulled into the station as she was leaving. *Better luck next time.* On the right side of the road, past the Wendy's, was a sign that read MAPLE LODGE with "Bed and Breakfast" painted below. An arrow underneath pointed left.

On an impulse she didn't understand, Shirley maneuvered

into the left lane. She felt compelled to explore. Her hands weren't her own. After turning at the light, Shirley drove a quarter mile to another intersection. She saw a smaller sign that read MAPLE LODGE with another green arrow indicating the way. She followed the sign.

Shirley hadn't gotten away from the gas station as cleanly as she'd thought. She didn't enjoy television, so she didn't watch it. She preferred more intellectual pursuits—reading or word puzzles—or doing fun crafty whatnots with her hands. The television with its incessant droning, flickering images, dull personalities, and hollow entertainment held no interest for her at all. Not even as background noise. If she wanted background noise, she'd listen to music.

Because she didn't watch television, Shirley had a blind spot: the power of mass communication. She didn't think about all the people who did watch television and had seen the news stories about her—people who were all around her. People vying for their fifteen minutes on the box searched for Shirley in every town, at every stop. The police tracked her across the country and were aware of her general area not because she wasn't careful—she was—but because she didn't watch the news.

Shirley had never been arrested. She never expected capture. Atoning for her crimes had never entered her mind. She felt charmed, protected, increasingly so since leaving Warren. She was simply better than her pursuers.

* * *

Deputy Roland entered, cup in hand, for his usual black coffee before heading to Route 11 to run radar. Roland wasn't even inside before Clem was up in his face, as excited as Roland had ever seen him. Clem was the kind of guy whose pulse you might need to check to make sure he was still alive. Customer service wasn't his priority. He'd never aspired to anything, didn't do much, but didn't cause trouble either. Roland knew Clem spent his time either at work or at home—not exactly the excitable type. But today, something had sure rung his bell.

"Deputy! Officer! Deputy! I seen her! I seen her! If you hurry, you'll catch her! Catch that bitch! I get the re-ward 'cause I seen her first!"

"Clem, slow down. Reward for what? Who'd you see?"

Clem stank. His breath was foul—probably the rotten teeth —and he had body odor, sharp, rank, intrusive. His work shirt was stained and greasy. A mustard stain covered the W in Wilco. The shirt had other spots of varying sizes, textures, and colors, but the true champions were under Clem's arms. The stains there had turned the gray fabric of the shirt a sickly yellow. How many moons had passed since Clem last washed his work shirt? Roland had to force himself to stand still, not back away from the man's offensive funk, to not yell, *Back up! Back up! Please, for the love of God, back away from me!* He managed to keep his composure. Dealing with Clem behind the counter was bad enough. An excited Clem exhaling so close made him somewhat nauseated.

"Ain't got time for explainin'. I seen that Shirley lady, the murderer! Hurry, you can get 'er! Fuckin' black widow!" Clem pointed at a Corvette turning at the light.

"McGreggor? Here?" Deputy Roland was naturally skepti-cal, but there was no denying Clem was wound up. He was practically hopping up and down, pointer finger stabbing the air with manic intensity.

"Yep! That's her! The Vette turnin' toward town! Get 'er and get my re-ward!"

Deputy Roland hustled back outside, not quite jogging, coffee and radar forgotten. He'd seen the Corvette when he first arrived. Car was an attention grabber. If Clem was right and McGreggor indeed was here and Roland slapped the cuffs on her, a serious promotion waited for him. He should call for backup—it was standard operating procedure for the apprehension of a dangerous wanted felon—but then it wouldn't be his collar. He would have to share the credit for the arrest—if he was even mentioned at all—with everyone else involved. And when it came to McGreggor, every cop in the county would want some. Town, staties, feds, not to mention the sheriff, would all jump. Plus, if Clem was wrong, Roland would look like a fool. He wasn't going to stake his otherwise unremarkable career on the word of a guy who couldn't even change his shirt.

No, he'd follow up alone. Probably bullshit anyway.

On the corner of Fifth Street and Prospect Avenue, overlooking downtown Summit Valley, sat the Maple Lodge. Local legend stated the house was originally built in 1751 as a gift for the town founder, James Viscot, a rumored nephew of Count Pulaski. No real ties had been established to link him with the father of the American cavalry, but the story was repeated so often it was generally accepted as fact.

After James Viscot's death, and with no heirs to claim the land, the house—a large Early American five-bedroom that watched over the valley below—was donated and expanded to support the workers of the budding logging industry. The site was abandoned in 1787 for unknown reasons, though possibly due to trouble subduing the local Cherokee or Shawnee, who weren't fully settled until the early 1800s.

In the early nineteenth century, during the expansion of Summit Valley, the Viscot house reopened to migrant workers and homesteaders intent on making a living in the Appalachian Mountains. Access to Peak Creek and the New River saw a population boom; however, the house was mysteriously abandoned, while home construction continued to the north and west of the property. Few migrants stayed for long.

Rumors of accidents, disappearances, and ghosts, demons, or worse, kept the townsfolk away. The 1870s saw the home restored by a Yankee businessman transplanted from New York by the name of Solomon Drury. Solomon reopened the home as an inn and renamed it the Maple Lodge. The inn operated with modest success until his death in the early 1900s.

Solomon passed the hotel on to his son, Solomon Jr. Although not as successful as his father, he kept the doors open. Four more generations of Drurys kept the inn operating in one form or another for over two hundred years, always managed by the eldest male member of the family.

A town grew around the Maple Lodge, but townsfolk rarely ever stayed within its walls. They kept their distance, looked away as they passed, and didn't speak about it. If asked about the Maple Lodge, a local wouldn't give much of a response. Most would say they didn't know the place, or they'd direct you instead to the Red Carpet Inn on Route 11.

There was a general feeling of wrongness about the lodge. Even the tax collector didn't send requests for taxes, make threats, or put liens on the Maple Lodge for nonpayment. People from Summit Valley knew not to poke a sleeping bear. So, the house sat on its corner, keeping silent watch over the town.

Solomon Drury VI was as much of a mystery as the rest of his family before him. He could sometimes be seen at the farmers market or walking down Main dressed in his peculiar old-fashioned way. No one spoke to him, and most people experienced a sudden urge to continue their business on the other side of the street, moving away from Mr. Drury's slow, sauntering walk. No one met his eye or otherwise did anything to get his attention. The people of Summit Valley knew better.

* * *

Shirley pulled into the gravel parking lot beside the bed-and-breakfast. A neon sign at the edge of the parking lot read MAPLE LODGE. Though the lodge was a large Early American, sometime in the past, additions had been made to the structure. Two long and rather ugly extensions, presumably for guest rooms, sat on either side of the main house in rough juxtaposition with the grace of the original home. Tacky. Shirley's lips drew thin in disapproval. Tacky row houses.

What a horrible thing to do to such a beautiful building.

The house itself was painted a bright off-white. The windows, polished and clean, gleamed, reflecting the sun happily. Two large maple trees sat on either side of a spacious light-gray front porch. A metal roof had been recently painted a cheery green. Aside from the ugly additions, the place looked wholesome. Shirley knew she had been right to come. The place felt safe. She left her bags in the car and went in to meet the proprietor of such a fine establishment.

She lingered a moment on the porch, enjoying the cool shade of the maple trees. Slow, inconsistent traffic passed. No one looked at her. Two boys in jeans and bright jackets raced by on bicycles, whooping cries of prepubescent joy then vanishing down the street like youthful ghosts.

Twin rocking chairs shared a table, and Shirley imagined the delight spending an afternoon rocking, sipping tea, people-watching. The front door was inlaid with thick beveled glass; the words MAPLE LODGE embossed in gold paint in the middle. A discreet wooden sign read COME IN. Shirley opened the screen door, pressed the handle, and did just that.

The interior was every bit as lovely as the outside. On her left was an actual parlor, similar to the one her mother had, complete with proper Victorian chairs lined with small brass buttons twinkling in the sun. A gleaming dark wooden table sat between the chairs. Perfect for traditional courting when men were gentlemen and knew how to treat a lady.

The living room had been converted into a reception area.

The front desk stretched along the far wall, and Victorian chairs and couches sat on lovely throw rugs. Even though the weather was warm, a fire burned in the hearth, and various knickknacks sat on either side of a large clock built into the mantle.

Best of all, a gentleman stood beside the front desk smiling at her. Dark, naturally curly hair was combed back from his forehead and held at the base of his neck with a strand of leather. His pristine shirt blazed white, the collar starched and flipped upside down to frame his perfect jawline. A patterned maroon silk ascot contrasted with his fine pinstriped waistcoat, which was accented with a gold chain Shirley knew held a pocket watch. A morning coat, black and sleek and trimmed in the same maroon silk as the tie, hung down to the knees of his pinstriped trousers. One hand held a top hat in front of his waist; the other rested lightly on a cane topped with a polished maroon stone. He was every inch the Victorian gentleman Shirley had dreamed of in her youth.

He walked over, bowed slightly at the waist. "Good afternoon, madam. How may I be of service?"

Her breath caught. Her mother had taught her better than this! Fawning over a man was beneath her.

"Are you quite well, madam? Perhaps you'd care to take a seat and have some iced tea? This climate can be unexpected to one not acclimated. I'm afraid the fire doesn't help, but I do love the atmosphere."

She nodded, allowing herself to be guided to one of the stiff-backed chairs. Climate? The chill nipping at any exposed skin was forgotten. The room seemed warmer than it should have.

The man stepped away from her once she was seated. He turned, disappearing down a hallway beside the reception desk, giving Shirley a moment to compose herself. She wasn't a schoolgirl who'd never seen a man before. Yes, he was handsome, but there was no need to lose her mind.

He reappeared as if by magic. She never heard him approach. "Your tea."

He handed her a cold sweaty glass, which she concentrated on. *Iced tea. Isn't it a bit late in the season for iced tea?* She banished the thought. He really was handsome in a way you didn't see anymore. Charming.

"Perhaps, Mrs. McGreggor—though it's Ms., isn't it? —you will be so kind as to tell an old innkeeper how he can be of service."

"I—I'm not really sure." When had she told him her name? "I didn't mean to stop here, but I followed the signs. I was going to Florida. I meant to winter at the beach."

He sat opposite her, sipping his tea. He set the glass down on a gold lace doily. "Delightful! And I'm ever so glad you decided to visit."

Shirley couldn't quite determine the color of his eyes. At first, she thought they were green, but now they appeared golden. He was fascinating beyond all reason.

"Please! Pardon my ill manners! My name is Solomon Drury VI, and I bid you welcome to the Maple Lodge."

* * *

Deputy Roland found the Corvette parked outside the Maple Lodge.

Ah, fuck. It would be parked here.

Roland's radio crackled to life. "Leave. Nothing to see here. Continue on your way, Deputy." Static hissed through the speakers.

Did I hear screaming?

Roland lifted the mic. "Say again, dispatch."

"Negative call, unit ninety-one. Do you require assistance?"

"Negative, dispatch. I must have caught a random signal. Ninety-one out."

He pulled in, tires crunching on gravel, and parked his cruiser beside the muscle car. It certainly matched the description of the one missing from Warren McGreggor's garage. The

Indiana tags matched the BOLO. He couldn't recall the number, but he'd bet his pension they matched. If he called dispatch, he'd have to stand down and wait for backup.

This run-down place gave him the creeps. The peeling paint, the broken window on the second floor—just the general wrongness of the house. From the dead maples out front to the warped porch, everything about the grounds screamed, GO AWAY. Roland had been a cop long enough that he trusted the heebie-jeebies when he got them. This place was all kinds of wrong. The smart play would be to call in, wait for help to arrive.

Roland stepped onto the porch.

* * *

"Shirley, may I call you Shirley?"

"Of course, Mr. Drury."

"And please do call me Solomon. All my friends call me Solomon. I think we're going to be very great friends."

Shirley smiled, slow and lazy. Her head was fuzzy, and the world spun the way it did when she'd had a bit too much to drink. Solomon's voice was so soothing, confident. She could listen to him talk all day. "Yes, that sounds nice. But oh! I don't intend to stay."

Solomon smiled. "Shirley, dear, as it so happens, I have need of someone with your particular talents. I think you're exactly what I've been looking for."

Shirley's brows drew together. "No, I really can't stay—" The words felt thick and foreign on her tongue. Solomon hadn't moved, though he seemed to be looming over her. His eyes were larger now, his torso curved toward her in a peculiar angle. Were his teeth looking sharper? Was it getting darker?

"What a magnificent creature you are! Truly remarkable!" Solomon purred.

Shirley smiled. She enjoyed praise. "Really, Mr. Drury, I

simply cannot stay. There are complications that I will not have a gentleman of your obvious caliber involved in. Personal issues. I'm sure you understand."

Why had she thought he'd changed? The atmosphere remained as bright and cheery as ever. Shirley passed it off as fatigue. She set her empty glass on a coaster. It would be criminal to leave a ring on such beautiful wood. She stood, intent on leaving this magical man, this wonderful place, when the door opened behind her. A sheriff's deputy stood blocking the exit. He looked directly at her, hand on the firearm at his hip.

Solomon stood, smoothly moving around her. "Good day, Deputy Roland. Always nice to see one of our local law enforcement officers. Shame you've never visited me before, but you're here now! What can I do for you?"

"Step aside, Mr. Drury. I'm taking her into custody." Roland nodded toward where Shirley stood.

* * *

Clem was right! Deputy Roland's initial rush of excitement at seeing the nation's most wanted fugitive eight feet away quickly died as Solomon Drury walked toward him. The man had a shark's smile—all teeth, so many teeth, too many teeth. He extended a hand, pale and blotchy, fingers tipped with ragged sharp nails—a corpse's hands.

Roland took an involuntary step backward. He had been nine when his grandfather died of a massive heart attack. Roland had stood with his father beside his grandfather's open casket. Mother had been against him attending; Father had insisted. His father didn't usually go against his mother's wishes, but on the rare occasion when he did, she knew not to fight.

Father thought it important that Roland be at the funeral, dressed in his suit, shaking hands as mourners came by to pay their respects. Roland hadn't forgotten Pappy lying in his casket. He'd died with a grimace on his face, which the mortician had tried to correct into a look of resting peace. Pappy was still snarling though. He'd died fighting the eternity come to claim him.

Worse than his face were his hands. Those loving hands had been the source of a thousand sticks of Juicy Fruit. The hands that had taught Roland to shoot, dig potatoes from the ground, drive a tractor, and move slowly enough to take honey from a bee's nest, were pale and liver spotted. Roland had reached out, ignoring the horrible snarl and the awful way the spots stood out, to squeeze Pappy's hand one last time. The hand was cold —colder than the room. It felt fake, plastic, not flesh at all. Pappy had groaned. Later, the mortician would say there was air in the lungs, and when Roland touched the hand, it disturbed the gas enough to emerge as a groan. He said it was fairly common.

Nine-year-old Roland never believed any of it. Pappy had squeezed back. He'd moaned. Pappy was in pain, looking for help. Roland had screamed, jerking away, pulling Pappy with him, and overturning the casket. Urine stained the front of his suit trousers when his bladder let go.

Nightmares about those hands gripping his haunted Roland the rest of his life. In the dreams, he would be pulled into the casket with a monster resembling his pappy, who only wanted to chew on boy flesh. In others, Pappy had been buried alive and clawed for help as his air depleted. Years later, Roland no longer woke up screaming, but the dreams never went away. Not completely.

Now he was grown, a deputy, and those hands were coming toward him anew. Guilt and shame flared up before being washed away by a rising tide of fear. Deputy Roland screamed, staining the front of his pants again. Another tide cascaded down his leg onto the warped floorboards of this horrible place. He no longer cared about getting the collar; all he wanted to do was leave. He'd forget he'd ever seen Shirley McGreggor.

Roland staggered backward and fell over his own feet. He crashed through the open doorway and onto the porch. Solomon advanced on him, smiling with those terrible teeth and his Pappy's dead hands. Solomon appeared a thing long dead, suit stained with mud and rot from the grave. Clumps of freshly turned earth fell from the sleeves of his suit, and sickly green-black grave mold lined the ragged fingernails grasping for Roland.

Screaming incoherent denials, Roland scuttled backward across the warped porch. Splinters he didn't feel embedded in his palms. Roland flipped over and somehow managed to get his feet underneath him. Thanking whatever powers watched over him he'd left the motor running, Roland crashed into his cruiser hard enough to dislocate his shoulder. He didn't notice that either.

Deputy Roland accelerated away from the Maple Lodge at better than forty miles an hour. At the hospital, he would later say a bear near Woodgate Park had chased him through the woods. He never mentioned to the sheriff that one of the nation's most wanted fugitives sat sipping iced tea at the Maple Lodge.

* * *

Solomon turned back to Shirley. "How curious. I suppose the good deputy had somewhere else to be. My dear, care to reconsider my invitation?"

Shirley was stunned. The deputy, who seconds before was ready to arrest her, had fled screaming. He had pissed himself too, unless she was mistaken.

Solomon looked her in the eye, all charm gone. "No police will ever touch you while you're in my employ. No law of mortals shall apply ever again. Work for me and you'll never leave another garden behind. You'll be as safe as in your mother's care."

Safe. Home. It sounded exquisite. "Solomon, my dear, I'd be delighted."

"Excellent." Solomon clapped his hands together. "Let's get started, then."

And the lights went out for Shirley McGreggor.

CHAPTER THREE
APPALACHIAN ARISTOCRACY

Early spring snuck into southwestern Virginia like an illicit lover. Cool mornings gave over to warm, pleasant afternoons, which fled winter's chill after the sun went down. Clem spent many hours rocking, watching the trees, drinking.

Brooding.

Two weeks. It had been two damn weeks. He needed to call RayRay. Clem sat in his rocking chair watching a line of large black ants work industriously to carry the remnants of a bag of pork rinds back to the nest. The pork rinds—Clem's dinner—sat forgotten on a small table beside the rocking chair.

The ants didn't bother him. He didn't bother them. Ants gotta eat too.

Plus, Clem's mind was on Shirley McGreggor. Or rather the reward for her successful capture. Two weeks had passed since he told Roland to go get her. Two weeks of nothing. Finally, Deputy Dumbass had come back. Clem couldn't stop thinking about the encounter. Playing it over in his mind again and again, unable to let go.

When Roland came into the Wilco yesterday with his arm in a sling, Clem had hustled around the counter. "Where ya been,

Roland? Did you get 'er? What about the re-ward. I got money coming to me," Clem said in a rush.

Deputy Roland had leaned away, pulling a thermos from his sling to fill with coffee. Roland didn't respond. He filled the cup and walked over to the counter to pay.

"What is it? Deputy?"

Roland busied himself gathering a couple of crinkled one-dollar bills from his wallet, completely ignoring Clem. Then he left the money on the counter, not waiting for change.

"What the hell?" Clem had money coming. He intended to collect. And Clem wasn't above whipping a lawman's ass if he tried to get in the way.

Roland paused at the door to speak for the first time. "There isn't going to be any reward, Clem. You were mistaken. It wasn't her. Let it go. You're from here; let it go."

Without waiting for a response Deputy Roland left the Wilco, probably heading for Route 99 to drink his coffee, catch a nap, and laugh about fucking Clem out of his rightful reward!

Mistaken, hell.

Clem *knew* it was her. Knew it. No doubt about it at all. Hell, she'd been on the damn television when she walked in for real! Can't make mistakes like that. Worst part was Clem knew Roland was lying. Clem took another sip of his Pabst Blue Ribbon—the other half of his dinner and probably breakfast tomorrow.

Why would the law lie to him?

He was scared. No other reason fit. Shirley had scared him good. *Shouldn't be law. Man's too cowardly.* Staring down the hollow from his front porch, Clem could just see the roof of RayRay's house steadily disappearing behind budding spring trees. Soon, it would be lost from view, hidden behind new foliage.

He needed another beer. Clem crushed the empty and threw it onto an impressive pile—close to chest height—beside the door. Passing through into the kitchen, he retrieved another can from the aging mustard-colored Frigidaire.

If I had that re-ward, I could replace the damn thing. I could fix up around here.

Built by Clem's great-great-grandfather, Jedidiah Farris, the house had sheltered five generations of Farrises. Various room additions added over the years masked architectural style for practicality. As the family grew, more rooms were necessary, and as home technology advanced, renovations were done to accommodate those advances. Clem could remember his grandfather, so proud when he'd brought indoor plumbing to his family. They were one of the first families on Caseknife Road who didn't need to go outside to pinch one off.

The Farrises were kings once, Appalachian aristocracy, running a successful dairy business. Since the Great Depression, their empire had fallen to ruin. Wooden siding needed sanding and painting. Shingles needed replacing. The porch sagged. Exposed nails snagged unwary knees or elbows.

There weren't so many Farrises left in Summit Valley. The bulk of the family had died or moved on, Summit Valley forgotten, and Clem had the house to himself. No real desire for a woman—women were trouble he didn't need—Clem kept to himself. If not for property taxes and beer, he'd quit his shitty job at the Wilco.

Beer in hand, he made his way back around the kitchen table, its surface masked by bottles, cans, empty chip bags, pizza boxes, and drive-through containers. Clem neither noticed nor cared. He'd clean it all out eventually. Another good reason not to have a woman around: no one to nag about the mess. RayRay sure didn't care, and he was the only one who ever stopped by.

The can cracked open with a satisfying *chunk-hiss*. Taking a long pull, Clem headed down the holler to see what RayRay was doing. His shoes crunched on the gravel driveway as he strolled down the hill toward his cousin's house. RayRay moved from the house to the yard and back again.

Probably getting the garden ready.

RayRay didn't see Clem until he crossed Caseknife Road and made it halfway through the yard. RayRay nodded, flinging a hand trowel into the dirt at Clem's feet in greeting. Clem stepped around the tool— blade buried halfway in the ground, handle still vibrating— unconcerned. RayRay would never hurt him. Showing off his skill with any kind of blade was an aspect of his character, not unlike his brown hair, constant five o'clock shadow, or cleft chin.

Clem accepted RayRay as he was. He loved his cousin, and he was the only family Clem had left.

"What you know good, RayRay? Getting any mud for your duck?"

"Clem! Thought you was workin' today. That place's gonna shut down without you."

"Nah. Say, RayRay, I need to talk to you."

RayRay's eyebrows drew down. "Something wrong, cousin?"

"Let's go on in the house. I'd like to talk in some privacy. No telling who might be listening out here." Clem cast a wary eye at the budding trees. Few cars ever made their way so far back along Caseknife Road. None were on the road now. Early season insects buzzed in the grass. Rustling wind whispered its secrets to the trees, and the trees kept silent.

Clyde Raymond "RayRay" Hall grunted his assent and turned to go inside. Anyone might be watching in Summit Valley. "Long as you don't mind the fumes, we can talk in here. I got the windows up to air the place out a bit. No one comes back here anyhow. Don't expect no law."

RayRay had bags of fertilizer stacked against the wall next to the front door.

"Jesus! Smells like you've been burning plastic bottles full of cat piss in here."

Color flushed RayRay's cheeks. "Yeah, I'm doing a little side cook for some extra cash."

"Why didn't you set that shit up in the woods away from here? Stinks to high heaven!"

"Too cold out there at night. I cook at night."

"Fuck. I guess. Anyway, you still got your internet?"

"Yeah, fuckin' Comcast shut it off for a while. S'why I had to break out the barrel." RayRay nodded over to a crude, albeit creative methamphetamine production lab.

Clem didn't understand the chemistry behind it and didn't really care to—that shit led to too much trouble. RayRay learned to cook meth during a five-year stretch in King Mountain for burglary. Out in the world his former cellmates introduced him to a few people who bought the small amounts of meth periodically produced. RayRay didn't use it; neither did Clem. They decided they could share an occasional joint while drinking beer, but no more.

Leave the hard drugs for hard addicts.

Besides, it wasn't wrong to make a little profit by giving people what they wanted. Times were hard. Clem and RayRay helped each other out as family should, but neither of them ever had much money. Two broken-down homes forgotten in the depths of the Appalachian Mountains represented the extent of their family wealth. The cousins, last of their line, struggled to hold on.

The pair made their way across the living room to RayRay's computer, and Clem said, "Good. We could use a little more cash around here. But I got something better than meth. Best part, it's legal. Might even be heroes."

"Yeah?"

"Yeah." Clem nodded. "Get on the Google and go to the FBI's most wanted list."

"Why?"

"You want to see this or not?"

"Yeah, but—"

"Then shut the fuck up! Google!"

RayRay sat down at the small desk shoved against the wall and shook the mouse to wake the computer. Immediately, a pornographic video began to play. A beautiful blonde woman moaned as she buried her face between the legs of an equally beautiful redhead, tongue working industriously. RayRay watched for a moment before pausing the video.

"Sorry. Was watching porn."

"Really? That what that was?"

"Fuck you, Clem." RayRay smiled up at him.

"We can get back to the girls later. Google! Now!"

RayRay brought up the FBI's Ten Most Wanted Fugitives. On the screen were pictures of nine rough-looking men leering at the camera, and one woman. She was smiling, completely out of place on a page about the most wanted felons in America. The picture had been professionally done, clearly taken from her home and used for this awful profile.

"Yeah, that's her! Click on her!" Clem jabbed his finger at the screen.

RayRay dutifully clicked on the redhead's picture.

SHIRLEY DURITZ MCGREGGOR

Unlawful Flight to Avoid Prosecution – First Degree Murder (14 counts), Arson of an Occupied Structure, Assault with a Deadly Weapon, Capital Fraud, Insurance Fraud

DESCRIPTION

Alias: Unknown
Date(s) of Birth Used: January 30, 1967
Place of Birth: Eugene, Oregon
Eyes: Green
Hair: Red
Height: 5'7"

Weight: 140 pounds
Complexion: Light
Build: Medium
Sex: Female
Race: White
Nationality: American
Occupation: Housewife
Scars and Marks: Shirley has pierced ears.

REWARD
The FBI is offering a reward of up to $5,000,000 for information leading directly to the arrest and conviction of Shirley Duritz McGreggor.

REMARKS
McGreggor is physically fit, an accomplished chef, and avid gardener. She tends to bury her victims in her garden, fertilizing her plants with the remains.

CAUTION
Shirley Duritz McGreggor is wanted in connection to a string of violent crimes across the United States. She is believed to be in possession of weapons, poisons, and lethal toxins.

SHOULD BE CONSIDERED ARMED AND EXTREMELY DANGEROUS
If you have any information concerning this person, please contact your local FBI office or the nearest American Embassy or Consulate.
Field Office: Portland

"Okay. So what?" RayRay didn't bother to hide his confusion.

"Here's what. What would you say if I told you there was $5 million dollars walking around unclaimed in Summit Valley?

That woman is here, Clyde! Collecting her reward fixes all our problems. We'd be rich! It'd put things back the way they used to be. We can make it right!"

Clem never called him Clyde. No one called him Clyde. Only a handful of people even knew his first name, and he hated it, but Clem used it when discussing serious points. Clem was serious, desperate. Hell, RayRay was too. Something about this reward felt wrong. RayRay never experienced a time when police ever did anything good. Cops made things worse, not better.

As tempting as an opportunity to get such a phenomenal sum of money for doing little to nothing was, RayRay doubted a good end. Happy endings didn't happen for the Farris clan. The Hall clan either. Things went bad—real bad—for people like them. Nothing worked out; nothing improved. Their line was cursed. Better to let it die out. RayRay had been raised with all the same stories Clem had. The difference between the cousins was RayRay never believed life could get better. Clem did. RayRay knew that once you were poor, you never escaped. When the monsters got their claws in you, they never let go. They piled up until your strength failed, dragging you into their depths.

The Farris clan arrived in Summit Valley near the time of its founding. While raising dairy cattle, their forefathers prospered. Farris milk and cheese shipped and sold all over the state. The farm expanded, taking up seventy-five acres between Summit Valley and Nilbud. Almost everyone in Summit Valley had an ancestor who worked for Farris Dairy, directly or otherwise.

Farris Dairy required blacksmiths to shoe horses and make barrels. Carpenters built barns, expanded the compound, constructed wagons to ship the products. Field hands by the score tended to the needs of the cattle—feeding, milking, breeding, making sure there was enough water available. Next to the budding lumber industry, the second largest contributor to the economic growth of both Summit Valley and Nilbud was Farris Dairy.

William Michael Farris, owner of Farris Dairy and head of the Farris clan, enjoyed tremendous wealth and influence in the area. According to the family, William became arrogant with his successes. He retained a seat on the newly formed Summit Valley City Council. William desired to expand his empire across the eastern seaboard. He pushed to make Summit Valley a center of trade.

Family legend said William entered a heated debate with another council member over the direction of the town. The owner of a local hospitality house, said to be from New York, didn't want the town becoming another metropolitan den of sin and vice. William saw profit and prosperity for the people here. Sin and vice made money. With enough money, William reasoned, the family could isolate themselves. Profit by and still remain apart from urban hedonism. The argument escalated. William ended up stabbed in the heart, dead on the council chamber floor.

Thus began the Farris curse.

Shawn Farris, William's brother and new head of the family, came out to the fields one day to discover his cattle dying. As far as he could see, the cattle couldn't support their weight with their hind legs, sagging and collapsing. Cows lay paralyzed, unable to even cry out, dying in the sun, dead where they fell. Shawn looked in horror at his herd, dead or dying, eyes glazed, tongues hanging out. Field hands panicked, too scared to help, and left the dairy. Many cast the twin-fingered sign of the evil eye toward Shawn, hoping none of his curse followed them home.

Modern science eventually solved the mystery. A rainy season had led to wet feed being stored, then eventually fed to the herd. The entire herd died from a botulism outbreak. Neither the Farrises nor the surrounding countryside knew anything of *Clostridium botulinum* or the lethal toxin produced.

Cattle dead by the score, entire generations of dairy producers gone.

Shawn tried his best to replace the lost herd, but believing the Farris line cursed, no one in the community bought their product. The farm, too large for the family alone to work, sold off bit by bit until nothing of Farris Dairy remained. Summit Valley retained its small-town stature instead of becoming the trade metropolis William Farris had envisioned.

Over the intervening years, the Farris clan moved on, leaving the Summit Valley area forever. Forgetting about their dairy farm, their past, their curse, they slowly migrated west. Only a small number struggled on in the mountains surrounding the town. Eventually, the line consisted only of one gas station attendant and his part-time methamphetamine-making cousin.

Chapter Four
In the Halls of Justice

D etective Aron Weaver stood before the Roanoke County Force Review Board alongside his lawyer.

"This commission finds the officer-involved shooting of Benjamin Stockmore a case of justifiable homicide. Based on physical evidence, as well as corroborating eyewitness testimony, we find Detective Aron A. Weaver justified in his use of lethal force. Furthermore, we commend Detective Weaver on his swift action and eye for detail instrumental in the timely rescue and return of four-year-old Jaren Banks to his family. This board will make a recommendation of no wrongdoing to the chief of police and the district attorney's office based upon the results of our investigation into the incident. And Detective, on a personal note, if I may"—here, the chairman of the Roanoke County Force Review Board leaned forward— "the Bankses are personal friends of mine. I thank you for your heroic actions in defending their child and protecting our community from a deranged serial murderer. You have my personal gratitude for your years of faithful service to the city and county of Roanoke. You, sir, are a credit to the force and a model for all officers to aspire to. This meeting of the Force Review Board is adjourned."

Detective Weaver couldn't believe they weren't prosecuting. Further, he was amazed the board had been so personal, so generous, in their praise. He was standing, hands clasped loosely behind his back, fully expecting the recommendation to pursue criminal charges against him for his unlawful actions. He deserved it.

Only his years of police discipline kept him from sagging when the verdict had been read. The headache from his hangover throbbed behind his right eye—the light in the courtroom too bright, too judgmental. No one could blame a guy for needing a drink on what he'd thought would be his last night of freedom. Weaver kept his head up and his shoulders back even though he wanted to collapse into the chair.

He'd shot Stockmore above the right eye, removing a large chunk from the back of the killer's head, and had pulled Jaren Banks away from Stockmore's nerveless fingers before the body ever hit the ground. SWAT had quickly closed ranks around him, blocking the boy's view of the carnage, for which Weaver had been grateful.

Before taking the boy and carrying him outside, Hill had patted Weaver on the shoulder and said that he'd done a great thing and had nothing to worry about. Now, outside of his combat gear and dressed in a conservative blue suit, Hill was a stranger to him, out of place in the sterile courtroom. A soldier at a tea party.

Weaver didn't regret Stockmore's death as much as he regretted his impulsive actions. He had been so angry, and allowing his anger to take control, he'd damned himself. He was paid to uphold and enforce the law and help prosecute those who didn't. He wasn't a hired gun delivering street justice however he saw fit.

Hill was true to his word, and SWAT told the same story of Stockmore preparing to kill the child, leaving Weaver no choice but to administer lethal force. Every officer on the team repeated the same.

Now Weaver wasn't prison-bound for putting down a rabid animal.

SWAT came up to Weaver, patting him on the back, congratulating him. His attorney, Mars Sanderson, shook his hand then began packing legal documents into his briefcase. "I told you," Mars said with a wink. "They'd never prosecute a hero cop. Even if they believed you were wrong, which they don't, they'd never put you away. This one was easy, Aron. You got the bad guy, saved the kid. Let's go get drunk."

Mars was a childhood friend that felt the call of civil service as Weaver had but lacked the necessary physical gifts. Mars had a sharp mind and would have made a fine detective in his own right, but a congenital heart defect kept him from the ranks of the police. The defect didn't require treatment, but police admissions felt it might be detrimental to Mars's long-term health in the stressful career of policing. So, Mars became a lawyer with cops as his primary clients.

He represented police in brutality lawsuits, civil rights violation allegations, or in this case, officer-involved shootings. More than one of Roanoke's finest had avoided legal trouble thanks to Mars's efforts on their behalf.

"Come on. We'll head down to Schooners and use your hero cop bit to get laid." Mars grinned at him. They had been friends since the fourth grade. Weaver couldn't help but grin back at him. Mars, always cool, acted as if Weaver's life and career hadn't just been on the line.

"I think I need to go home and work through the fact I won't be needing your services anymore."

"Aw, come on, Aron." Mars pretended to pout. "Let's go get some ladies. You're not too decrepit for fun. You're what? Sixty-seven? You know I can't get any without my hero buddy."

"You know I know that's a bunch of bullshit. Your mouth could talk the pants off the pope. And I'm forty-nine. Dickhead." Mars was handsome. He still had the same thick black hair he did as a boy and a solid jaw. Weaver always thought

Mars wasted his time being a lawyer. He should have gone to Hollywood and made some real money. Mars was educated, sophisticated, charming, and certainly didn't need Weaver to pick up women. Their bond had strengthened through time and trials beyond memory or concern. Neither had ever married, but there'd been plenty of girlfriends along the way. No one enjoyed their company the way they enjoyed each other's.

"Ew, why would I want the pope's pants? I'd much rather have some nuns."

"They ain't had none, don't want none." Weaver smiled at the familiar game. They'd been talking about *nones* and *somes* most of their lives. Mars was one of the few people Weaver joked with. Most thought he didn't have much of a sense of humor.

"Well, if we ain't getting none, I'll come hang at your place and get drunk. Either way, we're getting drunk. Again. My head is killing me, by the way. Thanks for that."

The courtroom was almost empty. SWAT was gone, and Mars and Weaver stood by the defendant's table. Weaver looked at Mars and said, "I fucked up, Mars. If it weren't for you, I'd be looking at prison time."

"Nah." Mars shook his head, sobering. "You were never going to face a jury for shooting that sick fuck. Especially with SWAT backing your story. And you saved the kid. Straight-up career suicide for a prosecutor to press charges. He'd have been vilified by the press, the public, probably even his mama before he could say, 'What the fuck was I thinking?' You're golden, my friend. A hero. This was a simple formality."

"I killed him. Didn't even think about it. Heroes don't murder."

"Yeah? Hooray. Fuck that guy. Aron, he was eating children. He wasn't building a better tomorrow; he was preying on the smallest and weakest of us. He was a cannibal, a coward, and if there's any justice, the devil is poking him in the balls with a pitchfork. Don't you waste another second thinking you've done wrong here."

Surprised at the heat in Mars's voice, Weaver decided to drop the subject. "All right, then, brother. Let's hit the bricks."

Mars smiled, shifting gears quickly. "Women?"

"Nah, I don't think I can manage the effort."

"You are upset, huh?"

"Let's go get drunk."

"I'm with that."

Weaver and Mars left the courtroom to the silence and dust, careers and honor intact.

Chapter Five
Besties

"Dude, you ever say a word so many times it loses its meaning?" Caden Quesenberry asked his best friend, Logan Burdette.

"What do you mean?" Caden hated when he answered questions with questions, so Logan made sure he did it as often as possible.

"You know what I mean, doofus." Caden recognized the grin on Logan's face. His friend was trying to aggravate him—still a favorite of their games, even if it was an old one.

"How would I know what you mean? All I know is you need to use your armor shout. You're about to get us both killed."

The two sat playing *Diablo III*, battling legions of the undead on Logan's new PlayStation 4 Pro. Logan used the Witch Doctor, and Caden's favorite character was the Barbarian. Since Logan's dad got a new job, Logan had received all kinds of cool new toys. Caden still had the better bike.

"Relax. You keep throwing your spiders. Leave the real work to me. We both know my Barb is doing the work here. Fighting skeletons with spiders is stupid. Enjoy following me around getting free experience. You're welcome," Caden said.

"Your toon sucks. If my Witch Doctor didn't keep mobs under control, we'd have died a million times already. Zero skill necessary to run and smash." Another old argument, neither boy willing to give any ground. Their play styles complemented each other, not unlike in real life.

Logan Burdette used to live across the hall from Caden. Dodging dangers at Edison Square Apartments together had cemented their bond, and they'd become best friends. Then Logan's family moved to a house on Seventh Street once his father found work. Caden missed his friend terribly. Seventh Street wasn't too far away from the Edison Square Apartments, separated by a scant few blocks, but their neighborhoods were worlds apart. Police maintained a presence in the Edison Square parking lot. Drugs, theft, and prostitution, among other crimes, kept officers busy. Fist fights and gunshots weren't uncommon.

Anger at their neighbors, at their lives, at themselves, and the inescapable soul-crushing poverty weighed on hearts and pulled corners of mouths toward cracked dirty pavement. Bills went unpaid. Collectors called and threatened. Children of broken homes gathered in sullen groups in the parking lots and basketball courts. Logan had Caden; Caden had Logan. The two had kept each other safe.

But Logan had been gone for over a year, and Caden never stopped feeling lonely.

Sometimes Caden got permission to ride his bike over to Logan's house. Away from the parking lots of Edison Square and across Prospect Avenue—the only truly dangerous areas— Caden found himself in a completely different world. Large maple and oak trees lined the streets. Houses had actual yards. Green was everywhere. Green grass, green trees, and green bushes grew fat and happy.

The houses might've been dated, but their owners took pride in them. Brightly colored flowers Caden couldn't identify lined walkways and porches. Lawns were neatly manicured, and there always seemed to be someone outside to throw up a hand as he rode by. Trash and cigarette butts no longer lined the streets once Caden crossed Prospect.

Caden dreamed his parents would one day leave the hell of Edison Square and move into a house next to Logan. Caden kept his dream secret, close to his heart, thinking about it in bed during the warm fuzzy hours before drifting off.

Their parents often talked about unemployment, assisted living, or food stamps. Caden and Logan had vague notions of what those things meant in the abstract way children view adult concerns. Logan said it was better at his house with his father working. Caden agreed. Logan's dad had found a job, and his parents had gotten "back on their feet." All that seemed to mean was Logan's dad was gone most of the time. His mom wasn't as angry anymore. Logan had a PlayStation 4 Pro.

Caden wanted his parents to be happy too. Back when his dad worked at Summit Valley Furniture, they'd had a house too. Caden didn't even know Edison Square Apartments existed back then. His parents had even bought him the BMX— easily the greatest present he'd ever gotten.

"Poop. Poop. Poop. Poop. Poop. Poop. Poop. Poop. Poop," Logan chanted.

"Your Witch Doctor?"

Both boys giggled. "No. I'm trying to say a word so many times it loses its meaning. You brought it up."

"That's the word you chose?" Caden progressed from giggles to outright belly laughs.

"Your breath inspired me."

Logan's dad passed by the pair, zipping up his coveralls, preparing for work. "Inspired what, pal?"

Both boys laughed hysterically, the way only young boys can, rolling around, their game momentarily forgotten. Logan's mother poked her head in. She raised her eyebrows at her husband, who shrugged.

"Boys," Mrs. Burdette said, "Caden's mother will be here in a few minutes to pick him up. Better get your things together."

At this news, Caden sobered. He'd spent the previous night with Logan on the promise that he'd be dressed for the Saturday farmers market with his mother. Caden didn't understand why he needed to go. He was perfectly fine here with Logan playing *Diablo*.

Logan paused the game, and the pair went to pack up Caden's things. He had his bookbag because he'd ridden the bus home with Logan after school yesterday. He stuffed his dirty clothes into it, put on yesterday's socks, and laced his shoes. Outside, a lawn mower started up.

Logan looked toward the sound filtering through his window before commenting, "All that guy does is cut grass. When can you come back? We didn't play any Magic. I want to try a new deck build, beat your butt in a refreshing new way."

Caden grinned at his friend. "I don't know. You always beat me at Magic anyway. What's the difference?"

"I want to see if I can make you cry."

"I cry every time I see your face." Caden flopped back on Logan's bed and groaned. "The farmers market sucks. Can't I stay here?"

"Maybe your mom likes you. Stranger things have happened."

"I guess so. I know *your* mom likes me. Better than you, anyway. Did I bring anything else?" Caden asked. Looking around, it was hard to tell. The floor was a mess of Lego pieces and Beyblades. To an outsider—specifically Logan's mother—his sanctuary was a chaotic mess. Lego pieces waited to be constructed into castles or tanks, and bedding from the bunk beds lay in crumpled piles—the perfect cushion for a well-aimed leap off the top. Stacks of Magic: The Gathering playing cards intermixed with Pokémon and Yu-Gi-Oh, forming games whose complex rules were unintelligible to anyone other than boys.

The lawn mower got close, then turned away, the sound retreating from a roar back to a background buzz. Neither boy wanted the other to go, but Caden's mother was on her way, and school was close to ending for the year. A whole summer of sleepovers and campouts awaited them.

"If you leave anything here, I'll take it to the Spot. I'll drop off whatever I find by this afternoon," Logan said. "If, you know, I find anything."

"Fine. I don't really care. It's whatever," Caden responded with a shrug. Leaving soured his mood.

Caden didn't think he'd forgotten anything. If he had, Logan had his back. Best friends looked out for each other. Besides, it was an excuse to meet up at the Spot: a hollow in an ancient maple behind the Deli Mart on Prospect. Since it was roughly halfway between their homes, the boys had decided it made for a perfect meeting point. Finding a hollow spot they could leave drops for each other had been a bonus.

Logan had told him how spies used to leave information for each other when it was too dangerous to meet up. Caden was enamored with the sound, the feel, of dead drops. A secret place to leave secret things. Logan always came up with the coolest things.

Logan had placed a faded blue ribbon, the kind attached to balloons, in the hollow, which could be tied to a branch. Logan said ribbon was hard to see unless you knew what you were looking for. The ribbon was thin, discreet. You had to look hard in order see it dancing on the breeze. Caden thought the pale blue would contrast against the green of the leaves, be too visible. He'd been mistaken though. It blended surprisingly well, the sinuous movement all but disappearing in the foliage. Caden watched for the ribbon every time he rolled by in his parents' beat-up Mazda truck. The ribbon meant something cool or important hid within the tree.

Comics, Magic cards, notes, action figures, games, the occasional DVD, or anything else small enough to fit, had been passed over the last year. Caden had even hidden a *Penthouse* magazine he found, but it'd disappeared. The faded pictures had made him feel both dirty and excited at the same time. His twig and berries—well, his twig—stood up for an hour afterward, and there wasn't anything he could do about it. Logan claimed he never saw the magazine, and Caden hadn't seen it since. Still, he wondered if Logan had it stashed somewhere in his bedroom. He bet he did.

A horn honked outside. Caden said goodbye, slightly embarrassed his mother hadn't knocked. Honking in the driveway was rude, he thought. Besides, his mother knew Mrs. Burdette. They used to be neighbors. Sheesh! Caden apologized for his mother's manners, then said goodbye to Logan on his way to pick a fight. Time to fuss with Mom. She knew better, and she'd taught him better.

CHAPTER SIX
AN INTERLUDE: SETTLING ACCOUNTS

Hannah Baenziger crept down the back stairs of the Maple Lodge and snuck through the emergency exit in a panic, careful not to make too much noise. She didn't want the crazy bat—or worse, *him*—knowing she wouldn't be staying another night. Wishing she'd never stopped at the nightmare that was the Maple Lodge, Hannah backed toward the car. She dropped her room key in the gravel, unlocked her car, and floored it away from the same parking lot Deputy Roland had fled a few days before. The stolen Bonneville rolled past the Corvette that had shown up that day. Even in the dark, the burnt rubber tracks left by the deputy's cruiser were obvious.

The Vette was the only other car in the lot. Hannah didn't want anything flashy, so switching vehicles here wasn't an option. The more mundane, the better. She wanted as little attention as possible. The Pontiac was invisible in this rural part of the country.

Sweat beaded on Hannah's forehead as she checked her mirrors to make sure he wasn't watching. Adrenaline flooded her system, making her hands shake. The cold hovering over the parking lot further chilled her. She shivered. Hannah wasn't going to be a victim tonight. She wasn't staying in his house of horrors for another minute.

She stayed off main roads. She was driving a stolen car with stolen tags. Getting arrested tonight was not part of her agenda. Hannah shook her head at the absurdity of her situation. Death or prison. No one would ever believe her.

According to her map—an honest old-fashioned road atlas—she'd stay on Route 11 until she hit 100. Afterward, she could stay on 100 until it ended, then hook a right into wild and wonderful West Virginia. Once across state lines, she could disappear into the myriad of back roads while she figured how to find safety.

Hannah had gotten the phone call from Rigo. Get the bag. Get out of the house. No time for questions. Get the bag. Run. Ditch the car. Head north. He said he would be in touch in a day or two. He said he would find her.

That had been four days ago.

She'd thrown a few clothes in her suitcase before leaving their Miami apartment forever. They'd planned to meet at an equestrian school Rigo once worked at in Waverly, West Virginia, if things went wrong. Isolated and located near the Ohio border, Waverly was a nothing-there-but-locals kind of town you wouldn't find unless you were looking for it. Such was Rigo's hope anyway.

Things must have gone completely sideways.

He was so stupid. Stupid, stupid, stupid! Hannah had known better than to get with Rigo, but he had great abs, was great in bed. His irresistible grin caused her nothing but grief. Rigo was constantly in trouble. Hannah had never outgrown a taste for bad boys. She should have settled down with someone stable, someone with an actual career—a dentist maybe. She should've been going to PTA meetings, gardening, grocery shopping, or whatever the hell else suburban wives did.

Truthfully, the thought of attending a PTA meeting bored her to death. Hannah would have rather opened a vein.

Rigo was as domesticated as a wild cat. He cheated on her, came home drunk or sometimes not at all. He had never held a day job for longer than a few months. He had no credit, or his credit was so bad he no longer tried using any, dealing strictly in cash. Or drugs. Or stolen goods.

Rigo was a minor criminal who fancied himself a business-man. There were always people he needed to meet. Contacts. It was always, "Baby, this guy has serious contacts," or, "Baby, this new contact is gonna make us rich."

It was all bullshit. Usually. But Hannah would smile and pretend she was excited about their upcoming life of wealth and luxury. Secretly, she feared one of his contacts was going to get him killed. They had set up this emergency plan in case things went wrong. You didn't need emergency evacuation plans in the PTA. Rigo had never said outright that she was in any danger because of him, but she knew. Sure she did.

He was a small-timer with a big ego.

Hannah didn't blame him. She never pointed a finger. She accepted him. She was no angel herself. She knew what Rigo was, and she stayed with him anyway. She'd taken part in his various cons and had watched his back while he bought or sold marijuana, cocaine, or meth. She'd helped him, followed him willingly, spread her legs for him. Ride or die.

Then he'd walked in with the bag. *Stupid fucking bag*! Black leather with a blue stripe. Larger than a gym bag, smaller than the ones she'd seen soldiers carrying off to war. Rigo threw the bag on the couch, where it hit with a thud before flopping onto the floor. Then he swept Hannah up close. They tripped over the thing and collapsed on the couch, breathing hard, laughing, happy. Hannah asked why he was so excited. Holding her eyes with his own, he opened the bag. Inside, five indistinct pack-ages tightly wrapped in cellophane sat on stacks of neatly bundled one-hundred-dollar bills.

"Oh my God, Rigo! How much is there?" Hannah couldn't

help feeling a bit scared. Things like this didn't happen to people like them—not without a price.

But Rigo had just flashed his cocky smile, which always melted her resolve. "With the H, close to a million dollars. Without, it's still over $800,000 in cash. I'm not exactly sure. I haven't counted it yet. I was waiting for you, babe!" They stared into the bag, half on her lap, its leather cool against her thighs, half on his. A million dollars. They'd dreamed about this kind of money, but Hannah had never expected she'd see it.

Hannah had wanted to flush the drugs, keep the cash. An extra $200,000 or so didn't matter in her opinion; they had enough right there to keep them comfortable for a good long while. Longer still if they were careful. Apparently, Rigo had contacts who could help launder the money for twenty cents on the dollar. He explained that they needed to have a story to explain their newfound wealth in case the IRS came knocking.

"That's how they got Capone, you know," Rigo had told her.

Hannah had a quick mind and ran the numbers in her head —$160,000 to clean the money, leaving them $640,000, plus the drugs. As much as she wanted to flush them, Rico would've never gone for it. He wouldn't have seen it as gaining over a half million, but the loss of $360,000. Rigo needed it *all*.

Hannah counted it later that night after Rigo had fallen asleep. He always fell asleep after sex. The grand total was $838,000 tax-free dollars. The gravity of the situation set in. She knew Rigo hadn't just *found* a bag full of cash.

Hannah felt the first twinges of fear worming around in her gut then. She trusted Rigo, but they were little fish. Bags of heroin and almost a million in cash was a totally different league. Before she fell asleep, she'd moved the bag from the couch, where she could see it, to the closet, where she couldn't. Her earlier joy was steadily being replaced by a creeping, biting fear.

At breakfast, she'd asked Rigo where the bag had come from. He told her a contact had tipped him off to a serious score if he was fast enough. A cartel plane had been forced down by the coast guard and lost in the swamps. Police were actively searching; cartel presumably were too. No one had managed to locate the downed aircraft.

A cartel-owned plane. Cartel. Jesus.

"No worries, babe. We were one and done, unsuspected, undetected, gone. Ghosts." Rigo's dark eyes sparkled while he told her his story. At some point, she'd stopped eating, breakfast forgotten.

The contact, a part-time burglar and full-time meth addict named Carlos Matanzas, was fishing when he saw the plane crash. Fishing probably meant either high or scouting a tourist to rob. Possibly, he'd been poaching. Carlos had been known to poach alligators.

He'd surveyed the wreckage and saw cash and drugs. For some reason, he'd been scared off. He'd called Rigo straight away with the location, hoping to settle a debt. Rigo rushed to the Miccosuke Casino to meet Carlos. He let Carlos see him load a pistol into his shoulder holster in case Carlos had any plans of robbing him. The two drove the flat stretch of Highway 41 West toward Carnestown.

At some point, Carlos had turned south into the swamps. The flat swampland crowded up on both sides of a narrow dirt road, trees allowing only dapples of sunlight to poke through. Stagnant water, cypress, and mangrove surrounded them. The road—if it could be called a road—eventually opened into a clearing. At the far end of the clearing, a raggedy boat shack with a rusted tin roof perched beside a dock Rigo didn't trust to support his weight. The shack was built over an open channel.

Carlos had parked the car, and the pair walked to the boathouse with Carlos jabbering the whole time about how happy Rigo was going to be. Lots of money, lots of drugs— they'd be even for sure. This was the fuckin' big time!

At this part of the story, Rigo did a passable impression of Carlos, which made Hannah smile. Rigo said he'd been more concerned with the helicopter in the distance, but Carlos assured him the helicopter was closer to Miami and searching in the wrong direction. They were going west, not east. According to Carlos, they'd be at the plane and gone before the cops—or anyone else—knew anything.

And even if they were caught, Carlos kept fishing gear on the airboat. They could claim to be a couple of tourists doing some fishing. Carlos had formulated a plan: Rigo would clear the plane of goodies, settling Carlos's debt, and there would be enough for Carlos to have some playtime. He didn't need much. A tiny taste would do.

The mosquitoes attacked as soon as they'd exited the vehicle. Must have been waiting for them. Rigo showed Hannah several bites on his neck. Inside, the boathouse was no better— open to the channel for the convenience of the airboat, so the bugs simply followed them inside. Rigo noted large wasp nests dotting the ceiling and wasps doing what wasps do. Carlos suggested it wasn't a smart idea to fire up the fan in the confined space.

"Fucker'll prolly blow the walls down and drop the ceiling on our fuckin' heads." Carlos had nodded sagely.

Rigo doubted Carlos's engineering abilities, but it didn't seem like a good idea to him either. Besides, he wouldn't have wanted to be trapped under the roof with his face in one of those wasp nests. Rigo boarded the boat and sat on a metal bench. Tackle and poles rested amongst dirt and shallow puddles of water. Rigo tried not to get his shoes wet.

Carlos pushed the boat into open water with a long pole. He set the pole back on the opposite side of the fishing poles, then mounted what Rigo thought of as the captain's seat. Carlos sat a solid four feet higher than Rigo, fronting a giant fan that propelled the boat.

Carlos started the fan motor while Rigo slapped at mosquitoes biting at his neck. The motor roared to life, and the boat lurched forward. The shallow draft allowed the craft to pass over inches-deep water, thick grasses, and debris at high speed. Even though Rigo had ridden on airboats before, he'd never gotten used to the noise.

After getting himself situated, fastening his belt, and whatever the fuck else Carlos did while dicking around up there, he shouted something Rigo didn't understand, following which the boat bounded forward. Rigo grabbed at the railing to keep from falling backward. Forty-five minutes of primal landscape, wind, and droning motor noise passed while Rigo waited impatiently. Carlos turned indiscriminately down random channels before he found the combination of grass, water, and mangrove he was looking for. Rigo's ass ached by the time Carlos eventually slowed.

Closer inspection of their surroundings told Rigo—who'd never been much of an outdoorsman—that great violence had happened near there. Trees were scored, burned. Swamp grasses were flattened, blackened. Broken stumps with gouges in the wood lined their path. Closer to the wreck, manmade debris appeared alongside the carnage of nature.

Metal shaped then reshaped from heat and impact formed an obscure arrow pointing at the wreck of a Cessna. Rigo had never owned a plane, although he wanted one. Not much remained of the Cessna—an aluminum tube trapped in a stand of mangrove.

The wings had shredded off somewhere in the swamps behind them along with the tail section. Part of an engine attached to a broken propeller lodged in the mangrove. Three arms had broken off completely, even with the trees, and a fourth, broken in half, stuck fast in the wood. Rigo imagined the thing shattering on impact with the thicket. Spinning at six thousand revolutions a minute, a manic chainsaw of the gods trying vainly to pull itself back into the sky, already dead, refusing to admit it. This plane's days dancing on the winds were forever gone.

Mosquitoes and no-see-ums were even worse here than

they'd been at the dock, but Rigo had forgotten their intrusive hunger with his own worry gnawing at him during the ride over. Carlos guided the airboat alongside the downed aircraft. Rigo leaned over, one hand braced on the plane, peeking at whatever remained inside.

Despite how chewed up the exterior looked, the interior was full of treasure.

Rigo didn't see any bodies inside the craft. He assumed the pilots had bailed during the crash or the swamp had taken them. In what remained of the cargo hold, two pallets were neatly stacked and wrapped. Wiggling inside, no longer thinking of wet shoes or what might lurk within, Rigo crawled over to the pallets.

Swamp water soaked his shoes and the front of his jeans as Rigo scooted closer to the pallets on his knees. Carlos tossed a large pocketknife through a broken window. Rigo used it to cut through a thick layer of protective plastic wrapping. Both pallets were stacked four feet high with bundles of United States currency. Hundreds, fifties, and twenties were piled as neatly as when they'd been loaded. Millions of dollars in cash just sitting in the middle of a Florida swamp waiting for someone to find it.

Rigo looked at the big idiot who had driven him there. If he'd had an idea of what was there, surely he would have taken the money for himself. Rigo considered shooting him as he knelt grinning in the doorway. Methamphetamine had ruined Carlos's remaining teeth.

"See, Rigo? Didn't I tell you we'd be square?"

Carlos's expression reminded Rigo of an eager puppy. He couldn't bring himself to draw the weapon from under his shirt. Plus, there was no way he would be able to find his own way back before the boat ran out of gas. Carlos was a swamp rat, albeit an extraordinarily useful swamp rat.

There wasn't a way they could successfully transport that much cash from the wreck to Miami. They would need a box truck and who knew how many runs between the wreck and the dock before they got it all from the plane. The only option was to grab as much as they could now and fucking bail.

"Carlos, how in the fuck do we transport all of this?"

Carlos's eager expression fell. "Rigo... Aw, homes. I thought you'd be happy."

"Why would I be happy knowing I had to leave millions of dollars to the alligators because my partner was too fucking stupid to bring something we could load the merch on? Got an extra boat up your ass?"

"I figured you'd know what to do."

"You figured I'd know what to do," Rigo repeated. "I know what I want to do. I want to shoot you in your stupid fucking face. We'll have to leave most of this shit here. Fine job. Pass me your damn bag."

Hannah looked over at Rigo's treasure. She didn't see the freedom he'd talked about. A travel bag wasn't an escape to a soft life of coconuts, massages on the beach, and room service. She thought of the bag as the end of the world. She no longer felt the exhilaration she had when first sitting in bed counting their money—the last night she'd spent with Rigo. In the morning, he'd gone to meet a contact about money laundering or buying the heroin. She couldn't remember which.

Very few lights dotted the landscape here in rural southwest Virginia. An occasional streetlight marked the long driveway of a house sitting at the top of a hill far from the road. Almost all the houses were ranch houses, which Hannah hated. Ranch houses reminded her of trailers. Immobile homes with two-car carports. Always plenty of additional parking available on the lawn when friends come over. Trashy. Poor.

The trees grew close, crowding the road. Going off-road here could strand her. Finding another car to steal would be difficult. Houses were few, far from the road, and across too much open ground. It was dark, quiet—completely different from her life in Miami, where life went on at any time of day or night. She missed the beach. All these trees hunched over the road were creepy.

Who knew what was in those woods?

She drove slowly. The unfamiliar road twisted back and forth and often back on itself in a series of steep switchbacks winding through the mountains. *God, you could kiss your own butt coming around some of these corners.* She didn't laugh at the thought. Instead, she glanced over at the homewrecker sitting in the passenger seat.

Rigo had brought that bag home and ruined their lives. She hated the bag, and as much as she didn't want to admit it, she hated Rigo for bringing it home. He'd spoiled everything. It should have stayed in the swamp, in the slime, where it belonged. Her Maple Lodge key sat on the bag.

She stopped the car in the middle of the road.

Hannah had dropped that damn key in the parking lot. She *knew* she had. Trees lit by her headlights resembled people trying to shield themselves from an unseen attack, skeletal branches raised in defense. The trees behind her looked drenched in blood. She sat in between, staring at an object that could not be there.

She didn't want to touch the key, but she couldn't leave it. It felt akin to having a dangerous snake in the car with her. She felt paralyzed, too scared to drive because she couldn't stop staring.

Lying there reflecting the green glow of the dash, looking like it had all the business in the world being back in her car. A wooden tab with a number four burned onto it hung below a metal key. When she'd arrived at the Maple Lodge, she'd thought the key was quaint. Not many places maintained physical guest keys; most used those magnetic key swipers.

Her numb finger pushed the button to roll down the window. She pinched the key between her forefinger and thumb, touching it as little as possible. With a quick flick of her wrist, Hannah tossed it into the night. She heard the rustle of leaves as the key skittered into a ditch. She wiped her hand on her jeans, feeling like she'd touched something nasty, like she'd shoved her hand into rotten meat. The tips of her fingers were hot where she'd handled the key. Hannah rolled the window back up as fast as the motor allowed, afraid the key would chase her down and jump back into the car.

With the window rolled back up and the doors locked, she put the car back into gear. The night remained calm and quiet, as before, but Hannah had the distinct feeling a presence was coming through the woods, rushing through the dark and right for her. She needed to move. Now.

Hannah stepped on the gas, and the Bonneville leapt to task. She kept checking the rearview mirror. There was nothing there —only trees fading into darkness—but her feeling of pursuit remained, growing stronger.

She wished for the millionth time that Rigo had left the damn bag in the swamp.

Hannah began a steep curving descent toward some place called Pearisburg. Past the town—if it could be called a town at all—the road ran beside a river. Moonlight shone on the water. It might have been pretty if not for all the dead trees lining the bank.

A noise drew her attention from the road back to the bag. Her key had returned to her.

Hannah slammed on the brakes. It should've been forgotten, lost in a ditch somewhere in her rearview. She'd thrown it away miles back. She'd heard it hit the leaves piled in a roadside ditch. What had drawn her attention was the sound of metal falling onto leather. Hannah rolled her window down. Time to throw it out again. An uncomfortable warmth radiated from it, as if it had recently come from inside someone's pocket. She recoiled from the nasty feel of the thing. In her surprise, she flicked it between seat and door.

Ah, fuck!

For a moment, Hannah was tempted to let it lie forgotten

beneath her. But no, she couldn't leave it. It would be like trying to drive with a poisonous viper in the car. The thing had to go. Fumbling between the tight gap and unable to find it from her spot behind the wheel, Hannah was forced to get out and search.

There it is!

It lay amongst Dorito crumbs, dirt, a wrapper from a Snickers she'd eaten in North Carolina, and tiny rocks that had hitchhiked on her shoes to the mat. Reluctant to touch it, Hannah scooted the warm key into her grip using her fingertips.

She stood and hurled her unwanted cargo over the Bonneville's roof with a force driven by fear and frustration. The key spun end over end before vanishing into the night. Wiping her hand on her shirt, Hannah got back behind the wheel.

Route 100 paralleled the New River before becoming Main Street of a small town called Narrows. Coming to a T-junction, Hannah followed the signs for Route 460 toward West Virginia. The big Pontiac swung a wide right turn across a bridge. She tried to relax, her feeling of pursuit diminishing with the increase of streetlights. This wasn't civilization, although it certainly seemed to be more civilized. Her attention shifted to the bag every few seconds, making sure the key hadn't returned.

"There is, of course, the troublesome matter of your bill. We must settle your account."

Hannah screamed, jamming on the brakes for a third time. Her stolen Bonneville stopped at an angle near the bridge's midpoint, blocking both lanes. The land had fallen away sharply, the bridge suspended hundreds of feet above dark water. Hannah noticed, in a distracted way, headlights on the twisting road she'd recently traveled. Solomon Drury, proprietor of the Maple Lodge, sat in the passenger seat, the bag on his lap, twirling her room key around his index finger.

"Really, my dear, you should let us know you're checking out. A simple farewell would suffice."

"T-Take the bag," Hannah stammered. "There's a lot of money. I don't w-w-want it anymore."

"You don't w-w-want it anymore?" Solomon mocked her. "Who said anything about money? I said your account needed settling." An impossible grin with far too many sharp teeth spread on Solomon's face.

Hannah jerked the handle. She fell onto the asphalt, making her teeth click, then crab-walked backward. The passenger door opened and Solomon stepped from the car, smiling his horrible smile at her. Keeping her eyes on him, she somehow managed to get to her feet. Solomon continued his slow stroll around the car toward her, his polished leather shoes clicking against black-top. Each step saw him taller. His grin grew more horrific.

Hannah turned to run, stumbling on the curb. A painful misstep on the sidewalk caused her ankle to turn. Pain roared up her leg. She fell into the handrail, and her breath exited in a "Umpf!" as she felt ribs crack. There was nowhere for her to run. Icy water flowed beneath her, indifferent to her struggles above. He was on her then, holding her against the handrail with arms colder than river water and hard as death.

Solomon leaned over her to whisper in her ear. "He died screaming two days ago. You know that don't you? They put him in a barrel and set him on fire. Then they dropped the barrel into the ocean. Crabs are picking at his corpse now. It's not nice to take what isn't yours."

She did know it. Hannah heard the fear in Rigo's voice when he'd told her to leave. In her heart, she'd already known Rigo wouldn't be meeting her in Waverly. The cartel had killed him for taking what wasn't his. It didn't matter the police were fast closing in on the location of the wreck. Rigo had beaten them there and winning that race cost him his life.

Hannah tried to struggle free from Solomon's grip. No good. He was too strong. He turned her to face him and lifted her up over the handrail by the neck. He brought her close. His mouth distorted into something resembling a lamprey. Rows of razor-sharp teeth glistened in the cold light from the streetlamps. At any moment, he would attach himself to her head, shredding her face and sucking her vitals out. She thought he'd eat her right there on the side of the road.

Hannah tried turning her head. Impossible. She closed her eyes. Hadn't she seen some headlights moving her way? Where the hell were all the people? There was no one to come to her rescue. No traffic. No help. Tremendous carrion stink wafted from Solomon's open mouth in cloying waves. It was like coppery blood in rotting garbage—a repugnant miasma that choked away her oxygen no less than his grip on her throat. She threw up down the front of her shirt. Some dribbled into Solomon's leering mouth.

He lifted her higher still, her feet free of the handrail and moving over empty space. "We'll consider your account settled," he hissed as he let her go.

Hannah screamed until she hit the water eighty feet below. Ice-cold river water shot up her nose, choking her. She couldn't feel her arms or legs, and she thought her back might've been broken. She felt she'd been thrown through a brick wall, but she was alive. Still alive.

Solomon watched her fall, his features melting back to normal. When she didn't die upon impact, he made a dismissive gesture toward the Bonneville with a miffed "Humpf!" He always had to do everything himself! The tires screeched as they fought for purchase. Smoke rolled from the wheel wells as the tires accelerated faster and faster while being held in place. Another hand gesture, this time toward the river, sent the car crashing through the guardrail where Hannah had dropped.

* * *

Hannah floated back up to the river's surface, amazed she'd survived the fall. Her face broke the water's surface just in time for her to recognize the headlights of her stolen Pontiac coming straight at her. Before the threat could register in her pain-wracked brain, the sedan landed on her. The river underneath the bridge was only ten feet deep. The grill of the Pontiac drove Hannah into the mud at the bottom, cutting her neatly in two.

Solomon walked back across the bridge, whistling a jaunty tune of his own making and twirling the key to number four around his pale finger.

* * *

The headlights Hannah had seen came across the bridge a few minutes later. They belonged to a state trooper, who stopped to assess the fresh damage on the bridge. He'd been following a stolen car when he heard a crash. Trooper Manlosa ran to the gap in the railing and saw the trunk of the car sinking into the river.

As he waited for backup, Manlosa thought he heard whistling. Nah... Probably just the wind, but backup could hurry. It was creepy here.

Outside his line of vision, a leather bag floated free of the wreck. Pulled by slow winter currents, the bag traveled down the river a way before becoming waterlogged. Rigo's treasure sank to the bottom of the New River, lost in pondweed, buried in mud.

Manlosa stood with his hands behind his back and his face burning. Crisp winter air did little to cool his flaming cheeks. Behind him, crime scene techs were now busy taping bright yellow caution tape over the hole made by Hannah's Bonneville. He'd been debating over whether he wanted to remain a police officer for the rest of his life. He was young; it wasn't too late for a change of career. Anywhere was preferable to where he was.

Virginia State Police had sent an inspector to investigate the death of Hannah Baenziger. His findings would determine if her multistate crime spree merited notifying the FBI. Staties hated handing anything off to the feds, and Manlosa's statement couldn't be the truth. No way could it be the truth. "This is the story you're sticking to, Trooper? Do you expect me to believe this garbage?"

Manlosa stood solid with his hands clasped behind his back, staring over the inspector's head. "Yes, sir. That's what I saw."

"Let me get your 'facts' straight." The inspector made condescending quote marks in the air with his fingers. "You saw the deceased throw something from her car approximately eight miles back on Route 100. In the dark. Where there are no streetlights. You must have the greatest vision in the history of police work."

"I was parked in a driveway running radar. She stopped directly in front of me. She was facing away, toward the passenger seat. She threw something, then drove on. I exited the cruiser to find what she'd thrown. My efforts were unsuccessful. I returned to my cruiser intent on pursuit."

"Your efforts were 'unsuccessful' is the greatest understatement I've ever heard. Your effort tonight was a complete failure."

Manlosa nodded, thinking the condescending prick could use a kick in the teeth, rank be damned. Instead, he stood there and kept his mouth shut while the inspector humiliated him. Other cops—state and local sheriff's deputies—had given the pair a bubble of relative privacy. Men stood far enough away to remain respectful but close enough to eavesdrop. Several officers smirked, making quiet jokes. Manlosa grit his teeth together, squared his shoulders, and struggled to maintain a neutral expression.

"You began an initial pursuit to discuss the littering you observed with your miraculous night vision when you realized the car in question was reported stolen and the driver was wanted for questioning. Not wanting a high-speed pursuit, you followed at a distance, planning an arrest when she—what? Crossed the state line? When were you going to make your move? When she drove outside our jurisdiction? One little girl, alone, too scary to apprehend? If you weren't such a chickenshit, she might be sitting in a cell. And she might still be in one piece."

Over the inspector's head, Manlosa noticed not all who were present were laughing at him. Some of them seemed ashamed of their senior leadership's behavior. A few even looked angry at the treatment Manlosa was receiving. But nobody corrected the inspector. Nobody wanted their climb up the law enforcement ladder to come to a grinding halt. Manlosa appreciated the solidarity if not their silence.

After calling it in, Manlosa had secured the perimeter. It wasn't an especially difficult task as he was in the middle of a bridge. The next on scene were local sheriff's deputies. Without much for them to do, they'd waited mostly in silence until the crime scene techs arrived. Soon after, a detective was dispatched. No traffic, pedestrian or motor, needed to be controlled. The morning commute remained several hours away. That said, there would be a traffic jam. The river muck wouldn't be releasing its prize anytime soon.

"It is your professional opinion, then, that the deceased"— Trooper Manlosa hated the sneer the inspector put on—"noticed your headlights behind her. Knowing she had only moments before she was arrested by you or West Virginia police, she decided to do a couple of donuts in the middle of the road, skip around in the street, puke on the sidewalk, jump off a bridge, and still somehow rig her car to crash through the exact point she jumped from and land on her fucking head. By herself. That's your theory?"

Manlosa ignored the sarcasm. "I'll give you my full report in writing, sir."

"You're goddamn right you'll give me your full report in writing. And it will happen before end of shift. Today, Trooper. Now get the fuck off my crime scene."

Manlosa groaned to himself. He had been on for over fourteen hours. He wouldn't be getting home for at least the amount of time it would take him to write this up. Two hours? Four? And what was he going to say in the report? He'd told the inspector what had happened. The only thing he'd withheld was the whistling. No one would believe him anyway.

* * *

Giles County Sheriff, Buck Whitland, watched the trooper walk away from the crime scene. He hurried over to catch him. A quick word with the first responder might help Buck gain some perspective on this mess.

"Trooper Manlosa! A word please," Buck called.

Manlosa turned. A look of relief washed across his face when he realized it wasn't the inspector coming for another round. "Yes, Sheriff?"

"You were the first on scene, correct?"

Manlosa appeared wary. "I was."

"What happened?"

"You didn't hear my…debriefing?"

"Well, I'm hard of hearing. Especially when I'm listening to a crock of shit." Buck smiled.

Manlosa smiled back. Buck was winning him over. "Honestly, I don't know. I was following her. I saw her discard an object—a key perhaps, it glinted in the light—some miles back. I tried unsuccessfully to find it. While continuing my pursuit, I heard a crash."

Buck nodded. "The Bonneville crashing through the guardrail, I reckon." Buck studied Manlosa's mannerisms for any sign of deception. Manlosa was direct, maintained eye contact, didn't fidget, pause, or look away. Buck had conducted hundreds of interrogations, possibly thousands. He was convinced Manlosa was telling the truth.

Manlosa nodded back. "I think so too. I ran from my cruiser and looked over the side in time to see the taillights sinking. I called for backup. That's it." He looked away.

"Sure that's all?"

"Well…"

"Well, what?"

Manlosa looked uncomfortable, shifting his weight from foot to foot. "I heard—" He left the thought unfinished.

"What did you hear?" Buck pushed.

"As the car sunk, I heard…whistling."

"Whistling? I thought you said there wasn't anyone else around."

"There wasn't. I know it's impossible, but I heard someone whistling."

Buck nodded. "I believe you. Inspector Walsh doesn't. Son, if I can help you, I will. This whole thing stinks."

Manlosa shook Buck's hand. "Thank you, Sheriff. I have a report to file."

Whistling. How about that? "Best get to it, then, Trooper."

Once Manlosa was in his cruiser and backing away, Buck moseyed over toward Inspector Walsh. A third-generation lawman, Buck had been sheriff of Giles County for twenty years, nearly unopposed. Buck had seen damn near everything there was to see in this line of work.

He'd seen the body of an infant child left to starve by drug-addict parents, diaper full, belly empty, tiny face still screwed up in its final cries for help. Buck had wanted to shoot the mother so bad that he'd departed the scene. He'd seen a coworker—a friend—jailed for running one of the state's largest methamphetamine rings. Buck had even worked a case where the deputy mayor slaughtered his family after discovering his wife had been unfaithful with a local fireman. He'd allowed his wife to live because he couldn't bear to kill her after murdering her lover. Nasty business, that.

Buck had arrested all manner of pimps, druggies, wife beaters, child predators, drunks, and other kinds of human scum. One of his local children had even fallen prey to Ol' Snapper. His former protégé bagged that bastard up nicely.

This mess on the bridge, however, was beyond all reason.

None of the physical evidence here made sense. Baenziger had stopped her car, thrown up, then jumped off the bridge. Somehow, her car had laid twelve feet of rubber before following her down. Two divers each hauled a half of Hannah Baenziger from the water once the car had been winched to the riverbank and then finally to the road, where it was loaded onto a flatbed. It would have been an operation worth remembering even without the body.

The discovery of Hannah Baenziger had elevated the status of the investigation and mandated the State Bureau of Investigation be informed. Inspector Walsh had taken the case and notified Buck there was a multistate felon being hauled from the New River in pieces.

"What are you thinking, Walsh?" Buck asked. He wasn't the least bit intimidated by Inspector Walsh of the Commonwealth of Virginia Bureau of Investigation. There wasn't a damn thing Walsh could do to him, and they both knew it. Buck had been elected. He enjoyed how the forced familiarity seemed to grate on Walsh's nerves.

"I'm thinking we got a serious cock-up."

"Eeehhhllllluup." Buck nodded in affirmation.

Inspector Walsh cut his eyes over to the fat hillbilly beside him.

"What sort of shitstorm are we talking about, Walsh?"

"You know good and hell well what kind of shitstorm, Buck. A state trooper tossed a girl off this fucking bridge. Then he dropped a Bonneville on her. Killer cop. Press loves a killer cop."

Having seen multiple murderers in his time, Buck knew killers. Trooper Manlosa was no killer. The only thing Buck had seen in his eyes was the shame of public embarrassment and lack of sleep. He would've been willing to bet Manlosa had been on for twelve hours at least, but he wasn't a murderer.

Damned if that was the only way the pieces fit together.

"I'm not one to tell another cop his business"—Buck hitched his belt up—"but that trooper ain't no killer. I know killers, and my gut is telling me he ain't packin' the gear. There's another explanation here we ain't seein'."

"Yeah? No disrespect to your gut, Sheriff, but the only way this works is if Manlosa pushed that bitch off the bridge. Personally, I think he did the world a favor, but the law is the law, and now I have to take down a cop because he aced some junkie whore."

"Why in the world would a young man—an LEO—kill some woman he didn't even know? Don't add up."

"Who cares? Maybe when he lit her up, she wouldn't blow him. What's it matter?"

* * *

At the trial of disgraced State Trooper Amos Manlosa, a jury of his peers found him guilty of first-degree murder. Hannah Baenziger's death was ruled a homicide, and the person convicted of killing her was the one who'd called the crime in. It was theorized in barbershops and beauty salons across the region that he had killed her in self-defense.

No one really believed Amos Manlosa killed Hannah Baenziger, despite rumors of a rejected sexual advance. Sheriff Buck Whitland's sworn deposition, which had been read in the courtroom by Manlosa's defense team, conveyed his belief that an as-yet unidentified person or persons had played a role in the death of Hannah Baenziger. He believed Trooper Manlosa to be a fair and competent law enforcement officer, not a killer or a sexual predator.

The judge in the case sentenced Manlosa to the maximum penalty allowed under the law: death.

CHAPTER SEVEN
A PLAN

"The law ain't gonna help us none. No way we get that reward. No way," RayRay said, crossing his arms across his chest. "They'll find a way to fuck us. You know it."

"RayRay, fuck the 'curse.'" Clem made quote marks in the air when mentioning his family's unfortunate stigma. "I already know local law ain't gonna be any use at all. I told that idiot deputy about her the day I seen her. He didn't do *shit*."

"So, what the fuck do we do? Call this here number? You know feds'll fuck us. Seems a good way to lose out."

"Nah, we ain't gonna call no one. Least of all their damn hotline." Clem leaned down in his cousin's face. "No one. We ain't gonna tell no one."

"Jesus, Clem, back up. Your breath stinks."

"All the same. No one knows other than us. That's how we got to keep it."

RayRay leaned back in the desk chair, interested. "How do we collect if we don't tell no one?"

Clem smiled. "We're going to deliver her is how."

"Deliver her where? Local law? Shit, Clem, we're for sure fucked if we do that. They'll probably lock us both up. I don't want to spend the next ten years sharing a cell with you. No offense."

"Get up. Let me have the captain's seat."

RayRay stood so his cousin could sit in front of the computer. Clem opened a new tab, bringing up Google Maps. "See, RayRay, we know local law ain't worth a fuck. Also, we can't tell no one, else we won't get paid."

Clem brought up a map of Roanoke and zoomed in on an ordinary office building in the city center. "What we're gonna do is take her to Roanoke. We can drop her right the hell off at the FBI field office downtown. No way to deny us then. Plus, once they verify our bounty, boom, instant heroes. Collect our check, then do whatever the hell we feel like. That's how the cow chews the cabbage."

"You want to kidnap a serial killer and deliver her to the FBI field office in Roanoke? Could work, I guess. You know where she is?"

Clem closed the window displaying downtown Roanoke. The browser popped back to the FBI's ten most wanted. "Only that she's still in town. Drives an old Vette. Fifties style. Not many cars like that cruising the streets. I've seen it a couple of times at the Wilco. Wait, what the fuck is this? Where'd her wanted page go?"

Shirley's picture had disappeared from the top ten list. The list was now comprised completely of men, no women—no woman—and no offer of five million dollars for her capture.

"Did they change the fuckin' list?" RayRay asked. "Wouldn't that be just our damn luck."

"Hell, I don't know. You stood there watching me refresh the page a dozen times. The window with her wanted page is gone too. Closed out when I closed out the map. Shit's not even in the browser history."

"How the hell do you know about browser histories?" RayRay asked.

"Gotta hide my porn on the machine at work. Late nights

are fuckin' *slow*. I pass the time best I can." Clem made a jerk off motion. "Don't want to get fired for rubbing one out on company time."

RayRay laughed. "Yeah, that'd be a hell of a thing. Be our luck they took her off the list right when we was looking at her."

Clem glared up at his cousin, annoyed at the off-handed way RayRay brought up the curse. "RayRay, there ain't no curse. McGreggor's been all over the damn news. The website fucked up is all. Don't be stupid."

"Actually, Clem, the website is fine. The Federal Bureau of Investigation has forgotten their former interest in Ms. McGreggor. Leave Shirley alone. The lady is spoken for."

Unbidden, the browser changed tabs back to the video RayRay had paused. The redhead smiled on the screen, swinging her leg over the head of the blonde and sitting up in a graceful motion. Her heavy breasts jiggled with the spent momentum. The blonde stretched out on the bed behind.

Leaning forward, she spoke again. "And there absolutely is a curse on your pathetic line. Better for all if you forget this ridiculous plan. There will be no money."

Clem pushed back from the computer, unable to look away. All the color drained from his face. RayRay, hair standing up all over his body, gauged the distance to the door. "Clem, what'd you do? What's going on?"

"Hush, you. Let the grown-ups speak," said the redhead on the monitor. "Nothing will come from this. The lady is spoken for."

A buzz began in the speakers. The word *mine* repeated over and over, a thousand voices chanting in a disorganized cacophony. Screaming, whispering, insane. Growing louder by the second into intolerable agonizing volume.

Clem clutched his ears, falling out of the chair. The sound brought RayRay to his knees beside him. On the screen, the redhead laughed, pointing, and the blonde shook her head, the two clearly amused by the cousins' pain. The monitor began to smoke. The screen blackened, the two nude women lost to a sparking darkness. Plastic melted and ran down the desk. The smoldering screen burst into flame, enlarging the puddles of molten plastic forming beneath.

RayRay recognized the fire first. Dragging his cousin toward the door, he shouted, "Clem, get up! If that fire ignites the meth, we're dead!" but Clem showed no sign of hearing him over the noise.

While the monitor was completely engulfed in flame now, the noise continued to grow, and Clem's hands did nothing to block the assault. He rolled over, trying to get his feet underneath him as RayRay pulled him by the collar.

RayRay continued to drag him along. Giving up on trying to be heard, he pointed with his free hand toward the barrel of chemicals. Clem got the picture. If the fumes lit, they'd be blown to hell. Nodding his understanding, Clem shook free of RayRay's hold.

RayRay had managed to haul him most of the way to the door. Thick smoke billowed from where the computer sat. *Only a matter of time before the walls catch,* Clem thought. Tremendous heat baked across the living room, making the air that much more noxious. Clem's throat closed as he tried to draw a breath. The noise from the ruined monitor was worse than ever now. RayRay screamed as the doorknob blistered his hand.

The pair fell into the yard. Sweet cool air filled their lungs, and as they tumbled across the threshold, the noise fell mercifully silent. RayRay staggered to his feet first, screaming, "Come on, cousin, before we get blown the fuck up!"

Clem stood, casting a wary glance back into the house. The melted monitor no longer burned. Pools of plastic had hardened into viral-looking growths, with tendrils stretching down the legs of the desk in little globs. Small plastic stalactites had formed over the edge of the desk. No fire burned. No smoke billowed out the front door.

If not for the melted remains of the monitor, Clem wouldn't have believed the fire had happened.

RayRay called from across the street, still believing they were in imminent danger of an explosion. Clem dusted himself off before crossing the street to join him.

* * *

The pair sat on the porch, each looking down toward RayRay's house. Late evening spring fog settled on the mountains and crept into the holler below. Soon the fog thickened, obscuring their view down the drive. For a time neither cousin spoke.

"You, uh, want to talk about it?" RayRay ventured, breaking the oppressive silence.

Clem stared at the late evening fog. RayRay's house was all but hidden in the mist. "Every time we try to do something. Every single fuckin' time!" Clem wasn't talking to RayRay. He was speaking to whatever held his people down. Clem wasn't scared; he was furious. "We ain't responsible for whatever our kin did hundreds of years ago. Can't put it on us. No more. This shit just ain't right. It ain't *fair*. Goddamn it all to hell. I'm tired of always havin' to struggle for every fuckin' inch!"

RayRay drank his beer in silence, watching the fog. Clem didn't get angry often. When he did get riled up, it was best to let him vent it off, cool down. The entire situation *was* completely fucked. His computer caught a haint that damn near burned the house down. Clem ranting all night couldn't compare to fuckery of this degree. Plus, the more he raved, the less RayRay had to think about how and what had just happened. They could have died. Easily.

"We deserve more. I'm tired of always being at the back of the fuckin' bus. Ain't you tired of it?"

"'Course I am. But what can we do about it? Nothin'. There ain't no re-ward now. It's over."

"Ain't nothin' over. There's a whole world outside this valley. Seems to me this thing, whatever our family's been fighting, don't stretch much farther than this valley. Bet you we get clear of here, and there is a re-ward. Bet you we drag that murderin' heifer to the FBI in Roanoke, and we get paid." Clem stopped to take a long pull on his beer. "Yeah," he said, speaking more to the mist than his cousin. "I bet we get paid no problem."

RayRay shrugged. Clem had made up his mind, and RayRay would follow.

"Best we bunk together up here," Clem said. "Ain't no telling what we're in for."

"Sounds good. What are we gonna do now?"

"Well, we get us some good sleep, then in the morning, we see about finding that Corvette. Can't be that hard in a town this size. Bet that fuckin' idiot Roland found it but got scared. We ain't gonna do that. Get scared, I mean. We find her, bag her, and give her a smooth ride to Roanoke. Keep her in the trunk while I go inside to get a feebee. They come out to collect her; we collect ours, then take off for a topless beach somewhere. A couple rich bachelors. We ain't gonna pay no attention to some fuckin' haint tryin' to chase us off. I don't care how big her tits are."

RayRay's eyes glassed over thinking about being rich on a topless beach. Miami had those. He'd been to Florida once—a lot of fine women in Florida. Blue sky, warm water. Being rich in a place like that would make up for a lot of years being poor in southwest Virginia. RayRay rolled a joint, lit it, inhaled deeply, and passed it to Clem. "Rich bachelors, huh?"

"Damn right. And all we need to do is find a woman and take her for a car ride."

"I think we can handle that," RayRay said, sealing his fate.

* * *

Clem woke up to the sound of tires crunching on his gravel driveway. A quick glance at the clock told him it was 3:21 a.m. The first squiggles of fear in his stomach grew as the crunch drew closer. It had been a fucking weird day, and after finishing the joint, the cousins had elected to go to bed. Clem had hit the pillow feeling more contented than he had in years.

He had a plan. A real plan. Roland, being a lying chicken-shit, had set him up to get the hell out of there. A sense of peace he rarely knew had settled over him. Hope. Clem felt hopeful for the future. Confident. Self-assured. An unusual state of mind for someone who usually tried to get through the day without too much hassle.

Clem lived far back on Caseknife Road. No one came back here unless they lived here or had relatives. And no one visited at 3:21 in the morning. Except cops. Cops came knocking at odd hours in hopes of catching you asleep.

The car stopped halfway up the drive, concealed in the shadow between porchlight and streetlight.

Clem grabbed his pistol—a .357 with a nine-inch barrel—from underneath his pillow. He navigated his house easily in the dark, out of his bedroom and into the basement where RayRay slept. Clem crouched next to the couch. RayRay snored on, oblivious to their late-night visitor.

"RayRay! Wake up!" Clem hissed, shaking his cousin's shoulder.

"Huzzat?"

"We got company. Some asshat is parked in the driveway."

At this RayRay came fully awake. Late-night visits were never good. Most ended with someone going away in hand-cuffs. "Cops?"

"Don't think so. They parked halfway up the drive. Just sitting there. I'm going upstairs to get a better look." They could hear a powerful engine idling. Whoever was in the car hadn't made any further move up the driveway.

Clem hustled back up the stairs, pistol gripped in his sweaty palm. Fear tickled across his guts on feathery feet, light and quick. In the darkened living room, Clem crouched beside the couch pushed up against the window, which afforded him cover and concealment. He could see down the drive, but they couldn't see him. From his vantage point, the kitchen door was covered, in case anyone tried to come in.

A heavy thud followed by RayRay cursing announced his arrival. He grabbed the shotgun from underneath the couch. "See anyone yet?"

"I don't."

"Can you make out the car?"

"I can't."

"Me neither."

In the driveway, the car's engine revved—a methodical build from idle to thousands of screaming revolutions per minute and back again. A tide of noise, swelling, peaking, and falling back, over and over. Engine noise echoed off the hills, seemingly magnified by the night mist, and bounced around the houses surrounding it with a mechanical roar.

"Big fuckin' engine," RayRay said.

"Yeah, but they're going to have to do better than waste gas if they're going to scare me. Hang on. Watch the kitchen door. I'm going out there."

Clem snuck from the cover of the couch. Throwing the front door open wide, he stepped onto the porch, arms in the air, pistol clearly displayed. "Hey, motherfucker! You feel like dying tonight?" Clem screamed with a bravado he didn't feel. His balls had drawn up tight, and he had a sickly crawling sensation in his stomach. His thighs shook with adrenaline.

"You gonna fuckin' do something?" Clem forced himself to step off the porch. It was too dark to tell the make and model of the intruder's vehicle. Clem took another step. No sooner had his bare feet landed on his wet lawn than the car's headlights blazed forth. Blinding high beams, flashing hazard lights, even brake lights and reverse lights flared in the darkness, effectively blinding Clem.

The car horn began to blare and then mutated into screams of pain. Thousands of people screaming. Clem's nerve broke. He ran back into the house to see RayRay had not moved from his position on the other side of the couch, only now, he was hunkered below the window. With the shotgun across his chest, he appeared to be praying. The chaos in the driveway intensified as the tires screeched, throwing gravel. Light invaded the house, painting insane patterns on the walls as the car spun out of control in the yard. Rocks thrown from underneath the tires crashed against the siding, adding an unnerving rattle to the deafening scream of the horn. Clem slammed the door and bolted it, as if that offered any protection from the screaming metal demon in the yard. Sinking against the wall, Clem joined his cousin in prayer.

Stop, stop! Please, God, make it stop! Clem chanted to himself over and over.

Then it was dark again. Quiet. Still.

Through silence almost as unnerving as the previous cacophony, Clem stood and unlocked the door.

"Don't do that. Don't let it in," RayRay whispered from his place on the floor.

Ignoring his cousin's plea, Clem stepped back onto the porch. The car sat idling under the streetlight in plain view. A Corvette. An old fifties-style Corvette. Clem stared as the car drove off. Another warning. She knew where they lived. Must have been her who hacked RayRay's computer. Somehow, she knew they were onto her.

Once the Vette cruised out of sight, Clem turned back to the house. The yard was torn all to hell. No biggie. Once he had his re-ward, he'd never set foot on this property again.

"Wh-Who was it?" RayRay asked.

"Same bitch that hacked your machine this afternoon. She'll

be fuckin' sorry she messed with us once she's bagged up in my trunk."

"Shirley did that?"

"Or some bitch driving her car. I'd know that Corvette anywhere. Must have been her on the computer. Bet she has some kind of monitor on the FBI website. That has to be how she knew we was looking at it. Figured we was looking to cash in and traced us. Showed up tonight hoping to scare us off. Ain't happening."

Even as he said it, it sounded impossible to Clem, like a crazy television show. But his story seemed to be calming RayRay down, so Clem stuck with it. How the hell this could have happened was beyond him, but he was determined to collect his reward, and nothing on earth was going to stop him.

"Come on. I don't think she'll be back. Probably rolling down Caseknife laughing her tits off. Her time's coming. Let's head back to bed. Tomorrow, we'll start hunting her."

RayRay nodded, not quite as pale as he had been.

Clem went back upstairs. He'd had a strange damn day but passed off the experience with a logical, albeit thin, explanation. He set his .357 back underneath his pillow within easy reach, glancing out the window at his ruined lawn. From this higher vantage point, he could clearly see a message dug into the grass that had been invisible from the ground level. Clem went cold as he stared at the word: *MINE*.

CHAPTER EIGHT
THE SATURDAY FARMERS MARKET

S hirley had never been happier and had never enjoyed a job as much as she did working for Solomon at the Maple Lodge. Solomon was ever the gentleman, always a witty conversationalist. Always polite, friendly, and never tried to get any special attention from her. His appetite didn't seem to extend past their professional friendship. Solomon was a bit unusual, but Shirley found his quirkiness refreshing nonetheless.

They'd talked about the killer police officer who had apparently attacked the harlot who'd stayed in number four when Shirley first started working. Shocking! Shirley recognized her type right away from the way Solomon had described her: a dirty girl about dirty business. He'd known she'd try to skip on her bill. He tightened her right up. Solomon wasn't one to be cheated by some hussy.

Shirley woke at 4:00 a.m. and began the process of preparing breakfast for the guests. Solomon—bless him—didn't seem to sleep at all. The poor dear spent most of his time near the fire, and she wondered if he had a chill. He was awake when Shirley went to bed and was there when she woke up in the morning.

Maybe she would get him a nice chamomile tea. Tea always helped her sleep.

After breakfast, Shirley would tidy the rooms or prepare the shopping list for the evening's meal. A trip to the grocery store was on her to-do list for this morning. Solomon never seemed to have much of an appetite either, but he obviously recognized her superior palate and left the entrée selection entirely to her sophisticated culinary sense. This was one of the things Shirley enjoyed the most: her autonomy. Solomon trusted her with every aspect of the business despite only knowing her a short time.

Well, like attracts like, as her dear mother used to say.

After cleaning up the breakfast dishes, Shirley went back to her lodgings. Employee quarters weren't as nice as the guest suites at the lodge, though they suited Shirley. Her room was homey, and even better, it was hers. Sure, she'd lived in larger places, had more square footage, but Solomon Drury and his Maple Lodge radiated an otherworldly air previously missing from her life. Solomon was respectful, charming in a cultured, civilized way. Funny without being crude. Being near him felt as if she'd returned to a better place in time. She loved sitting on the porch overlooking the quaint downtown of Summit Valley. Working there didn't feel at all like work to her. She felt she was taking care of a large extended family. Her family.

Shirley felt she'd come home. Finally.

She put on her face, not noticing how her earring slid through the flesh before dropping to the floor with a *tink,* as she prepared to do the morning errands.

* * *

Caden Quesenberry prepared for a champion fight with his parents. "You could have knocked the way a human being is supposed to!" Caden jerked open the passenger door and threw his bookbag on his mother's feet, then pulled up short. He was surprised to see his father behind the wheel. Dad almost never left the house since losing his job.

Before Caden's mother could speak, his father growled, "Boy, who do you think you're talking to? You forget what your mother looks like?"

Caden didn't want to deal with Angry Dad. The dark circles under his eyes told Caden Dad hadn't slept much last night. Mom had probably gotten him up before he was ready so they could have some family time. There was already enough family time for Caden. They were home together all the time unless Caden was in school.

His father loved him and never beat on him. Caden thought of his father as a force of nature. Mighty. Terrible. Eternal. A mountain of a man who never compromised, never negotiated. His father expected immediate obedience and wouldn't tolerate anything less. Caden did what he was told, or Dad would make him do what he was told. Simple.

His mother tended to give him a slap with the fly swatter if she couldn't find the belt. Dad relied on pure threat, which was somehow worse than Mom's actual violence. Caden's house wasn't a dangerous one. He knew kids at school and lots of kids at the apartments whose parents beat them routinely. His parents loved him. They cared enough to expect better from him. Standards must be maintained. Hard times for the family didn't change that.

She could have come to the door.

Caden stepped back after retrieving his bookbag from his mother's feet. She raised the lever so her seat would slide forward. Caden tossed his bag to the far side and crawled into the back. Small seats, normally folded into the wall of the cab, faced each other instead of facing forward. Caden started to sit down in his usual spot behind his mother but reconsidered the wisdom of his seating. He moved his bag to sit behind his father instead. Probably better to remain hard to reach. Those dark circles warned of trouble.

As he buckled his seat belt, his mother waved to Mrs. Burdette before sliding the passenger seat back into place. "Did you have fun with Logan, honey?" Mom asked, completely ignoring the gathering tension in the car.

Caden didn't want to go to the market. Staying with Logan and playing *Diablo* would have been a fine way to spend his Saturday. Family time was completely overrated. Most of the time, they didn't even talk to each other, so what was the big deal?

"Honking in the driveway is rude. You embarrassed me!"

"Dad wanted to surprise you. No one was being rude. I'm sorry you feel that way." Mom was using her patient tone. Caden didn't know the word *condescending*, though something in her tone frustrated him. He imagined her saying, *See, we're really all good here. You'd know that if you weren't so dumb!*

Caden wasn't dumb. He might not have been as smart as Logan, but he wasn't dumb. "How did Dad being here prevent you from walking up and knocking?"

"Boy," his father warned, watching him in the rearview mirror.

His mother placed a soothing hand on his father's forearm. The truck still sat idling in Logan's driveway. "Let's not do this," Mom pleaded. "Can't we have a nice day as a family?"

Caden grunted a response and folded himself up as tight as he could. Maintaining an angry posture was difficult in the tiny seat, but Caden gave it his best. Dad stared at him in the rearview mirror for another long moment before putting the truck in gear and driving away from Logan's house.

* * *

Sheriff Buck Whitland wasn't happy with the way things were shaping up for Trooper Manlosa. Guy was getting railroaded, and Buck needed the why of it. It didn't make sense to ruin the life of, by all accounts, a decent trooper.

Buck's dedication to the truth could end up costing him the job of sheriff. The papers were painting Manlosa as a devil, a killer cop. It wasn't right, and Buck was determined to find out what really happened. He had enough of a reputation that he could ask some questions and people would give him the truth. Buck was counting on name recognition to aid in his investigation.

And he planned to call in a celebrity investigator.

* * *

Five million dollars is a powerful incentive. For two weeks, Clem and RayRay's fantasy of being rich motivated them to take nightly drives throughout the streets of Summit Valley. Every night, they drove deserted avenues, side streets, and alleys; passing houses, inspecting driveways, and searching parking lots.

Two weeks of unsuccessful searching. Nothing.

RayRay, who still hadn't gone home after the incident with his computer, brewed a new batch of meth in the woods behind Clem's house. Clem, grateful for the extra income, went to collect supplies from RayRay's living room. He had called off sick frequently from the Wilco in his desire to find Shirley.

Probably be fired soon, if I'm not already.

RayRay's house smelled of burnt plastic and stagnant cat piss. The monitor seemed to be the only casualty. RayRay's keyboard stuck to the desk in a plastic pool along with the mouse. The mousepad was buried beneath a layer of melted monitor, but Clem could still partially make out the picture of a random bikini model forever preserved beneath dark plastic. Clem shrugged and walked over to the lab to pack up the essentials his cousin needed to make his product with a list RayRay had left on the kitchen table for reference.

Car loaded with supplies, Clem drove up his driveway, bypassing the house. He drove through his damaged yard and stopped at the tree line. RayRay met him, helped him unload, and went back to whatever it was he did. The area stank of chemicals. Two weeks, and the smell was tremendous! Clem, grateful to leave him to it, turned the car around. This time, he parked in front of the house.

He took a map off the passenger seat and moved to his usual spot on the porch. After scooting his side table around in front of his chair, Clem spread out his map of Summit Valley. Heavy red X's drawn through outlying neighborhoods, apartment complexes, and side streets marked out previously searched areas. The two main areas he had left to search were downtown and Dora Highway. Less highway and more residential drive, Dora skirted Summit Valley and followed Peak Creek out to Route 99, which eventually met up with Interstate 81.

Several promising neighborhoods branched south, their houses dotting the hills and overlooking the creek. Lots of places a fugitive could hide. Not from Clem though; he was determined. He was less concerned with downtown. There weren't many places to hide there. The old furniture factory might've been a good spot to check, but Clem doubted his quarry would rough it in an abandoned factory.

No, a lady like that slept on a mattress in a proper bedroom.

While Clem was involved in tracing out the evening's route to cover the most area in the least time, he never noticed RayRay leave. Never heard RayRay say he was off to sell the batch of product he'd made.

* * *

Tires grinding gravel brought Clem up from his map. He'd highlighted one route that covered half of the neighborhoods sprouting off Dora Highway and had worked out a second for tomorrow night's search. Glancing up from the map, back cracking painfully, a sliver of fear shot up Clem's spine that drew his testicles up tight. The Corvette cruised toward him, intent on crushing him between the grill and his house. Blinking the sun out of his eyes, he jumped to his feet to dodge the Vette.

"What the hell is wrong with you, cousin?" RayRay asked, his face a quizzical mask of concern. RayRay stood beside his old pickup, pulling a fat wad of greasy bills from his pocket. "We got paid today! My little bit of whoop chicken sold for $1,500! Got me a bigger, better quality batch cooking right now worth a lot more! Red said I'm the best small batcher he knows."

Clem nodded, failing to catch his cousin's enthusiasm. Residual fear made him grumpy. "You scared me 'bout half to death! Thought that fuckin' car was back."

Nodding like he understood, RayRay said, "We should forget this bounty thing. Red'll buy everything I bring him. We could cook our way out of here."

Stupid bastard doesn't understand anything, Clem thought but didn't say.

"RayRay, you made $1,500 for two weeks' worth of work. How many weeks do you think we'll need to make $5 million? All at once."

RayRay's expression fell. "Sorry, Clem. I didn't think—"

"Exactly. You didn't think. I'm doing the thinking for us both. Long term. Your cooks can keep us going in the meantime. I'm grateful for 'em, but we're going to need real money to get out of here. Plus, how do you explain your income to the tax man? They got fuckin' Al Capone on taxes. You ain't no Al Capone. We get this bounty, that's long-term money. Legal."

RayRay dropped the money on Clem's map before sulking his way to the kitchen. Clem sat back down, feeling much better. RayRay paused at the door. "Yeah. Legal. Whatever. By the way, I saw the damn car."

Clem's head whipped around. "Where?"

Enjoying the sudden role reversal, RayRay took his time walking into the kitchen. He pulled a beer from the fridge, opened it, and took a long pull. Casually, he turned back to the porch, where Clem was blocking the doorway.

"I said where, goddamn it!"

"I heard you the first time. Since you want to be such an asshole, maybe I'll forget where I saw it. Maybe I'll tell Red about the bounty and go get it with him. Gotta think about the future, 'cause I ain't no Al Capone."

"RayRay, we're family. I swear I'm being like this for us. Help me."

"Apologize."

Five million dollars. Five million dollars. Five million dollars. Clem repeated the mantra in his head. Swallowing his pride for such a sum was a small price to pay. If RayRay needed to feel like a boss for a moment, Clem would oblige him. *I can always drown his stupid ass in a hot tub once we're rich.*

"Fine." Clem sighed a drawn-out exaggerated breath. "I'm sorry I'm trying to bring us to better days."

"No. Not good enough."

"Sorry I was being a sandy butt-reaming asshat. Better?"

"Better."

The cousins stared at each other across the yellow light of the kitchen, each fighting not to smile.

"Where the fuck did you see it, you big baby?"

"Saw it parked outside the factory." RayRay pronounced it *fac-tree.*

"Tomorrow is the farmers market. Let's take us a ride into town."

"Clem, we should let this go."

"Stay here, then. I ain't letting five million dollars go 'cause you're a big pussy."

* * *

RayRay's cheeks flushed. The whole deal stank. Couldn't Clem feel how bad this was? He ignored the danger in favor of obsessing over the reward. RayRay had lost interest back when his monitor burst into flame. This shit was weird. Wrong. What good did $5 million dollars do a dead man? Being the richest motherfucker in the cemetery made you just as dead. Still, the thought of Clem believing him a coward pushed him beyond his own good sense.

"Saw it parked near the loading docks. I'll be ready when you are."

"Good." Clem smiled. "Tomorrow, we'll go buy some veggies."

* * *

At the shrill ringing of his phone, Aron Weaver woke from a familiar nightmare in which he pulled the trigger on an innocent. Stockmore hadn't been innocent, but that minor fact didn't seem to slow down the nightmares any. Weaver's drinking was worse; the house was a wreck. Whenever Mars came around, he gave these concerned glances whenever he thought Weaver wasn't paying attention.

Where the fuck was the damn phone?

He'd crashed on the couch. Bottles of beer sat in clusters around an empty pizza box. Dead soldiers. He'd killed them too. Weaver didn't remember ordering the pizza, couldn't remember the last time he'd eaten. The phone fell mercifully silent.

Weaver sat up and rubbed his face. He couldn't remember the last time he'd showered either. *I'm getting ripe here. Jesus, the couch is even starting to stink.* While checking the empties around the coffee table for some hair of the dog and finding them empty, Weaver managed to locate the phone.

A shower, four Aleve, and some different clothes had Weaver feeling almost human. The clothes might not have been fresh from the laundry, but they passed the sniff test. *Fuck it. I'm retired.* While waiting on a K-Cup to top off his brandy, the phone rang again. This time, it was in his pocket, and Weaver managed to find it before losing the call. The screen read *Old Fart*. Buck was calling.

Weaver had worked for Buck as a rookie. Buck was a mentor and a friend, and the two had kept in touch as Weaver moved on to other assignments and departments. Weaver wasn't a bit surprised the old man's career had outlasted his own. Buck was a warhorse. They didn't make 'em like Buck anymore.

Per the papers, Buck's opinions about a killer trooper were causing the community he'd served for twenty-odd years to finally turn on him. Another sheriff might finally be elected in Giles County.

"What are you calling me for, you mean old bastard? I got troubles enough without you."

"Weaver, my boy! How's retirement treating you?"

Rubbing his temples, which were beginning to throb, Weaver replied, "Can't complain. No one would care if I did."

"You sound drunk. I interrupt a bender? Did I wake you?"

Weaver could imagine the line of concern forming between Buck's eyebrows. Weaver thought he was doing all right; he was upright and had even showered. But Buck knew. Somehow, he always knew. Knowing made him such an effective sheriff. You couldn't lie to him. Buck saw the lie before it ever crossed the lips. Apparently, he could do it over the phone too. Weaver wondered if Mars had called him. "I don't sleep much. Hell, Buck, I killed a guy."

"Couldn't be helped."

"Think so? I killed him because I was mad. I couldn't stand to see him get away with killing children. You know he would have. He knew it too."

"Son, someday you'll have to come to grips with the fact that in this job"—Buck spoke as if Weaver were still police—"there are times you'll have to do the wrong thing for the right reasons. Doesn't make you a bad guy. It doesn't make you one of them. You're protecting the prey from the predators. That's all you did. You put down a rabid predator. It's the job. Can't say I'd have done any different."

Weaver wanted to believe his friend. He wanted to believe Mars too. But he couldn't. They weren't there.

"Aron, you still there?"

Weaver imagined that wrinkle between Buck's eyes deepening. "Yeah, Buck, I'm here. I guess you're right."

"'Course I am. Anyway, I didn't call to listen to you piss and moan. If you're done, Suzy, I have some work for you."

Back to business. Weaver laughed in spite of himself. Buck was that kind of guy—tough, fair, oddly gentle in a rough redneck kind of way. "All right, you dusty fart, what do you want?"

"Be a shame to have to tell your boyfriend how you got your ass kicked by a wrinkly old man. He wouldn't ask what happened, he'd ask—"

"How in the hell I got away." Weaver finished the familiar joke.

"Right. You remember the Manlosa case?"

"The trooper who pitched some hooker off a bridge when she wouldn't give him any?"

"Well, yes and no. He's probably going to be convicted of it. I don't believe he'd drop anyone off a bridge, much less an interstate felon. Whole damn case is hinky, and I can't stand seeing an honest man on death row. The Commonwealth takes a dim view of police who kill, and they're going to execute him, innocence be damned."

"Good. We have enough trouble with our reputation without psycho cops killing civilians."

"Are you still drinking, or are you trying to piss me off? I need you to listen. Manlosa didn't kill the Baenziger woman. She was dead before he got there. Someone else was there, and we need to find out who that someone is. Manlosa told me the night it happened that he heard someone whistling. Who was whistling? I've called in a few favors, and I've managed to track

Hannah's movements through the last week of her life. She ran from Miami and her small-time dealer boyfriend, ditched their car in the Carolinas. She stole another—the Bonneville that ended up cutting her in half—and abandoned the interstate in favor of the highways and byways of Virginia. I have her on security film filling up at a gas station in Summit Valley two days before Manlosa found her."

"A whistle? Pretty thin, Buck. Summit Valley is a nice town. She stayed a couple of extra days to enjoy the small-town charm."

"Are these the actions of someone looking to soak up the country ambience? She was running, Aron. She was hiding. The boyfriend was found burned to death in an oil drum, by the way. Fisherman dragged the barrel off the bottom of the ocean. You know who burns people in oil drums and drops them in the ocean?"

"Someone awful mad."

"The cartel, Aron. The cartel burns people in oil drums. The cartel can cause someone to run so scared they leave everything they own. A woman whose boyfriend does a stupid thing and gets on the wrong side of the cartel could very well have been running for her life. She could have thought she was safe in Summit Valley, but then something tipped her off that her boyfriend's killers were close. So, she runs, but not quite fast enough. They catch her right down the road in Pearisburg and throw her off a bridge. She isn't dead, so they drop her car on top of her."

Weaver zoned out when Buck began ranting about the shadowy fingers of conspiracy murdering insignificant hoods. Even if Buck was right, there wouldn't be any way to prove it. Colombian death squads running amok made for a tough sell to a jury. International crime rings weren't typically the root of criminal activity in southwest Virginia. Why bother? Manlosa would wind up just as dead.

Instead of antagonizing his mentor—the old guy still

deserved respect—Weaver asked, "Okay, assuming this isn't pure conjecture, and there is some conspiracy—and that's a big damn if—what can we do about it? Where did the bad guys go? Manlosa never reported seeing anyone else."

Brightening, Buck said, "Glad to hear you're thinking like a cop. I'm on my way to Summit Valley to see if anyone there remembers her. She probably stayed at the Red Carpet since it has the closest access to the interstate. I bet she saw someone, and it scared her. I'm also willing to bet someone will remember another person asking questions about her. I want you to help."

"Buck, I'm not a cop anymore."

"Well, yes and no."

"No, just no. There isn't a gray area here. I have zero legal authority to conduct investigations. I bet I'd get arrested for impersonating an officer."

"Are you going to help me, or am I dealing with a drunken washed-up nut suck?"

"Ouch. Harsh."

"Then get your ass off the couch and help me. Meet me at the railway station in Summit Valley. There's a farmers market held there every Saturday when the weather's warm. I'll deputize you so you don't have to worry."

"Fine."

"That's my boy. And Weaver?"

"What?"

"Leave the booze at home."

* * *

Buck hung up the phone, feeling supremely pleased with himself. Mars had called to tell him that since the retirement, Aron had lain around the house wallowing in guilt and alcohol. Apparently, Aron wasn't listening to Mars, wouldn't even talk about it, and Mars was scared Aron might graduate from depression to worse. Possibly suicide. Police and military had significantly higher rates of suicide than Joe Public, as Buck well knew. Buck wondered, not for the first time, if the two were queer for each other. Not that it mattered to him, but still, who pitched? Who received?

Satisfaction from motivating Weaver to get off the damn couch quickly turned sour when Buck's search at the Red Carpet didn't yield any leads. No one remembered seeing the Baenziger girl. The clerk even got snippy about answering questions, asking, "Don't police talk to each other?" Buck decided to go early and ask around at the farmers market.

Nah, this is thin. I'm chasing shadows here. Cartel at the Saturday farmers market? I'm getting daft in my old age.

Buck parked the truck—an ancient Ford F-150 with almost as much mileage as the owner —excited to see what the market had in store for him.

* * *

Shirley went to the Food City first because they were having a sale on meats. While she preferred a competent butcher, there didn't seem to be one in this tiny town. People seemed content to buy their meat at Walmart; Shirley was not eating meat from there. The grocery store would probably be the best cuts she could get until she became familiar with the area. With any luck, she'd eventually locate a farmer willing to butcher a cow. Solomon might have a suggestion should she remember to ask him. After stocking up on some rather thin steaks, she headed over to National Linen for crisp new tablecloths and napkins.

A rude clerk shoved a bag of linen wrapped in clear plastic into her chest before she could even say what she wanted. Solomon must have placed the order. The clerk disappeared into the back before Shirley could speak to him about his poor customer service.

Someone in the back exclaimed, "Jesus! What the fuck is that smell?"

Another—presumably the rude clerk—answered, "Shut. Up. He's hired another one."

The voices fell silent, and the workers didn't reappear from wherever they were hiding. No one else was around, so instead of standing at the counter feeling offended, Shirley decided to leave.

Oddly, there wasn't a receipt. Perhaps Solomon had an account. Business was handled differently in small towns. She would have never handed a bag of goods to someone with no way to track the inventory. Well, she had what she needed, anyway. Dinner was going to be spectacular. Solomon said there would be a new guest tonight, and Shirley was determined to make an impression with dinner.

On a whim, she decided to see what the farmers market had to offer. She was only a few blocks away. Managing to find some fresh peppers and onions or perhaps some baby spinach might salvage these criminally thin steaks. An outdoor market might have fresh goat cheese. Some grilled parmesan broccoli or roasted sweet potatoes with cilantro pesto would work with what she had planned. A farmers market would be the ideal place to pick up some fresh herbs. She couldn't very well make pesto without fresh basil. Everyone knew you needed fresh basil to make decent pesto.

Shirley was so involved in searching each vendor for the perfect ingredients, she never noticed the man staring at her. She turned, shocked as the rest of the crowd, when he screamed and started running, sweaty and red-faced, toward her.

Buck couldn't believe it. Shirley Goddamn McGreggor. Sipping bottled coconut water and shopping among ordinary regular people. Buck would have called it in. In fact, he was feeling for his cell but had forgotten it in his truck. A part of him knew if he went for his phone, she'd be gone, and he'd never find her. The first real taste of spring weather had brought a large crowd, and Buck had had to park three blocks from the market grounds. Three blocks down to grab the phone from the truck and call a uniformed cop. Then turn around, hustle three blocks back and try to locate her in the sea of people. Right.

Most of the nation's law enforcement community was looking for the evil heifer standing in front of him. Buck was confused as to why she wasn't reacting to his presence until he realized he wasn't in uniform. He'd thought dressing down would make people feel less intimidated, more willing to speak. He hadn't even brought his sidearm. He looked like anyone else. Cursing himself for leaving the phone charging, Buck looked around for someone to ask to use theirs.

If he went for a phone, he'd lose her. If he went to grab her, maybe he could hold on to her long enough for someone to call the police. But a woefully misinformed do-gooder, meaning well, might believe Buck was attacking a defenseless lady, and Buck didn't need a fight. Shirley would escape in the chaos and be in the wind. Where was Aron? He couldn't wait.

There wasn't a choice.

"Of course there is, dog. There's always a choice. You can't swallow losing."

Buck turned to the voice. There was no one there. Anonymous market goers flowed indifferently around him. Turning back, he saw Shirley had moved away from a stand, having paid for her basil. The crowd pressed in around him, moving him away from where Shirley had stopped to inspect broccoli.

"Things won't go well for you if you decide to pursue this. Shirley belongs to me."

The same voice, this time on the left. Turning revealed no one there. Buck was being toyed with. The voice was in his head, and yet, not.

Unsatisfied with the broccoli, Shirley moved across the aisle to another stand.

"She is not such easy prey. You're making a mistake, Sheriff Whitland."

Buck felt the breath on the back of his neck. A quick glance back confirmed what he already knew: no one stood directly behind him. Still, Buck had never seen crowds this thick at a Saturday market. He was bumped and jostled farther and farther from Shirley. His heart pounded, and he'd broken a sweat pushing against a relentless tide. Buck felt he was in one of those slow-motion nightmares where no matter how hard you run, you can't escape the monster behind you.

Except the monster was in front of him, and Buck was trying to catch her.

Finally, a gap!

Buck roared and charged, pushing his way through the crowd.

"Shirley! Stop!"

Belly jiggling and moving much too slowly, Buck charged toward the fugitive as fast as his body would allow. He'd tried to keep in shape, but too many rich dinners, too much politics, and not enough time in the gym had softened him. Amazingly, Shirley continued to watch his approach. She didn't run. She stood at the booth, broccoli in one hand, bottle in the other. A look of mild disapproval on her face pulled the corners of her mouth toward the ground. She could have been his wife standing there, slightly embarrassed but resigned to his shenanigans. Could have been, except that when he grabbed her upper arm—the broccoli arm—she broke the bottle she was holding and brought the jagged shards across his ample belly, then back, widening the gash.

She took a quick step back, dropping the bottle while keeping hold of the vegetables. Buck felt something wet and heavy land on his feet. *Those are my guts. She's killed me with a damn bottle.* He tried to pull his intestines back into his body. He stepped on a rope of his own small intestine and slipped. The slip jerked more of his insides onto the ground. The broccoli vendor threw up on his vegetables.

Buck was being rolled over with no clear memory of having fallen. The pain in his belly was intense, worse than anything he'd ever felt. Someone was whining, mewling—a sound not dissimilar to a hungry kitten. Buck realized it was him. Blood —*must be mine*—blended with the spilled remainder of Shirley's coconut water, forming pink splashes on the ground. *Hell, this place ain't crowded at all.* A boy watched, mouth frozen in an O before his parents jerked him away. Aron appeared, fighting through the circle of people gathered around Buck.

Surrounding noises faded.

"Buck! Oh Buck. Oh Jesus. What happened? Someone call an ambulance! Call 911, damn it!"

Aron was here. Good, that was good. Aron would catch her.

"Aron…"

"I'm here, Buck. I'm here."

"Should have listened. Should have…"

And while he was thinking of what he should have done, Buck Whitland, Sheriff of Giles County, died.

CHAPTER NINE
SECOND INTERLUDE: THE RUMPUS ROOM

Tyrell "TJ" Jackson was a playa. In this corner of Virginia, he was *the* playa. No one had hustle like Tyrell. He knew the game better than anyone. TJ had more game than Milton Bradley. Whether rolling in his Caddy, chillin' with the homies, or whatever the fuck, TJ believed he could walk through brick walls.

TJ sold weed here and there, had moved some stolen televisions, but he'd struck gold when he discovered ransomware. Drugs and stolen goods got too much attention. TJ didn't have a college degree, never needed one. He'd been working the streets from Miami to Los Angeles since he was a boy. Tyrell was smart—too smart to work a day job for shit pay.

TJ realized early the money-making potential of the net. He'd learned about networking, intercepting email, data mining through spyware or malware, penetrating networks, and of course, the selling of all that personal data. The work was solid, safe, and for years had been extremely difficult to prosecute. TJ might have made a comfortable living as an information security expert, but day jobs were for suckas. TJ did whatever the fuck he wanted whenever the fuck he wanted to do it, but he made sure to pay taxes. On paper, he looked like a moderately successful computer consultant.

TJ loved taking over someone's personal machine, then locking them out. Even small businesses usually had an IT person on staff, so he stayed away from businesses. He listed himself as a computer repair expert specializing in software issues and let the people call him to come undo his own work. If they didn't call, TJ would remotely search the hard drive for any personal or credit information and sell that instead. If he received a call from someone he hadn't locked up, he would go, pirate anything sensitive, collect a repair fee, then sell the information he found. It was glorious.

And no one shot at him.

The people who called him were usually elderly or not computer savvy. They stared at him as if he were Yoda raising the X-wing from the swamp instead of merely unlocking their computer. It's why TJ made house calls despite the danger. Usually, he entered a simple four-digit code into the Syskey, rendering the computer user unable to log on. After erasing the Syskey, he'd give the owner a lecture about websites they should stay away from. Husbands and sons would hang their heads, shamefaced, thinking it was their jerk-off porn habits that had caused the trouble.

TJ was a shark—or better yet, a spider, and the net was his feeding ground. The po-po couldn't touch him, and his savings grew larger every year. As soon as law enforcement began to catch on to what he was doing, he'd switch it up and disappear. Plus, he moved a lot because he dug the travel. He'd hustled in nearly every major city in the United States. TJ thought one day he'd make some serious money and move to Nigeria to live the life of the African king he was.

Recently, the Charlotte area had started heating up after the local ISPs began to circulate notices about his business. Better to be gone before those circulated warnings transformed into warrants for arrest, so he'd switched Charlotte, North Carolina, for Roanoke, Virginia. TJ was never going to jail. Only one thing better than taking a fool's money.

Pussy.

And he was rough. Thirteen inches and fat like a yam. With white girls, he didn't treat them gently. He choked them. He beat them. Here in trailer-park-land, there were so many cracker-ass snowflake bitches who couldn't wait to give him that ass. And the only thing better than a young girl was a married one.

TJ loved fucking married women.

No sweeter revenge than throwing the meat to some bitch and letting her husband know he'd wrecked her pussy with his fat black dick. Sometimes it was because of women, not the law, that TJ had to skip town. Angry and humiliated husbands had come looking for him before. TJ was a lover, a hustler, but he most definitely was not a fighter. Better to fuck and run, hit it raw dog and bail, than knuckle up. No thanks, fuck that shit. Besides, he'd never met a bitch worth carrying an ass whoopin' for.

This latest one was a peach. He'd gone to a town called Nilbud to "fix" a computer. Neighborhood was nice in a white bread Beaver Cleaver kind of way. His Cadillac blended in perfectly. His dark skin, not so much. The house was a brick ranch like the rest of them. TJ didn't give a fuck. Let the crackers live in their ugly fucking houses.

He rang the doorbell, and a sweet piece answered. Bored housewife irritated her computer wasn't working. When she saw him, TJ swore he could smell her getting wet. He was a good-looking guy, and he knew the right bullshit to say to make women drop their drawers. He checked the family photos in the hall and saw not only was Mama hot, but there were also two fuckable teenage daughters in the house as well. Fucking jackpot, baby.

He took his time fixing the computer. Her name was Wren—probably had dope-smoking hippie parents. She'd met her husband in college, then gotten pregnant and decided to leave school to raise babies while he went to work. TJ had heard this same bullshit story a million fucking times, but his ability to pretend he gave a fuck was one of his greatest assets. He listened to her talk about her daughters and then shifted the conversation back to her. Bitches loved talking about themselves.

He'd have to take care of this one. Three prime cunts were in desperate need of long dick lovin'. What a great day. He made $500 unlocking Wren's laptop. As he was getting ready to leave, she gave him her cell number and told him to call during the day when the hubby was at work. No problem. TJ was his own boss.

He fucked Wren all winter long. For a white girl, she wasn't half bad, taking everything he gave her, always wanting more. He probably wasn't going to get her girls in the mix though. Wren was extremely protective. Another growing issue for TJ: they'd used up most of the motels in the area. He was starting to be recognized at the Super 8, Holiday Inn Express, Dogwood, even the Red Carpet Inn. The rest of his usual places he took bitches to were starting to recognize him as well.

That wouldn't do.

In tight-knit communities, there was a serious risk of some maid or desk jockey recognizing one of his girlies, then telling her husband about it. Bitches loved drama. He'd heard of a brother fucking some girl up here. Her family came up from Tennessee, hung him in Woodgate Park. Rumor was they set him on fire, cut his balls off, ran over him, shot him, stabbed him, and dumped what remained of his body in the creek. TJ did not need that shit in his life.

Klan was active here too. Might be time to move on, even though he really wanted to fuck Wren's daughters before he hit the bricks. Even better would be to have them at the same time. But Wren was too protective of the girls.

TJ drove down a mountainside located in a low-rent neighborhood in a low-rent town called Summit Valley. He'd "fixed" a computer for fifty bones way back in the mountains off Caseknife Road. There wasn't enough money here to make his hustle worth it. Too much risk, not enough reward.

Caseknife became Commerce Street, and the Cadillac cruised along at twenty-five miles an hour. From a red light, he could see the park where the farmers market was held. Flashing emergency lights could be seen crying for attention. Radio said some fat cop got dealt with. Fucking tough luck for him.

The light changed to green. He made his turn. The park disappeared from both his rearview mirror and his thoughts as he settled into a pleasant fantasy of mother and daughters. Five smooth blocks later, he made a right on Fifth Street, intending to follow it all the way back to Nilbud when he saw it: the Maple Lodge.

Perfect.

No one ever went there. Guarding the lot was a lone Corvette gathering dust. A bed-and-breakfast couldn't be used more than once or twice. *Yeah. Once for the mother. Another round for the daughters? Not likely. But a guy can dream.* Pulling in, TJ decided reservations for two would be in order. Place wasn't the greatest, but what the fuck?

A creepy woman gave him the key—an actual key—for room number six after taking his information. Some fucking weirdo was staring into the fire. TJ ignored him. He always paid cash for his recreational activities. The creepy heifer behind the counter—not bad for an older lady —was happy to take the fifty he'd made earlier. Not a bad deal at all, really.

TJ drove to Wren's house next with a smile on his face and 2Pac's "California Love" blasting from his speakers. Wren had said her husband would be going to some truck builders conference in Las Vegas. He'd be gone for a solid week, but TJ wasn't allowed to stay the night because, as Wren put it, "*I have neighbors!*"

He could throw it to Wren one last time, send her husband a custom video of his wife enjoying his black magic at the hotel, and then find a new spot. She'd been fun for the winter, but TJ was feeling the urge to move along.

Afterward, he could give one of those neighbors of hers a phone call and get the rumor mill rolling. Or send one of them a video of how industrious Wren could be working a cock. Christmas cards for the extended family with Mama doing her thing were always fun. It would certainly liven up the next neighborhood block party. Breaking families was almost as much fun as breaking computers.

Wren's schedule didn't allow her to come to the Maple Lodge immediately—PTA meeting or some shit. She said she'd meet him at the Maple Lodge after her girls went to bed. With nothing to do except wait, TJ decided to drive back to the lodge and get things ready. He'd take a shower, maybe binge The Punisher depending on the Wi-Fi.

Pulling back into the parking lot, TJ noticed a back stairway he could use to access the second floor. Convenient, private, and discreet. TJ should have been coming here instead of wearing out his wallet on all those chain motels. The place was cheap, and he would never have to see another employee if he didn't want to. Next place he went to, he'd spend some extra time doing recon in the area. TJ had found this gem almost on accident.

TJ bounded up the back stairs and used his key to enter through a secured exit on the second floor. If his key worked on the outer door as well as on his room, TJ idly wondered if he could access other rooms with it. This might be the only night he stayed here, and from the looks of things, there wasn't a mad rush of guests.

Inside his room, a king-size four-poster bed sat maybe three steps from a whirlpool tub large enough for three. The décor was stylish and decadent. A spacious bathroom with a large shower, complete with bench seats and multiple showerheads, sat behind a glass wall on the other side of the tub. The textured marble floor complemented the tiling of the tub and shower area. In the bedroom, the thick carpets on the floors matched animal skins on the walls. A low-profile leather couch with a matching chair lined the wall opposite the tub. A large flat-screen television was mounted to the wall. The entirety was much larger and more impressive than TJ had expected, looking at the place from the outside. He could pass the time in bed until the pussy arrived. The place screamed sex, and TJ was hard just thinking about the possibilities.

To cool off, TJ decided to go downstairs. Maybe the redhead behind the counter had some grub. When he'd checked in, there had been some crazy white boy staring into the fire dressed like an old-school pimp. TJ could respect a man who took time to look good, even if his definition of that was batshit crazy.

Lady wasn't there, but TJ smelled food cooking. The pimp stood behind the desk. "Ah, our guest in number six. A most pleasant evening to you, sir."

Why did white people smile so much?

"Sup." TJ nodded.

"Indeed, sir. Solomon is my name, and I am the owner of this establishment. How may I be of assistance?" Dude gave a stiff bow when introducing himself.

"Uh, yeah, fo' real? This your place?"

"Indeed it is, sir. For six generations."

"Family business, huh? Cool. Hey, I wanted to talk about my room."

The innkeeper looked concerned. A slight line formed between his eyes, and he leaned across the counter toward TJ. "Is there a problem, sir?"

TJ laughed at the guy's seriousness. Dude took his job to

heart! "Nah, nothing bad. I wanted to say it's the nicest I've seen in a while. Didn't think it'd be that way from the outside."

The line between his eyebrows disappeared, and Solomon smiled. "Glad to hear you're pleased with the accommodations, as we do try. Sadly, we don't have the traffic here that we used to."

"Well, like I said, it's probably the nicest place I've seen."

"Thank you, sir. We at the Maple Lodge try to make each guest's experience here a memorable one. Is there anything I can do to improve the quality of your stay? Have you eaten dinner?"

Tantalizing aromas from in the kitchen made TJ's stomach growl. Dinner sounded like a fine idea. The afternoon had gotten away from him. "Yeah, what's that I'm smelling?"

"Ah, yes. I believe Shirley has a medium rare steak paired with roasted parmesan broccoli and grilled prosciutto-wrapped peaches with burrata and basil."

"I don't even know what all that shit is, but it smells good."

Solomon laughed, which made TJ uncomfortable for some reason. "I can have Shirley bring you a plate, or you're welcome to dine down here."

"How much for the steak?"

"Complimentary, sir. I think you'll not be with us for breakfast."

"Fo' real? Free?" If the dude wanted to serve him, TJ would let him serve. "Yeah, have her bring a plate to my room. And some coffee or sweet tea."

"Why not both, sir?"

"Why not?"

* * *

Solomon watched the meat go back upstairs. No, he certainly would not be with them in the morning. In the kitchen, he instructed Shirley to take some food upstairs. She pouted, but only a little.

"When you said we were having guests this evening, I didn't know you meant one of them." Shirley's racism amused Solomon—just one of the many facets of her character that enamored him so. She was simply enchanting.

"Shirley, my dear, we can accept the business of our darker skinned citizens too. They bleed as red as you do."

Instead of arguing with Solomon, who was right, even if he was toying with her, she showed her disdain with a small sniff. Before returning to the desk, Solomon also instructed her to take a pot of coffee and a pitcher of sweet tea up to six. Apparently, their guest was thirsty.

Shirley brewed a fresh pot, poured it into a silver carafe, and set cream, sugar, and saucers on the tray. She also placed a pitcher of sweet tea and a pair of glasses, along with a bucket of ice on the opposite side of the tray. It was much too heavy for her to carry safely up the stairs. She set the tray on a cart and loaded the cart into the dumbwaiter, then sent the entirety to the second floor.

She took the back stairs from the kitchen and opened the dumbwaiter once the ancient device had delivered the cart. She wheeled the cart into the hall and turned to find Solomon blocking her path. Wordlessly, he poured a cup of coffee from the cart and drank it in a single gulp. Shirley hung her head, and her cheeks began to burn.

He poured some tea into the same cup and downed that as well. "Cyanide? No. This won't do. While I admire your enthusiasm, dear heart, we are not poisoning our guests. Not this guest. Not tonight."

Shirley didn't say anything. Solomon had ingested enough poison to kill several men. She had loaded both the coffee and tea for the darkie to enjoy. She hoped Solomon wouldn't die.

"Shirley, take this back downstairs and do it once more. Correctly."

She wrestled the cart back into the dumbwaiter. When she looked up, Solomon was no longer in the hall. He moved so silently, like a ghost! Shirley sent the cart back downstairs to redo the drink order.

* * *

A knock let TJ know the food was here. He thought he'd heard a conversation in the hall a few minutes ago. When he'd looked, no one was there. Someone was here now, and she brought a cart loaded with goodies. He stepped aside, removing himself from Shirley's path. She wheeled in a cart with two silver trays on it. One had coffee, tea, and glasses; the other was covered with a stainless-steel cloche.

Shirley left the cart with instructions to wheel it into the hall when he was finished with dinner. She walked away without waiting for any kind of tip. TJ removed the cloche and was greeted with the heady aromas of grilled steak and peaches.

Dinner was delicious.

TJ finished the meal and wheeled the cart into the hall as he'd been instructed. There were still a couple of hours to wait until Wren arrived, so he flipped on the television and decided to doze off while listening to the local news. The anchor was running a story about the life and career of the fat cop that had gotten himself killed earlier.

A dead cop was a good cop as far as TJ was concerned. If the fat bastard was dead, then that was one less to be up in his business. One less made for a brighter world. If TJ knew who'd killed the porker, he would shake that dude's hand.

He was almost asleep when a subtle knock brought him immediately awake. It was dark outside, though still too early for Wren. Unless she'd managed to get away early. The girls were old enough to not need a sitter. Hell, they'd been doing the babysitting for years.

Maybe she brought them with her!

Hot damn! Tyrell rushed over to answer. It *was* Wren! She swished past him, all perfume, grace, and the promise of illicit sex. If TJ had a woman like this at home, he'd never leave her alone. Couldn't trust her.

He grabbed her waist. She twirled away while also somehow stepping free of her skirt. She smiled at his lust. Her incredible legs began right under the edge of her blouse. Her nipples poked through above. "TJ, I want to play a game." She maneuvered him toward the bed.

"Sure, baby." TJ was surprised when the bed caught the backs of his knees, causing him to fall backward.

Wren giggled at his lack of grace. It's hard to be graceful when there isn't any blood in your brain. He put his hand where the blood had gone, where he strained against his zipper. She straddled him as he centered himself on the bed, then pulled his shirt off, still not allowing him to kiss her.

His hands wandered over her body until she grabbed one and tied it to the bed with a silken scarf she'd produced from somewhere behind her. "Yeah, baby. Let's do this." TJ's voice was thick with lust, and the way she ground against his hard-on was driving him crazy.

Wren produced another scarf and tied his other hand to the bed. She jerked his pants and underwear off in a single savage motion. Her fine nails scraped his thighs, drawing blood, but he was so turned on he didn't notice. Two extra scarves appeared, and then he was strapped naked to the bed.

"Come on, baby. Come on. I can't wait."

Wren was back on top of him. Thrusting his hips, TJ tried desperately to get inside her. She continued grinding on him. Leaning down, she nipped at his neck, then worked down to his chest and lower still.

TJ's eyes closed. Her hands seemed to be everywhere, and her mouth nipped a hot line down his stomach. "Careful with the teeth baby. You know I can't handle teeth."

"Oh, I know," she answered. "Don't worry, lover, I don't

have any teeth." Wren's voice was off. Wrong. He looked down and screamed. His thirteen-inch cock rested between the mouth parts of a huge spider. Beside the fangs rubbing against his thighs, pedipalps rubbed his hips, maneuvering him farther into the thing's mouth.

"God! Oh God. Oh God! Oh Lord, please! Help me!"

"God? He doesn't live here, lover. Only creatures like me do."

TJ screamed, struggling to pull his hands free of the scarves. No, not scarves—his hands and feet had been webbed to the bedframe. He wasn't going anywhere. The sexy ambience was gone. He was trapped in a web. He felt her suck. Then his pride ripped off, disappearing down her throat. She moaned while she fed, like a well-pleasured lover. TJ groaned, strength waning, bucking against her, growing weaker as she drained his lifeblood. Before losing consciousness, TJ saw her babies, each as big as his fist, squeezing free of the walls, dropping from the ceiling on delicate silk to feed.

"Shirley, be a dear and come with me."

Shirley abandoned the desk and followed Solomon down the hall. The gem on his cane was a deep emerald and matched the silk on the inside of his jacket. He'd been particularly chatty during breakfast. Solomon was always a delight to be around, but Solomon in a chipper mood was particularly delightful. He looked a bit flushed in his cheeks, perhaps, but otherwise, Solomon appeared to be in high spirits this morning. He never mentioned the cyanide incident from last night or the elderly gentleman at the market. He didn't even seem to remember either had happened.

"We need to clean up six."

"Of course."

He opened the door, and Shirley surveyed the husk on the bed that had once been Tyrell "TJ" Jackson.

"Can we get this done by noon? I'm expecting another guest. What do you think, dear?"

Shirley looked from the husk on the bed to Solomon's flushed smiling face. "I think I need to start another garden."

"Capital idea, my dear. Absolutely capital idea."

CHAPTER TEN
FALLING APART SIP BY SIP

B uck was dead. Not sick or on vacation. Dead. No more guidance, advice, or the tough love Weaver desperately needed. His mentor and friend had been gutted in the middle of a marketplace, an animal to slaughter. A pig. No one even lifted a finger to help.

People had stood by watching him die. No one had called 911. No one had tried to stop Buck's killer. No one could even describe Buck's killer. Were they male? Female? Why had it happened? The official police report stated Buck was the victim of a robbery gone wrong. Weaver had picked up Buck's personal effects, since Buck had no next of kin. He'd had a wallet full of cash, a gold crucifix on a chain, his keys, and an expensive Citizen Eco Drive watch with diamond chips marking the hours.

Clearly robbery wasn't the motivation behind Buck's death.

Revenge? Certainly, a career sheriff would have plenty of enemies. There would be the obvious people he had busted over the years. Friends and family of those jailed must not be overlooked. Buck had conducted a staggering number of arrests over a span of two decades—far too many people to sift through. No, his idea about revenge sucked. It plain didn't feel right.

Weaver sat on the edge of his bed holding the crucifix that had recently hung around Buck's neck. A discreet plastic bag of personal effects lay on the nightstand beside his Seven and Seven. Golden light the same shade as the cross dangling from his palm filtered through the whiskey in his glass. Weaver stood, dropping the necklace into the drink. The chain broke the surface with barely a ripple. After sliding between the cubes, the cross settled on the bottom buried underneath a pile of chain. Same golden color, same empty promises. The same comfortable old lies and heartache. God had dropped the ball in Summit Valley. Weaver picked up Buck's keys. With an unsteady gait, he staggered from the bedroom. He would go in a minute. First, he needed another drink.

CHAPTER ELEVEN
UNRAVELED

*F**ucked. Oh RayRay! It was all wrong! Everything is falling apart.* Clem had gone to bed last night believing he and RayRay would be celebrating in Hotel Roanoke after the sun set the next day, newly rich men. Heroes who'd brought in one of the nation's most wanted serial killers. Clem had drifted to sleep, a smile on his face and a throbbing erection between his legs.

Staggering into the house, he pushed the door closed and fell back against it. A bloody streak followed his descent to the floor. Clem sat, knees drawn beneath his chin, holding his head in his hands. He shook his head, doubting his sanity, replaying the day's events over in his mind. No easy stretch of logic explained away what he'd been through. What they'd seen.

The morning had started out great. Perfectly according to plan. Clem woke with a grin. RayRay had come through with the Tasers, and Clem had picked up forty feet of nylon rope—more than they'd need—and a fresh roll of duct tape—pronounced *duck tape* in the South—from the True Value on Jefferson.

Clem's aging CRV was loaded before 9:00 a.m., a personal record for cousins who usually refused to do anything before noon. Five million dollars walking the streets proved to be a powerful motivator. Clem drove back into town and parked in the same space on Jefferson he'd occupied earlier. RayRay sat silent beside him, listening to Clem talk about the marvels their future held. Passing off RayRay's moodiness as RayRay's moodiness, Clem was happy to maintain the one-sided conversation.

Their planned route effectively circled the old furniture factory. If the car was there, they'd find it. Madison Avenue offered enough cover to enter the factory through the old loading docks. When they found Shirley, they'd knock her out with a Taser shot. Then, while Clem stood watch, RayRay would bring the car around to the loading docks. He would bring in the rope and tape to secure Shirley, then they'd load her into the CRV neatly wrapped for the FBI.

They walked down Main. Clem spotted her driving south on Washington in her fancy car. Her hair was tied up, and she had sunglasses on. Even still, Clem recognized her instantly. She passed by them, less than five feet away, never even glancing in their direction. She drove over the old train tracks and made an illegal U-turn before parking on the street. Clem and RayRay turned to follow. Clem's eyes never left the Corvette. When she'd parked at the farmers market, Clem began forming a new plan. After sending RayRay back to the car, Clem searched for a quiet somewhere to drag her.

Everywhere he looked, people. People who would see, call for help, try to stop him. *Calm down. We were never going to take her at a damn market anyway.* The thought helped some. This might even work better. Clem could follow her from the market back to her hidey hole. Might even be an opportunity to get her at a stop light. It all depended on where RayRay parked.

The light crowd made following her easy. She made her way from stand to stand, handling vegetables. Most didn't seem to suit her. Clem maintained a distance of two stands between them at all times. Another man, drunk from the look of him, appeared to be tracking the same quarry. Old and heavy, the guy didn't strike Clem as an immediate threat. Maybe a retiree, drunk at ten in the morning, looking to hook up? Whatever the situation, Clem didn't think much of him. Shirley would be in his trunk before lunchtime and in the hands of the FBI before the afternoon was out. Clem would be a rich man come suppertime, and this poor drunk bastard following her would have to rub one out all by his lonesome. Hard times. *Such is life, my fat friend.*

RayRay tapped his shoulder. "I parked two spaces behind her. No problem."

Clem nodded his approval, never taking an eye off her. She walked casually, sipping her coconut water. Shirley didn't look like one of the most wanted felons in the United States. She looked like money—expensively dressed, clean, pressed. Not rich, not like suppertime Clem, but upper middle-class money for sure. Gold hung around her neck, twinkled from her ears. Diamonds waved from her fingers. She'd found some broccoli that met her rigorous standard.

She's gonna miss that shit in jail.

"Who's the fat fuck following?" RayRay asked.

"Glad you've got your head in the game. I'm not sure who that guy is, but he doesn't matter. She'll chase him off or we will. I don't want to tase the old feller, but if he gets in our way, he's gonna be pissing sparks."

"Hope we won't need to zap an old guy in public. There aren't a ton of people here"—RayRay looked around at the stands—"but enough to give our description to the law."

"Shirley! Stop!"

The drunk charged her. Clem stared, mouth hanging open, as the old guy rushed her. Called her by name, even. Shirley stood, watching him charge. As he grabbed her arm, she broke the coconut water bottle and gutted the old guy! *Damn! She fuckin' killed him!* His guts hit the ground with a wet plop Clem would never get out of his head. Plop!

RayRay backed away. "No, no, no, this is wrong. We're wrong. We shouldn't be here." A small crowd gathered around the dying drunk, and Shirley walked away, leaving the broccoli where it lay. RayRay tripped over a table leg, and his teeth clacked as he landed on his butt.

Clem jerked him back to his feet. "We need to move!"

RayRay looked at him, expression blank, muttering, "No," over and over.

"Ray! Now! Quit fucking around!"

Clem jerked his cousin roughly by the collar, walking fast toward the car. No one tried to stop Shirley. No one seemed to even see her. No one stared. Clem dragged his useless cousin to their car near where she loaded her groceries into hers. Not a care in the world. She paid no attention to the men following her.

After tossing RayRay into the passenger side, Clem jumped into the driver's seat. Shirley walked around to the driver's side of the Corvette, tucking her hair under a scarf—just another well-to-do lady enjoying a top-down drive in her convertible. Clem wondered if the old guy's blood had stained her gold jewelry.

Refraining from pulling out exactly when she did, Clem allowed a blue Pacifica to pass. Better to have some cover, and the minivan provided plenty. "Where's the fuckin' ambulance? Fire station ain't but a couple blocks from here." But there was no time to worry about the old guy, dead by now for sure, when their meal ticket was pulling away.

She drove north on Washington, then turned east on Fifth. To Clem's surprise, Shirley didn't go far. From the intersection of Washington and Fifth, the cousins watched her unload her groceries. After tying the tops of three bags together, she hoisted them in one hand, her vegetables in the other. Bags of linen, which must have weighed fifty pounds each, were carried in without any visible strain.

Certainly didn't look like a woman who'd just gutted a man.

An impatient honk brought Clem back to the moment. The light had turned green. Turning east on Fifth, he drove a block over to Madison. A left on Madison and another on Sixth brought him behind the bed-and-breakfast.

The building didn't look like anywhere he'd want to stay. Run-down, peeling paint, a gigantic hornet nest built onto the door of a carriage house. The place reminded him of a horror movie. A place where a monster made its lair. Everything here felt wrong, including the Corvette sitting in the gravel lot waiting for the return of its owner.

* * *

Shirley carried in the linen, along with a few bags of groceries. Solomon met her at the door, opening it for her. Always such a gentleman! "Shirley, why don't you go wash your hands. You've brought some of the late sheriff back with you."

Her face blushed at the mild chastising. "Of course, Mr. Drury. Right away."

"And please, call me Solomon. No need for the formality. We're friends. We are friends."

"I think we might be the very best of friends," Shirley said.

"Shirley, did you know you have people following you?"

She paused, caught off guard by the change of subject. Was Solomon angry? Annoyed that she'd handled things in her fashion? Disappointed? Perhaps she'd been too rash. Her temper occasionally got the better of her. Character flaw.

It wasn't unreasonable that someone had followed her after her little altercation at the market. People were such busybodies! They couldn't wait to get involved in someone else's business. "That doesn't really surprise me, Solomon."

"I thought those two had learned their lesson." Solomon's

brow drew down in mild annoyance. "I do hate repeating myself."

"What was that?" Shirley asked from the kitchen. Scrubbing blood off her hands under the running water had garbled what Solomon said. Her hearing wasn't what it once was and seemed to be getting worse. He didn't seem upset.

"Nothing of relevance, dear. I need to step out for a moment. Keep an eye on the fire for me, please." Solomon stepped outside, ending the conversation. Any version of *watch the fire* was Solomon speak for *watch the desk while I'm gone*. He didn't often leave his spot and earning his trust humbled Shirley.

* * *

"We shouldn't be here." Clem looked over at RayRay, who'd finally decided to come out of his stupor. "He knows we're here. We should go."

"What are you talking about?" Clem asked.

"This is his home. We shouldn't be here."

"Cousin, I don't know what you're talking about. Five million dollars is in there. The only thing keeping me from going in there right now is that I'd have to pass right by that big fuckin' swarm." Clem pointed at the hornets.

"Clem, she killed that man—a sheriff—because he told her to. He's in my head now. He said he's tired of warning us. Shirley is spoken for. We can't have her."

"Are you feeling all right, RayRay? What sheriff? That old fat guy? Nah, he was just some old drunk who got handsy with the wrong woman. First time seeing blood like that?"

"She's bad, Clem. He's worse. We need to let this go. We'll never get her. He won't allow it."

The sincerity on RayRay's face almost scared Clem into driving home. Almost. But if he did, he knew he'd never be able to forgive RayRay. Besides, RayRay was just scared. Freaking out. Who wouldn't be? Only natural to be scared after seeing something so awful.

"RayRay, I don't know what's going on with you right now, but I need you. I need you with me. This is going to take both of us. Can you put this shit on hold for me? For our future?"

RayRay stared back, face sweating, pale, shaking. Clem didn't understand. "I can. Last I'll say about it: if we don't leave, we aren't going to have a future."

Clem stared at RayRay, unsure of what to say, and was spared from finding a suitable retort by Shirley making her way to the Corvette. Back in the driver's seat, she revved the engine a few times like she enjoyed the powerful mechanical scream. The Vette slunk away onto Fifth Street, low to the ground, careful on the curb, exhaust throbbing.

She headed south again, and Clem shadowed her movements. Carefully following from a quarter mile back, he slowed as she turned into the Summit Valley Furniture Plant parking lot. She drove directly to the loading dock, which had been closed for years now, got out, and went inside.

Clem parked the CRV beside her Corvette.

Summit Valley Furniture Plant occupied the entire east-west block between Madison and Washington. From Third Street, the plant stretched north most of the way to Fifth Street and was surrounded by parking lots with weeds peeking through the asphalt, surrounded in turn with barbed wire fencing, except on the Madison Avenue side where the loading docks were. The bankrupt plant had run out of money before securing the entire property.

The plant was a large brick-and-sheet metal monstrosity with opaque windows near the ceilings of each of the five floors. Raw steel support beams spiderwebbed from the ground to the roof. At the second-floor, sheet metal had been built out to hide the supports. A large stairwell, gripped between brick columns, rose toward the sky on Third Street. The stairwell provided roof access to the plant. The Summit Valley Furniture

Plant was the second tallest structure in Summit Valley behind the Summit Valley County Courthouse spire.

Painted a cheery sky blue at its construction, the color of the building had faded over the years, corrupted by weather and exposure to industry. Rust dotted the metal shell and slowly chewed into exposed supports. Once an economic boon and source of pride for Summit Valley, the factory now served as a reminder of better times. Industry had moved away, and Summit Valley was drying up—just one of the many small industrial American towns dying a slow death of stagnation.

Clem eyed the building looming over them. Despite it being a bright spring day, the factory's shadow fell upon them, heavy and oppressive. Daylight seemed to be diffused through some dark fabric, providing light but no warmth. Ignoring his growing feeling of foreboding, Clem hopped up onto the loading dock. All the shutters were closed. The employee entrance was chained shut.

"How did she get in?" Clem asked no one in particular.

RayRay stood by the open door of the CRV, reluctant to come closer. "He let her in."

"He who? What the fuck are you on about?"

"You know who. Him. The owner."

"The plant owner?"

"He owns that too."

Clem rolled his eyes, unwilling to continue this pointless conversation. Seeing that feller die that morning had apparently caused RayRay's cheese to slide right the hell off his cracker. Wondering if he might be better off leaving RayRay in the parking lot, Clem searched for a way in. Shirley was inside, and this was going to be a great day, despite RayRay wigging out. Five million dollars was sure to cure whatever ailed him.

Shirley didn't go around the building; he knew it. Either way, he would have spotted her. No, she used the loading dock. But how did she lock up behind herself? The chain and padlock hung undisturbed. A spiderweb stretched between chain and door, dotted with the dried corpses of past meals. Must not have used the employee door. Walking back down the line, Clem searched the shuttered doors. All were locked tight. Frustration began to build.

How did she get inside? Sure as hell didn't float through the wall.

If unable to solve the mystery, they'd have to leave and split their surveillance between the Maple Lodge and the furniture plant. Clem didn't want to do that. Who knew how long before RayRay came back to himself? He was completely unreliable right now.

RayRay moved from his place by the CRV to wait in the middle of the dock. Pointing to the door in front of him, he said, "Check this one, Clem."

"I checked all the fuckin' doors. All of 'em are locked."

"He opened it."

"The owner?" Clem asked. Sarcasm dripped from his words.

"Yes."

"Oh hell. Fine."

Clem bent over, gripping the cold metal handle, and jerked. The door slid up smoothly without a creak of protest. The room behind hid in shadow. Clem made out vague shapes within. Shipping boxes? Thick dust covered everything, and inside stank of stagnant air—musty with a sharp chemical undertone.

Deciding not to attract undue attention, Clem fetched two flashlights from their kit in the CRV. He handed RayRay one, as well as the backpack containing their rope, tape, batteries, and masks. Clem tried to close the door quietly, but the metal slammed down against the concrete, and a hollow boom echoed through the industrial space.

"Damn it!" Clem hissed. "Fuckin' thing got away from me. If she didn't know we were here before, she does now."

"It doesn't matter. We're never leaving this place."

"Jesus, RayRay, have faith. We'll be sipping champagne in the Hotel Roanoke tonight."

RayRay sighed as Clem moved farther into the gloom.

Packed with cardboard boxes, the room formed a maze. Dusty corridors led to dead ends, causing Clem and RayRay to frequently backtrack. Getting lost wasn't a concern as they followed their own footprints back. Clem wrote 'no' in the dust at the entrances to dead ends. He drew arrows indicating their correct direction.

Closer examination showed the boxes came from China. Wiping a layer of dust from the cardboard, Clem said, "You know, I'd heard they got furniture from China, repackaged it here, and sold it off as Summit Valley. Guess the rumors were true."

RayRay shrugged, indifferent to the shady business practices of a defunct company.

The maze ended before a large set of double doors. Undisturbed dust suggested there was nothing beyond—a clear indication that they'd somehow missed their quarry. Clem led the way undeterred. She'd come this way. He knew it. Opening the double doors proved to be a simpler matter as they were unlocked. Apparently securing the interior wasn't a concern.

In juxtaposition to the claustrophobia of the box maze, the openness of the factory proper shocked both cousins. They stood in the doorway. Dust motes danced in the filtered sunlight streaming through the windows and between the shadows above and below. To Clem's left was the entrance to the stairwell, which meant the windows must've bordered Third Street.

Large clusters of metal drums lined the walls. The chemical smell was much stronger here. Mounts that had held massive machinery in place when the factory was open hung in rows, a danger for the unwary foot or skull. Piles of metal scrap, whose purpose remained unidentifiable to Clem, caught the light only to bury it in thicker shadow.

"She isn't on this floor. Let's go up," Clem suggested.

The stairwell entrance was also unlocked. Better lit than the factory floor, the dirty glass here provided light for a much smaller space. Clem put his hand on the guardrail and looked up. Stairs and handrails spiraled toward roof access. No one lurked above them waiting in ambush. Other than their anxious breathing and hesitant footsteps, the silence remained undisturbed. Nothing moved.

"I thought this place would be a haven for homeless, drunks, and whatnot. Other than the dust, it really isn't that bad in here. A little clean up and you could move another business in, no problem," Clem said.

"He doesn't want anyone here. This place is his monument, a testament, his reminder to the town of what happens when they're good and what happens when they disobey. He likes it just like it is."

"What?"

"You can't hear him? I do. He's been speaking to me since the market."

"RayRay, I don't know what's happened to you, but I promise we'll get you all the help you need once we're done here."

"What I need is for us to leave before it finds us. He says it's loose in here. Somewhere."

"Only thing loose in here is us and a fat paycheck."

A metallic crash, metal clanging off concrete, boomed somewhere above, cutting the conversation short. The cousins listened to the echoes die.

"You know which floor that came from?" RayRay asked.

"Third or fourth. Maybe even the fifth. Sound was too far away to be on the second. Close to the stairwell though, so keep your eyes open." Clem sounded more confident than he felt. Part of him was starting to agree with RayRay. This place was wrong—bad wrong—and they should've been on their way out. Only the lure of reward kept him pressing on.

The cousins made their way to the third floor. Clem winced each time they set a foot down because their steps, no matter how slow or light, reverberated up and down the stairwell.

Clem felt like he might as well have been blaring a trombone. Thick dust covered everything, and each jarring step caused a mini explosion underfoot. Breathing became increasingly difficult and their ascent more dangerous with the slick coating underfoot. Both men donned masks despite the heat of the stairwell, attempting to filter out the filth floating in the air.

Sunlight baked through the windows, turning the stairwell into a makeshift greenhouse. The heat was tremendous. *At least thirty degrees difference between here and the factory. Incredible*, Clem thought. Sweat ran into his eyes, down his back, both Taser and flashlight slippery in his hands. Dust settled onto whatever sweat-soaked skin was exposed, mixing into gray mud that caused his flesh to burn and itch.

Five million dollars. Five million dollars. A few moments of sucking dirt will be worth every penny.

RayRay wiped a gray streak across his forehead. Having put his flashlight away, he used his free hand to scratch.

"Don't you worry, cousin; the hot tub is going to feel real good tonight. This time tomorrow, we'll be laughing about all this. We'll do a quick check at the doors on our way to the fifth floor. Then we can do a thorough check floor by floor. She's between three and five and has to use this stairwell," Clem said.

RayRay didn't seem to share his enthusiasm.

Passing the third floor, they continued their ascent. Clem wondered what it must have been like to work here—climbing these stairs daily, the heat, noise, and soul-crushing manual labor, then dragging yourself out after sucking sawdust for eight or more grueling hours, knowing it all needed to be done again tomorrow. No time or energy for anything except work. The thought made working at the Wilco seem almost pleasant.

A quick test of the handle on the third floor and Clem jerked his hand back, "Fucking thing's hot." A peek through the closing gap revealed more metal anchors in the floor and ceiling, concrete, dust, and open space stretching into the distance. The heat in the stairwell grew worse.

RayRay stopped to remove his backpack. After pulling two bottles of water from within, he handed one to Clem.

"Thanks, cousin. Hotter'n a half-jacked fox in a forest fire in here."

"Yup."

"Bet the bitch is on five. Let's hustle up, get this done, and get the hell out of here."

"Yeah."

Four was unlocked. Clem used his shirt to pull the door open enough to wedge his foot inside. The space was empty even of the metal anchors, which seemed to be everywhere else in the factory. A heavy residual chemical smell led Clem to believe this was where the wood was stained. Beneath a thick layer of undisturbed dust, the concrete, covered in splatters and discolorations, gave credence to his theory. The pair lingered longer than necessary as the temperature was so much cooler there than in the stairwell. Neither were excited to climb to the final floor in that heat.

A final push brought them before the open doors of the fifth floor. Administration and management had worked up here. Glass-walled offices lined the wall. Desks, file cabinets, and other assorted office furniture pushed into small groups formed little islands that broke up the tremendous amount of open floor. Clem passed a pile of telephones missing handsets stacked higher than his nearly six feet. Farther in, he found the handsets—hundreds of them—hanging from their respective cords like a bizarre art project.

Why would anyone take the time to do this?

Shirley could've been hiding in any of a thousand places. The two of them might've walked past her a dozen times without seeing her. Unlike the barren floors below, the cluttered chaos here unnerved Clem. This made no sense. Was this how Shirley spent her time when she wasn't killing people in the market?

Boom!

A blast that vibrated deep beneath their feet drew the cousins' attention back to the stairwell.

Boom!

Another blast, followed by a crash of metal. This one closer than the first.

Boom!

On the fifth floor now. An initial impact, followed by a slam of metal against concrete, this one close enough that they could feel the metal grinding beneath them.

"What the fuck is that?" Clem whispered.

"It's him. Coming for us," RayRay answered matter-of-factly. Water is wet, the sky is up, grass is green, and death is coming up the stairwell.

"Hide! Quick!" Clem ducked beneath a grouping of file cabinets near the edge of the hanging handsets. RayRay crawled underneath a desk pushed against a glass-walled cubicle. From Clem's vantage point, both RayRay and the stairwell doors were visible.

Behind Clem, a cool, slightly robotic female voice spoke from the handsets hanging from the ceiling. *"If you'd like to make a call, please hang up and try again. If you feel you've reached this message in error, please hang up and kill yourself. It'll be easier than what he has planned."*

Over and over, each handset spoke the same message slightly off from all the others, creating an insane babble. Clem scooted away from the swinging voices, trying to watch RayRay, the handsets, and the stairwell door all at the same time. "Oh God! What is this? Save me, save me, Jesus. Please, oh God, save me."

Boom!

The doors blew in with tremendous force, clearing a thirty-foot space in front of the stairwell. Cheap office furniture crumpled, groaning in protest as metal bent and wood splintered. Layers of dust disturbed into flight thickened the air, further masking the meager sunlight forcing itself through the opaque windows near the ceiling.

"Too late to run. You're fucked now." The handsets spoke as one behind him. Disoriented from the blast, choking on near unbreathable air, Clem crab-walked to his left, moving in a semi-circle toward the door. When whatever came in to search the room for him, Clem planned on being somewhere else, like moving down the stairs and away from this place.

Clem squinted toward the light streaming in from the stairs, but it was impossible to tell if anything stood in the threshold or if it had moved into the room to join them already. The open space in front of the doors made running a gamble. If he didn't wait for it—whatever it was—to move farther into the room, he'd be spotted. Problem was, he didn't know what he was hiding from, only that it was incredibly strong.

He almost screamed when a hand grabbed his shoulder. Turning, he looked into the frightened eyes of his cousin. RayRay had seen him move and had followed. Sweat carved little channels through the dust clinging to RayRay's forehead. Somehow, he managed to have both his flashlight and his Taser. Clem wasn't sure where he'd dropped his.

RayRay held a finger up to the filthy black fabric of his mask. *Shhh.* He nodded toward the offices. Puffs of dust rose from the floor, and footsteps sounded along the edge of the room. Something invisible stalked them. Disbelieving, Clem watched the steps move deliberately through the debris in the direction of the handsets—right where he'd been hiding.

Furniture scooted aside, bumped by an invisible something moving deeper into the factory.

Clem gave it a few more seconds to get farther away before he and RayRay crept toward the stairs. Intense heat radiated from the stairwell, much hotter than it had any right to be. Paint bubbled, smoking. "Don't touch anything in here, RayRay. We need to get the hell out of here. We can try again somewhere else," Clem whispered, holding a hand up to shield his face.

The cousins moved as quickly as they could through the baking heat. The soles of their shoes melted away, leaving greasy tracks. Breathing the superheated air sapped their strength. Clem was tired, his muscles heavy, but still he strained to hear if that thing pursued. The thought kept them moving ever on.

The doors on floors four and three had been smashed in like on five. On the second-floor landing, the doors had been knocked into the stairwell. One metal door lay propped against the handrail on the landing. The other door had landed down the stairs partially blocking the next landing. The former didn't pose a problem; the latter blocked their path to the final stretch of stairwell. Climbing over would be like crossing a griddle. Crawling under meant they'd need to scoot along the wall until clear. Neither option seemed appealing.

RayRay bumped into him, causing him to burn his arm on the handrail. "Jesus, RayRay, what the fuck?" Clem hissed at his cousin's carelessness.

"No, something knocked me into the wall." RayRay turned to display the scorched fabric of his T-shirt, his arm already blistering. An imprint in the melting paint showed where he'd hit. It had passed between them, pushing them aside. It wasn't on the fifth floor. It was in the stairwell with them. It had touched them.

No movement, no puff of dust, betrayed the creature's movements. Gripping their remaining Taser with his uninjured arm, RayRay led the way, trying to look everywhere at once. He gave the remaining flashlight to Clem. Around the second-floor landing and down the stairs he went, pausing only for a moment before using the handrail to vault over to the final set of stairs.

Clem followed, leaving the burnt flesh of his palm behind.

As they neared the entrance to the first floor, a noise behind caused them to turn. It stood on the door. Four distinct spots smoked, filling the stairwell with the smell of burning flesh. The creature didn't seem bothered that its feet were burning as it casually licked at the crisped meat clinging to the handrail. Smoke curled around an impossible shape. Claws ticked on metal.

It was in no hurry, enjoying the cooked meat they'd left behind.

"Oh, fuck this." RayRay stepped around Clem, firing his Taser now that he had a target. The darts hung in midair, having hit the thing. Instead of fifty thousand volts at twenty-five watts of incapacitating electrical current knocking the creature out, the Taser exploded in RayRay's hand. Clem watched RayRay's blood sizzle and smoke where it hit the walls. His fingers cooked like sausages where they lay on the stairs.

RayRay screamed, the strength leaving his legs. Clem caught him, holding him up, and dragged him into the factory and toward the loading dock. He glanced back to see the thing eating RayRay's fingers, licking up bits of palm and smoky gore. No hurry. It had all the time in the world. Don't think about it. Just get out of here. Clem dragged his cousin into the mercifully cool dark of the loading dock maze.

RayRay continued to scream about his hand, his hand, "Oh Jesus, my fuckin' hand!" His wound left a trail behind them. A gory splatter pattern for the thing to follow. No chance of losing it in here. Maybe the fucking thing couldn't see in the dark. Maybe they'd catch a little break…

RayRay was heavy and losing too much blood. As he went into shock, he was no longer helping Clem carry his weight. Clem dared to stop, kneeling in the darkness, his cousin propped against a Chinese box. Clem removed RayRay's belt and tied it around the elbow above the wound, a makeshift tourniquet. RayRay stirred some when Clem cinched it tight.

"RayRay, we got to go. That thing is still after us, and it's got a taste now. Get up, cousin. We have to leave."

"No…escape," RayRay mumbled.

"Yeah, fuck that noise. Time to go." Ignoring his blistered

palm, Clem hoisted his cousin up to stagger forward once again. The belt seemed to stem the cascade of blood pouring from the end of RayRay's ruined arm. Clem followed his markings on the dusty floor back the way they'd come, grateful he'd had that foresight. At the loading dock, he set RayRay down. Throughout his panicked flight, he'd expected the thing to land on his back and rip him open, saving RayRay for later, but they'd made it this far. "I have to get this door open. Should have left the fucking thing up."

Turning his back to the room, Clem crouched, working his fingers underneath the roll door. It slid up so easily the first time! Clem strained, pushing with his legs, until pain flared in his lower back. Somewhere in the dark behind him, he heard boxes moving, along with a wet slobbering noise. It was coming, licking its way along the blood trail.

The door slid up a few inches. Bright unfiltered sunlight, the sweet promise of freedom, pushed back the blackness. Renewed panic lent strength to Clem's tired muscles, and hope pushed him through the pain in his back and hand to raise the stubborn door enough to slide underneath. RayRay slumped over, falling facedown on the dusty concrete. Clem slid underneath the door, then turned around and grabbed RayRay by the collar. He pulled RayRay, completely dead weight, partway under the door. His cousin mumbled something about sunshine.

Clem pulled again, bringing RayRay a little farther into the sunlight. When he scooted back for a final pull, his cousin was yanked back into the dark. Clem grabbed for his hand—the only part of him still outside the factory. A second yank and nothing of his cousin could be seen. The door slammed shut.

Inside, the thing landed on RayRay's back, claws ripping through his backpack, clothing, and muscle in a single vicious stroke. It tore thick ropy muscle from the right side of RayRay's spine and slurped the hot meat down with greedy satisfaction. RayRay screamed, a sound of pure wordless agony, his ineffectual bucking doing little to dislodge his attacker.

It ripped another chunk of meat free, from the left side of his spine this time. RayRay's cries grew weaker, and it settled in to enjoy a hot meal.

Outside, Clem slammed into the door, beating his fists against it, screaming for RayRay. He yanked the handle, attempting to force the door back open. The handle broke off in his hand. Overbalanced, Clem staggered back and fell off the loading dock. He smacked his head against the hood of the CRV, then bounced off the car and hit his head again on the pavement.

He blacked out to the wet crunch of his cousin, the last of his family, being eaten alive.

* * *

Clem woke to near darkness. The sun had almost set behind the Appalachians, the spring sky the color of clotted blood, deep reds mixed in with sickly purples, the last of the light vanishing. A few stars poked faintly through, embarrassed to shine too early. Silence lay heavy around Summit Valley Furniture Plant. The wind moved hesitantly through the parking lot occupied only by his CRV. The Corvette had gone sometime while he was unconscious.

RayRay was dead, and Shirley had gotten away, if she'd ever even been here.

Clem stood in the parking lot, unsure of what to do. He was the last Farris. Last of the cursed bloodline. Eventually, he got in the car and went home.

CHAPTER TWELVE
DOING WHAT NEEDS DOING

Caden lay in the darkness, hoping *he* wouldn't be outside his window. Daddy said ten years old was too old to believe in the boogeyman. Daddy also said there was no way anyone could be outside his window because his room was on the second floor. No one was tall enough to look in at him, not even in the NBA.

But that was because Daddy hadn't seen him. He hadn't even looked. Not really.

The boogeyman came inside too. It didn't seem to matter if the window was shut or the doors were locked. Sometimes he stood behind Caden's bedroom door, watching as his parents tried to comfort him. Sometimes his awful smile, the only part Caden could really see, floated in the dark of his closet. He had even been under the bed, and Caden could feel him move around beneath the mattress.

No matter where he was, he was trying to scare Caden into keeping the secret.

Caden had seen what happened at the farmer's market. He'd seen the boogeyman whisper in the sheriff's ear. The sheriff had seemed confused. He must have been convinced to attack the lady. The boogeyman knew the old sheriff wouldn't be able to fight her—she was as bad as the boogeyman.

Mom had tried to hide his eyes. She'd tried to keep him from seeing all the blood. The sheriff had been hurt bad, cut worse than Caden had ever seen. Worse even than when he'd cut his hand last Halloween. Caden clenched his fist in remembered pain. He had removed the slimy pumpkin guts with his hand and a cereal spoon. Then he'd picked up the knife, hands covered in pumpkin slime, to start on the jack-o-lantern's eyes. Caden stabbed the pumpkin hard with a solid underhand swing; he'd already opened a hole in the top and knew how tough the pumpkin was to cut. The point of the knife stuck in the pumpkin's flesh, while Caden's hand, carried by momentum and slick with pumpkin slime, slipped down the handle and right down the blade.

The blade had sliced the flesh where his fingers met his palm. He opened his fist. The cut didn't bleed at first, didn't hurt. Until air rushed into the gap in his skin.

Then it hurt—it hurt a lot!—and began to bleed. Scary amounts of blood, stringy orange bits of pumpkin guts, and seeds set aside for roasting mixed together on the newspaper spread across the kitchen floor. Mom had rushed him off to the hospital, and Caden got eight stitches, two per finger. Daddy had said he was brave—tough stuff—even though Mom shouldn't have let him do it alone.

The sheriff had been cut so much worse. His guts had dropped right in the dirt! There was no way to fix him. Not even with all the doctors and all the stitches in the hospital. Mom had tried to keep him from seeing how badly the sheriff was hurt. Caden had seen it though. And he'd seen the boogeyman standing outside the crowd, smiling, as the woman walked away.

No one had tried to stop her. Instead, people had shuffled a couple of steps off to one side or another, as if they'd walked into a spot where someone had farted and were trying to clear the blast zone.

Caden sometimes played crop duster in Walmart, laughing at the folks caught by surprise and laughing even harder at Mom's disapproval. Daddy, on the other hand, thought it was funny. The people at the market that day had acted like they'd been crop dusted. Noses wrinkled, and they'd hurried to clear the lady's path. Then Mom had dragged him off after Daddy said, "Get the damn kid away."

As Caden was being led off through the crowd, he'd seen the boogeyman looking at him! The boogeyman wore a big Abraham Lincoln hat. He'd smiled and tipped one finger off the brim, then brought it down to his lips in a *Shhh!*

Sunday night following the disastrous Saturday Market, Caden was going to bed when he saw *him* looking in his window. He'd screamed, and his parents came pounding down the hall like when he'd cut himself. Caden had pointed to the window, but they didn't see. The boogeyman had smiled just like he'd smiled at the market and made the same *Shhh!* gesture. He was *right there*! Why couldn't they see him? Dad had stomped away, muttering that now the kid would need therapy.

Sometimes Daddy wasn't nice.

The boogeyman didn't show up every night, but even when he wasn't there, Caden couldn't sleep, afraid he might appear. Maybe one of these nights the boogeyman would spill his guts the way the woman had done to the sheriff. Or maybe he'd leave Caden alone and get his daddy or his mama instead. His terrible smile had told Caden that if he said anything about the lady at the market, he could expect a visit some night soon.

One of these nights it was going to get him, and no one would know what happened to him. Dad thought he was making stuff up, and Mom thought it was her fault, even though Caden had told them why he'd stopped sleeping. The only person who would be able to help him was Logan, because best buddies looked out for each other.

He checked the window—nothing there. With the sun still shining, Caden didn't expect to see anything on the other side of the glass, but you never knew. The sun had been shining at the farmers market when the sheriff was killed, so daytime didn't guarantee safety. Drumming up his courage, Caden lifted the skirt to check underneath the bed. The dark space beneath his mattress was clear as well. He was safe for now. With a couple of hours left before dinner, Caden sat down at his desk, picked up his pen, and got to work.

* * *

"Mom, can I go ride my bike? I'll be back before dinner," Caden asked while moving toward the door. Mom sat slumped on the couch playing with her phone. She didn't respond, and Caden was about to yell for her again when his dad walked out of the kitchen.

"Where you going, killer?" Dad had a peanut butter and bacon sandwich in his hand, his hair crazy from sleep. A rough shadow of beard made him look tired. Life was grinding Dad down, wearing him thin, a used battery almost devoid of spark.

"Outside. I want to ride my bike." Caden's cheeks burned bright red. He hated lying and was uncomfortable telling even this little white one.

"Dinner will be ready before long. Don't ride over to Logan's house. Be where you can hear me if I need you. Okay, pal?" Dad's eyes were flat and his words empty of love or warmth to lend them any weight. The absence was worst of all.

Caden nodded. "Okay, Dad." In truth, he would only need a few minutes.

Caden skipped down the stairs, one hand making sure the package hadn't moved and the other on the handrail. Summer was supposed to be his favorite time of year. Still close enough to spring and not overly warm, it was perfect bike riding weather. Caden unlocked his prized possession, a beautiful

BMX, from the rack underneath the stairs. He stared a moment at the empty space next to his where Logan's bike used to live, gone now, safe in a garage. It didn't have to be chained up underneath the stairs where it hopefully wouldn't be stolen.

A large bald-faced hornet sat on the rail. Caden couldn't shake the feeling the thing was watching him. Glossy wings hid the insect's thick black body, but the white stripes on the abdomen and its white head were unmistakable. Caden felt a minor prickle of fear worm through his stomach. Dad said they were aggressive, doubly so when someone was near their nest. Sitting unusually still, the hornet watched him as he pulled his bike from the rack.

Careful, boy. You're making a mistake. Go on back inside so you don't wake up one night to find your house filled with my sisters.

Caden wasn't sure where the thought had come from. The hornet stared, antenna flicking slightly over its black eyes. All Caden knew was the boogeyman had been haunting him since the farmers market at the end of the school year, and it was almost time for school to start up again. An entire summer without sleep.

Caden hadn't spent much time with Logan because he didn't want the boogeyman to haunt him too. The campouts and sleepovers hadn't happened. Logan thought he'd made Caden mad, and Caden let him think it because the thought kept him away. Kept him safe. And now this stupid bug was trying to scare him away from doing what needed doing.

"Fuck you, bug!" Caden said, both alarmed and proud of the ferocity in his voice. "You aren't stopping me!"

The hornet didn't respond.

Holding the handbrake for the rear tire, Caden turned the bike around, front wheel in the air. As the front wheel came down, Caden mounted the bike with the effortless unconscious grace of youth. As he pedaled away from the bike rack, the hornet took flight. It buzzed around Caden's head, causing him to panic. He tried to swat the thing away and lost his balance, dumping himself and his bike into the parking lot with considerably less grace than when he'd started. He hit the pavement hard enough to knock the wind from his lungs. Caden's palms were dotted with blood, bits of peeled skin, and dirt where he'd tried to catch himself.

Luckily, he wasn't hurt. Not really.

He picked himself up, looking around to see if anyone had noticed him, then turned to pick up his bike and stopped. The hornet sat on his handlebars. No doubt about it—it was watching him. It had dumped him on purpose! Caden wondered if it was laughing.

Foolish boy. Of course I'm laughing!

"Laugh at this." Caden took the package from under his shirt and swatted the nasty thing with it. Caden stepped over to where the hornet struggled to right itself. "Still funny?" he asked, feeling slightly foolish for talking to a bug.

The hornet was on the edge of getting airborne when Caden brought his foot down, relishing the pop underneath his shoe. He ground his foot on the asphalt for good measure, then righted his bike and pedaled for the Spot.

Chapter Thirteen
A Cool Drink

"What you're telling me is that it's all right to kill a sheriff?" Aron Weaver couldn't believe the indifference coming from the damn desk jockey in front of him. The name tag read ROLAND.

"Mr. Weaver. It's mister, right? You're retired? I've said nothing of the kind. Sheriff Whitland's death is a loss mourned by every sheriff and every deputy across the Commonwealth."

"In almost three months, you haven't even been able to determine if the killer was male or female. No one in a crowded marketplace saw anything?"

"I can't comment on ongoing investigations. All I can tell you is we are assisting the Summit Valley Police in pursing every lead."

"What leads?"

"I can't comment."

"Buck was my friend. He deserves better."

"Sheriff Whitland's death was tragic. We're doing everything we can to bring his murderer to justice." Roland felt for the guy, but he didn't get it. No one was going to pursue this. Yes, Summit Valley Police had ruled it a homicide, but without witnesses or evidence of any value gathered at the crime scene, there wasn't anything else to do. Suspects weren't dropping from the sky. Summit Valley officers were only human. The case wasn't officially closed, but no further work was getting done, nor was it likely to.

People in Summit Valley knew that sometimes it was better to leave well enough alone. This Aron Weaver, a retired Roanoke detective, might've been a hero—he'd saved some rich kid from a deviant, and all the papers had lauded his courageous actions—but he wasn't from Summit Valley. Some things in this world were better left undisturbed. Monsters existed— the kind of monsters immune to bullets. You couldn't put handcuffs on a nightmare. Roland shuddered. The phone rang. Grateful for a reason to end the conversation, Roland broke eye contact. "If there's nothing else, sir, I have to get back to my duties."

* * *

Weaver heard the fuck-you in the way Deputy Roland said sir. Rather than continue a pointless battle with an obvious bureaucrat, Weaver left the sheriff's office. Arguing further with Roland, who seemed like the kind of slimy career cop who got by doing as little as possible, would have landed him in jail. Weaver had known a million Rolands.

Weaver might have continued ranting but the situation here was hopeless. In a rage he slammed open the door hard enough to rattle the glass. Buck deserved better. Local law enforcement should have been falling over themselves to solve the murder of one of their own. Instead, they had closed the books and turned their backs. First Manlosa, then Buck. How could they be so nonchalant about a fellow law enforcement officer? It failed the logic test. Law enforcement in Summit Valley operated differently than any other agency Weaver had ever seen. He knew this desk jockey, Deputy Roland, was only giving the official statement, but Weaver no longer had the power to bypass sanctioned stonewalling. An ex-hero cop was still an ex.

* * *

Roland watched the ex-detective make his way back through the station's public entrance. Simone, who worked dispatch three days a week, came from the back, where she'd been listening to the exchange. Of all the people Roland worked with, Simone was his favorite. She was tough and spry with a foul mouth and a great sense of humor. Sixty-four years hadn't slowed her down at all. She still had her hair done once a week, drove herself to work, and took care of six grandchildren.

"Guy smelled like a brewery."

"Yeah. Believe he's the guy that shot the serial killer a while back?"

"That alkie did Ol' Snapper?" Simone seemed impressed. Impressing Simone didn't happen often.

"Yeah, fuckin' prehab ain't a hero no way." Roland, relieved the guy was gone, filled her in. "He wanted to pull that blue line brotherhood crap. Said we aren't doing enough to redress Buck dying on our watch."

"He's not from here."

Roland thought about his grandfather's hands dirty, molded, reaching for him. "No. He's not."

"Well," she said, "I'm going back to the phones. Shoot another text if you need me."

* * *

The heat, residual simmering rage, and the hangover had Weaver feeling slightly sick. A wave of volcanic air blasted free of Buck's raggedy truck when he opened the door. Weaver sat down in a seat worn in by someone else while sweat ran down his neck. He smelled sour, even to himself, and the sweat soaking his back smelled wrong. *I need to clean up, go to the doctor, get straight.* Similar thoughts floated through his conscious mind from time to time, though they carried no real weight.

The truth was, Weaver didn't want to get straight. What he wanted was to forget he'd committed murder. The commission said it was justified use of force. The news had called him a hero. The people thought he'd done a noble thing. He hadn't. The commission hadn't been there, the people hadn't seen, and the news didn't know the truth. Wrath had guided his actions. No way to atone for ending a life, even a life as deranged as Ben Stockmore's. He'd been cleared of any wrongdoing. What a fucking joke. Murder stained his soul. Weaver had gotten into policing naively thinking he was making a difference. Protecting the community.

An entire career spent trying to do the right thing had been lost with a bullet that couldn't be taken back. Weaver had always tried to enforce the law, while other officers he'd served with enforced opinions and were almost completely ignorant to the law. Officers who ruined lives with "contempt of cop" charges for the simple act of disagreeing.

Judges knew, but the accused were often convicted as a matter of routine. Weaver tried to give people a fair shake. Yes, there were times he'd wanted to run someone up with a "contempt of cop." Difference being he never did. He tried to respect people's rights. An oath to protect and uphold the Constitution of the United States was not an empty promise. Weaver took his oath seriously. But under Ben Stockmore's house, he'd thrown it all away. His life, his legacy, years he'd never get back were tainted. Ruined.

He put the keys in the ignition but didn't start the engine. Leaving the keys dangling, he retrieved his flask from under the armrest. His head throbbed. The temperature climbed in the closed cab, the hot air becoming difficult to breathe. His body demanded he cool down. The metal of the flask was warm to the touch, almost uncomfortable, a living thing. The liquid inside would cool him off.

Except it didn't.

Three long pulls numbed his mouth and set his throat on fire. Heat upon heat. His stomach cramped. When had he last eaten? He couldn't remember. He flung the door open, releasing yet another blast of heat, and vomited in the parking lot. *Hiss!* The asphalt was hot enough to make his sick boil. Hanging half out of the truck, eyes watering, stomach shooting pain and heaving, Weaver waited for it to end. His heart pounded. Here it came. Release. This time, his heart would finally say, "Fuck it. I quit. Pump your own fucking blood. I'm done," dropping him to the dirt. Weaver was only mildly alarmed by the prospect.

Gradually, his burning stomach relented. He opened his eyes. Snot choked his nose. Spots floated before his eyes as he tried to both breathe and puke through his mouth. Sweet, sweet oxygen flooded his lungs as the attack eased. *What the fuck was that about?* Weaver sat back up, instinctively looking around for anyone watching—a task made difficult by the tears blurring his vision.

The lot was empty of cars, devoid of spectators. Traffic passed by on Route 11, oblivious. Weaver spit once again to clear the taste from his mouth. He shut the door and started the engine, then sat back, savoring the air conditioning, which had fired up mercifully cool.

When his head quit spinning, Weaver put the car in gear and pulled away from the Summit Valley sheriff's station. A Sonic Drive-In across the street promised a treat that might cool the fire in his throat. Odd that a cheeseburger and milkshake sounded fine after his recent gastrointestinal display. Surprised by his appetite, Weaver shot through a gap in traffic to place his order.

Weaver's truck was one of exactly three cars parked in the narrow slots at the drive-in. He drove around the building where the greatest amount of shade was. Unfamiliar with the truck's wider turn radius, Weaver had to put the thing in reverse to properly line up. Brightly colored menus filled both driver and passenger side windows. The driver's side contained burgers, dogs, fries, tater tots, sodas, slushes, and limeades. On the passenger side, the menu was dedicated to dessert: soft serve cones, sundaes, banana splits, and milkshakes in a thousand different flavors. *Who the fuck asked for a pickle juice-flavored shake?*

Having no interest in sea salt-banana-fudge-peanut butter-pickle-smoked ham-whatever-the-fuck milkshakes, Weaver checked the driver's side menu. A simple cherry limeade would do the trick. At the bottom of the menu sat a talk box with a large red button. A silver-and-yellow polka-dotted arrow pointed toward it with the words *PUSH TO ORDER*.

Rolling down the window to do just that, Weaver discovered he had parked too far away to reach the button. There was no hope of pushing to order. Unwilling to move the truck to get the extra two inches he needed, he took off his seat belt. Weaver got on his knees on the seat to hang his torso from the window. He might've looked foolish, but he managed to order.

A light in the button began to flash. The light stopped blinking as a female voice came on the speaker. "Welcome to Sonic! How may I help you?" She sounded young, high school age, sixteen or seventeen. Probably her first job.

"I want a large cherry limeade and that's all."

"One Route 100 cherry limeade?" the box asked him.

"I thought it was a Route 44."

"No, sir. It's Route 100. As in carry your sorry drunken ass onto Route 100 and get the fuck out of my town."

"What did you say to me?" The raw aggression in the girl's voice shocked Weaver into near silence.

"You heard me, fuckin' murderer. There's nothing here for you except pain. Take your dead friend's truck and drive on before you get some of what he got." The voice from the box continued being bright, chipper, and sharp enough to cut.

Weaver felt his face flush red with anger and shame in equal measure. "Look here, you little bitch—"

"No, you look. Buck died screaming. You will too. Fuck off. Right this second. Before I decide to take a bite of your black heart."

Not content arguing with a speaker box, Weaver shoved the truck door open. *Let's see how brave she is face-to-face.* The door hit the menu, bouncing immediately back and hitting him in the forehead.

The voice from the box laughed, sweet, feminine, cruel. "How did that feel, dummy?"

Roaring his frustration, Weaver slammed the gearshift into reverse. The truck leapt back far enough for him to open the door. He could feel the goose egg on his forehead beginning to swell, and the voice box continued to taunt him. Stepping around the menu, Weaver found himself blocked by a portly balding man. In his cheap short-sleeve button-up shirt, blue polyester pants, and grease-stained black loafers, he obviously worked for Sonic. A gold name tag over the breast pocket proclaimed him *MANAGER*.

Weaver bet this greasy wad blocking his way would be pompous, self-important, and a sixteen-year-old girl away from jail. He wasn't disappointed on the first two counts. "*Sir*, you need to leave, sir. Right now, sir."

"I'm not going anywhere until you speak to the girl in the kitchen who's been abusing me."

"*Sir*! There's no one on the microphone. I told you. We're closed. You need to leave."

"You never told me any such thing. I never even spoke to you! Why are you protecting an employee who speaks to your customers this way?"

"There's no girl. I'm the only one here. I don't know what you're talking about. I told you we were closed when you pushed the button. You became abusive. Leave before I call the sheriff. They're right over there." *MANAGER* pointed a chubby finger toward the sheriff's station. His other hand was on his cell phone. Both were shaking. *MANAGER* was afraid.

Probably used to roughing up little girls. Telling off this cream puff has him pissing his pants. Weaver looked at the occupants of the other two cars. Both had food. Both were watching him, delighted to have an unexpected show. Deputy Roland would've loved an excuse to arrest him. He would've been over there before pus bucket hung up his phone, but going to jail wouldn't help Weaver find Buck's killer. He looked back to *MANAGER*. "Why are they eating, then?"

MANAGER ignored the question. "We're closed. Leave. Don't come back. I'll have you trespassed." Then, he turned on a greasy heel and waddled away.

The box squawked to life behind him. "Kick rocks, dickhead!"

Weaver got back in Buck's truck as the speaker continued its tirade.

"One Route 100 Special coming up! Get the fuck out of *HERE!*"

CHAPTER FOURTEEN
LAST OF HIS LINE

Sitting against the door, holding his head in his hands, Clem wasn't surprised to hear footsteps coming toward him. Everything else had gone wrong; why shouldn't he have an intruder in his home? And what did it even matter? RayRay was dead. Eaten alive by something he couldn't even see.

"My boy, you look terrible! If ever I saw a man in need of some tender mercy, it'd be you."

The last of the Farris line raised his head. Tear tracks cut through the black crust on his cheeks. The speaker stood between his kitchen and living room, leaning on a jeweled cane. He wore a suit a hundred years out of style, and under his arm, he held a bowler hat. The man smiled everywhere except his eyes. His eyes were cold.

"You Farrises are a stubborn lot. Anyone else would have heeded the warnings and left well enough alone. Clem, it didn't need to come to this, really."

"What do you know about anything?"

The man laughed, deep and hearty. "Oh, Clem! I know everything! I told you to leave Shirley alone. She belongs to me now. So do you. I know what awaited you in the old factory. I know what happened to poor sweet RayRay. I was with him all day today. You two were my special project."

"You're who RayRay kept talking about..." Clem said, finally understanding. "You're him."

"Solomon Drury VI. Pleasure to make your acquaintance." Solomon stepped closer, standing over Clem. "I must admit, I've been associated with your line for some time. Farrises are stubborn indeed. I stabbed William Michael through the heart with this cane when he refused to listen to reason. I drank his blood on the council chamber floor. I'm the guiding hand behind your every venture."

"Impossible."

"Is it? After what you've seen?"

Clem knew he spoke true. The originator of the Farris family curse stood before him.

Solomon crouched, leaning on his cane, to get to eye level. "I told you to forget about her. The lady is spoken for. There is no reward beyond what I've brought you."

"You brought a reward?"

Solomon smiled, and a shudder of fear ran up Clem's spine. "Of course I did. A reward for the last of the Farris line." Solomon stood, graceful as a cat. "Now, if you'll forgive my abrupt departure, I must be going. Much to do, much to do."

As Solomon opened the kitchen door, Clem called out, "Hey, what do you mean, a reward?"

"Forgive me. Slipped my mind. For you, Clem, as the sole surviving Farris, I grant unto you an end to the curse." Solomon tipped his hat, melting into the night before the kitchen door eased open again. Clem recognized the tick of claws on his kitchen tile. Drawing closer. Hot breath in his face.

A release from the curse. Death.

CHAPTER FIFTEEN
ILL OMENS FROM THE FLAMES

The fire from the hearth radiated unnatural heat. The temperature in the lobby of the Maple Lodge was only a few degrees cooler than the Summit Valley sheriff's vomit-stained parking lot. Solomon wasn't concerned about the temperature, even in his morning coat. The layers of clothing affected him not at all.

The lodge was as empty as it ever was. Shirley was busy performing the duties her position dictated. Mundane tasks were better left to the help. Solomon, in fact, insisted on it. From his usual spot on the side of the hearth, he could see lobby, the flames, and what lay beyond the fire. Solomon stood his vigil. Quiet, still, controlled. Hands resting lightly on the jewel of his cane. The jewel shifted through the spectrum of color, the matching silk trim of his coat keeping pace: red, orange, yellow, green, blue, indigo, violet. Steadily, almost imperceptibly, the jewel ran the spectrum.

Solomon stared through the flames.

Trouble was coming.

Solomon had maintained a vigil over the hearth since first arriving in this valley. At first, he'd been excitable, ravenous, taking too much, too fast. Lean times then birthed from his gluttony. Natives had learned to avoid his valley as tales of horrors spread, and settlers had refused to stay.

But Solomon learned. Quiet. Still. Controlled.

Eventually, the warnings faded to superstition. He'd outlasted, and the meat had returned. Solomon used them to build this town. His larder. Always, though, he kept an eye on the flames. This was his valley. He had guided its people's growth, kept its secrets throughout the many years.

The flames of Gehenna lit the blackened plains in the Pit. Twisted shapes, unrecognizable, wandered in their torment, casting their terrible shadows. Flames from the lake's ever-shifting shore washed over the plains. Unquenchable fire fueled by sin passed over tortured souls, searching for the one who'd escaped. Searching for him.

The tide of flames had never come so close to the hearth before. Something drew the fire. Drew *him*. Solomon read the signs of trouble. Caden's defiance would be remedied in short order. Tonight perhaps. And then there was Shirley's attempt to poison the guest—another disturbing attempt at free will. This would not do. The fire would be denied. Solomon had found his home and had no plans on returning to the Pit. These little rebellions would be suppressed, and life would continue as it always had.

Chapter Sixteen
Business Elsewhere

TJ's Cadillac sunk into the quarry, buried under black water, while his remains were buried under the black earth of Shirley's flourishing new garden. She watched the car sink. Solomon had assured her she could sink as many as she wished there. The quarry was aged, abandoned, and deep enough to pile up hundreds of vehicles that might never be found.

Solomon didn't want the carriage house—or worse, the parking lot—choked up with cars belonging to missing people. Best to keep everything in apple pie order. After dumping the Cadillac, Shirley had three cars in the carriage house to drop off and one in the parking lot. Business was picking up.

She waited until she couldn't see the headlights before turning away from the cliff face. Moonlight seemed to shine a little brighter here. Lightning bugs flashed their staccato messages across the clearing. The surrounding woods might have been creepy to some, but Shirley paid them no attention. The eight-mile walk back to the lodge promised to be arduous. It would take several nights to dispose of all the cars. She was grateful, at least, that the night air had broken the day's heat.

Two overgrown ruts passed as an excuse for the road leading away from the top of the quarry. Enough swimmers knew of the quarry to keep the weeds beaten back off the road. None of them seemed to have any interest in night swimming, at least not tonight. Tonight, business at the quarry belonged to Shirley alone.

Twisting around the hill from the cliff top, the road led to an ancient chain-link fence. A rusted KEEP OUT! NO TRESPASS-ING! sign hung defiantly by one corner on the outside of the double swing gate. Silver moonlight highlighted bullet holes, their edges frayed with time and corrosion, telling what some long-ago swimmer thought about the warning to keep away. One gate was missing. Hinges moaned as the wind rocked the remaining gate back and forth with invisible fingers.

Parked outside the gate, as if reluctant to enter, was her Corvette.

The engine was idle, the parking lights on. Shirley looked around for whoever had brought her car. *Must've been Solomon. Bless his sweet heart. I wonder where he went to...* With the convertible top down, she could see no one was waiting within.

The interior could use a cleaning. Warren's plush leather was getting grimy on the driver's side. Maybe all the travel had been harder on the Corvette than she'd thought. *I'll give it a good scrubbing tomorrow.* An envelope propped on the steering wheel caught her attention. Moonlight reflected from gold Maple Lodge lettering on the face. The envelope was otherwise unadorned. Inside was a handwritten note on a white wove correspondence card. Flowing script glowed under the moon-light, fine as the decadent stationery it was written on.

Dearest Shirley,

Although a beautiful night for a walk, you are far too precious to leave to the mercies of the roadside. I would be with you, but alas, I have business elsewhere. The Corvette will await you here to spirit you home as you endeavor to complete the evening's task.

–S.D.

A man that took care of his lady. She should have known Solomon would have never allowed her to walk back. Ashamed for ever doubting him, Shirley got behind the wheel and headed back to town. So much to do!

* * *

Caden sat in front of the television without seeing it. Instead, his eyes were on the sunset. The shadows grew longer, the light weaker. Tonight would be the night. He'd openly defied the boogeyman by squashing his messenger. Bug guts could still be seen on the bottom of his shoe. Mom and Dad sat on either side of him. For once, they weren't on opposite ends of the couch in antagonistic silence.

Caden felt grateful they'd had a happy day—a loving day— because their time was nearly up. The sun was setting. Something was coming. Caden felt it in his bones, knew it as completely as he knew his own name. He had disobeyed. What would the punishment be? Caden hoped it would be his alone, but felt sure the boogeyman would punish his family too. In his eyes, Mom and Dad were guilty of Caden's rebellion.

The morning had begun with Mom making pancakes and bacon. Bakey cakes. They'd called them bakey cakes since he was a baby. Dad had a phone interview for a janitor position at the elementary school in Nilbud and said it had gone well. Caden didn't know what a phone interview was. Could one go wrong? It made his father happy and, in turn, made his mother happy, so it made him happy as well. Caden didn't say anything about the boogeyman. No point in worrying them. Nothing could be done. After breakfast, they'd piled into the truck and driven down to Carter's Park.

While he and Dad swam in the creek, Mom had snuck off. She drove back into town to pick up a bucket of KFC extra crispy, with baked beans, mashed potatoes, gravy, biscuits, and macaroni and cheese. KFC was Caden's favorite, even better than McDonald's. Fried chicken was expensive, so he didn't get it very often. No one even mentioned the cost. Caden felt guilty they hadn't noticed she was gone until she yelled, "Lunchtime! Do I have any hungry boys?" from the bank.

They'd made a picnic of it by the creekside. Afterward, Dad had stretched, lounging on the grass, while Caden and Mom swam. Finally, they spent a couple of hours hunting crawdads. Mom taught him how to turn the rocks over gently so the crawdads didn't scare. The tiny lobsters, if grabbed behind the arms, didn't pinch, but he couldn't get his nerve up enough to really grab one. Mom caught way more.

Crawdads released back into the water, picnic cleaned up, and trash thrown away, the three piled back in the truck to drive home. Exhausted, sunburnt, and content, they took a family nap. Peanut butter and leftover bacon sandwiches were eaten for dinner as they sat in companionable silence watching television.

The sun was setting too fast. Anxiety built in his chest as Caden watched the shadows crawl across the floor. Bedtime was on him before he knew it. Mom brought clean pajamas while he was in the bath. Clean, teeth brushed, Caden stood in his bedroom doorway, reluctant to enter. Time was almost up.

"Come on, twerp. Time for bed." Dad scooped him up from behind.

Caden put his head against his father's chest, enjoying the coconut smell of suntan lotion mixed with Dry Idea deodorant and the Irish Spring soap his father favored. Warm smells. Safe.

Dad tucked him in, leaning down to kiss him on the cheek. He almost never kissed Caden on the face anymore. "Did you have a good day today, buddy?"

"I did. I love you, Dad."

"What about me? I taught you how to catch crawdads!" his

mother exclaimed as she walked into his bedroom. She leaned down and kissed him on the corner of his mouth—an act not unusual for her.

"I love you too, Mom." Caden wanted desperately to tell them what was coming, to warn them. But they hadn't believed him all summer, and Caden knew that wasn't going to change. It would only worry them and ruin the day. Caden wanted to remember them this way, standing by his bed, backlit by the hall light, looking at him, loving him. Loving each other. Dad had his arm around Mom's waist. She leaned into him, seeming comforted by his touch. Three against the world.

His parents turned, shutting the door behind them and cutting him off from the light. Nothing outside the window. His closet, empty. Nothing crouched behind the door. Relief washed through Caden. Had he been wrong?

Sleep came quickly despite his fear. Even with the nap they'd taken, the sunburn had sucked all his energy away. During the night, he heard his father ask, "Are those hornets? Jesus, don't move, babe." His mother's screams brought him fully awake. Caden sat up, pulling the covers up to his chin, hoping they would provide some type of protection. A slight movement underneath the mattress confirmed the awful truth. He was here.

A white hand with impossibly long thin fingers reached up to grab the foot of his bed. Another appeared beside the first. The hands gripped the mattress. Caden heard the fabric tear as fingers punched through the bedding. The boogeyman pulled himself loose from underneath the bed. His arms were too long, elbows bent at a strange angle near his ceiling. He perched on top of the footboard, looming over Caden. Impossible, still, there he was.

The legs were as malformed as the arms, knees and elbows near the ceiling like some horrible grasshopper. The boogeyman wore an old-timey suit, reminding Caden of someone from the

Old West; only the suit stretched to awful proportions to cover the boogeyman's terrible form. The top hat he'd been wearing at the farmers market perched over red eyes and too many teeth. Too terrified to move, Caden could only stare. The boogeyman leaned down to whisper in his face.

"Caden, we have some things to discuss, yes?"

CHAPTER SEVENTEEN
THE THIRD INTERLUDE: PRIVATE DINING

F inding the Maple Lodge didn't prove to be much of a task. It had been much less eventful than getting gas. An exit off the interstate onto Route 11 took him directly into Summit Valley. Calling this a town was a bit of a stretch. A row of fast-food places and a couple of gas stations surrounded by shitty houses. Big deal.

From the gravel lot of the Maple Lodge, Elliott checked the porch—cool and comfortable looking. Late summer heat bounced off the gravel, making the ground feel better suited for baking than parking. Late summer afternoons in the South were the worst. At the back of the property was an actual carriage house. He hadn't seen one of those in forever. This place was old; there was some history here. Maybe the Maple Lodge would turn into a happy accident after all.

Elliott Jensen had the best job in America. Tasked with finding new and interesting places to eat, he scoured the country looking for unusual food. Driving through innumerable small towns—and Elliott always drove—he had discovered a backlog of unique restaurants. His discoveries were divvied up amongst the network's top tier producers to be assigned to popular Food Network shows. Gordon, Guy, Alton, and Padma were a few of the hosts whose location shoots could be credited to Elliott. Although most people outside the network didn't know Elliott's name, much less his face, his talents for discovery were hotly in demand.

He loved to eat.

Chain restaurants dominated off the major travel arteries. Nobody wanted to watch a show set in an Olive Garden. Elliott found not only original dishes served in interesting surroundings, but unique personalities creating culinary art. Compelling television couldn't be found off the interstate, which was why Elliott rarely used them. Talent was discovered off the highways and byways.

After discovering a retired couple who sold gourmet hot dogs out of a converted school bus in West Virginia, he found himself traveling south on Interstate 77 toward Interstate 81. At the intersection of I-77 and I-81, he would head north to see if there was anything worth eating in Roanoke, Virginia. Rural areas rarely had hidden gems, but it never hurt to look. His recent success in West Virginia was proof enough. Now he sat in the parking lot of another triumph discovery.

His Chevy Colorado chewed up the miles at a comfortable pace. The low mountains of Appalachia slid by the windows cool and green. Traffic remained friendly and light. Standing at six feet, three inches and weighing in at over 350 pounds, Elliott loved the truck because of the space afforded to the driver's seat thanks to an extended cab. Although the 3.7-liter V6 wasn't the most powerful engine, he enjoyed sitting above everyone, looking down at the traffic, even if he wasn't speeding by.

People did the most interesting things when they thought they weren't being watched. Most of the time, he caught people picking their nose. Traveling on I-5 in California, he'd seen a woman reading a magazine while putting on her makeup—at eighty-five miles an hour. Sometimes they tried to hide the fact that they were texting. Once, he'd even seen a guy masturbating, feverishly working like he'd freshly figured out how, in traffic. He'd waved with a free hand when he noticed Elliott watching and kept on, never losing pace. Elliott could do without seeing that ever again, thank you very much.

He pulled off shortly after merging onto I-81 to gas up the truck. Elliott guided the truck in beside pump five facing the Love's. The gas station had a fair amount of traffic, though it couldn't be described as busy. A couple of eighteen-wheelers parked together in a far corner of the lot. The pumps toward the end of the row were occupied, but Elliott didn't have a neighbor on either side. A few cars sat parked in the spaces in front of the building.

Before he could turn off the engine, his phone vibrated. Food Network had forwarded an email. Leaving the truck running to keep both the music and, more importantly, the air conditioning going, Elliott read the message.

Isn't this fucking typical? Elliott thought, his anger growing. It was never enough. He'd discovered a little bit of gold in West Virginia for one of their no-talent hosts. Someone—not him, because he wouldn't ever get what he deserved for all his hard work—was going to make a ton of money off the hippy hot dog people. His material was guaranteed ratings gold. Elliott had raised a piddly little network doing stand and stirs to—let's be honest here—the international stage.

Now they wanted him to delve back into the land of backward bumpkin cousin fuckers. Did it matter that he had plans, *appointments*, in Roanoke? No. Roanoke, though not a bastion of sophistication, could at least claim to have a Starbucks. He'd been instructed to put his appointments on hold and head to some nowhere town called Summit Valley.

According to the tip, there was a bed-and-breakfast that had acquired a creative gourmet chef. The B and B had been run by the same family for six generations. The owner and the chef were both eccentric, though the tip didn't elaborate on exactly how. There was no mention of formal dining open to the public. If there wasn't any kind of sit-down service, it wouldn't be of much use. Unless the eccentricity of the staff made it worth his while, he would eat, stay the night, and run.

Elliott was torn. Part of him wanted to keep this cushy job. He was paid to find interesting places to eat. That pay could've been better, and for a scout of his ability, it should've been. At the very least, he deserved credit and a modicum of respect.

Summit Valley was close. A quick check of the GPS revealed he was less than twenty miles from the front door of the Maple Lodge. Another part of him—albeit a much smaller part—wanted to tell Food Network to fuck right off. He wasn't some nobody to be ordered around. Elliott wasn't a servant. He'd helped *build* the brand.

He might not have been there from the very beginning—

Honkkk!

An impatient customer lay on the horn. Elliott's anger flared, his cheeks hot and flushed red. Elliot's blood pressure spiked, and he dropped his phone and threw open the door.

He stepped from the truck, moving to face the asshat honking at him. Some guy in a backward hat and wraparound sunglasses threw his hands up at Elliott. *Probably thinks he looks tough*, Elliott thought. A female, probably the girlfriend, sat in the passenger seat looking embarrassed. Big men weren't known for their speed, and people always seemed surprised at how quickly Elliott covered ground when necessary.

Big men weren't known for their tempers either, but Elliott went nuclear at any perceived slight, no matter how minor. Like when some dipshit thought he was taking too long at the pump while he was trying to sort through a few work issues.

"If you're not getting gas, could you move—"

Elliott never let him finish. One day, his temper would get him into serious trouble.

The guy had his window down. His mistake. Elliott reached into the car, grabbing him by the tank top before the guy could register the danger he was in. "What the fuck do you want, junior? Am I taking too long? Fat man moving too slow for you?" Elliott yelled into the man's surprised face, jerking him sideways toward the open window. The seat belt kept him from being yanked free of the car. Elliott let go of the shirt and grabbed the side of his head, then slammed the honker's face into the car door. "This your personal pump? The others quit working? Hit that fucking horn again! Hit it again!"

The impact shattered the sunglasses, driving shards of plastic into the guy's temple and left eye. Elliott slammed him into the doorframe three more times to make sure the point was understood. The driver slumped in the seat, blood flowing from his mangled face. The ruined eye squirted red flecks onto the windshield in time with his heartbeat.

"Stop! Stop hurting him, please!" the girl begged, crying.

"Let me hear another honk. Let me see you on the phone. Give me any reason to come back over here, and I'll ruin both of you. Understand, missy?"

"Y-Yes. I—uh—I understand."

"You know what? Let me help you resist temptation." Elliott extended his hand. "Phones."

"W-What?"

Had fear made her stupid, or was she naturally thick? Elliott didn't know or care. He wanted their phones. "Give me your phone. Give me this dummy's phone. If I have to tell you again, you join him in the hospital. Don't make me repeat myself."

She scrambled to hand over the cell phones. Sobbing, makeup running, pale and shaking—it made Girlfriend hot. Too bad there wasn't time. Elliott had a fine hard-on straining at his zipper. This was fun. He'd almost forgotten about how annoyed he was with Food Network. He took the phones and casually threw them toward the street as he strolled back to the truck. The phones shattered, and broken plastic skittered across the blacktop.

He pumped his gas, oblivious to the stares he was getting, and listened to Girlfriend cry. A better woman would have checked her man before someone broke his face. Elliott had taught them both a lesson. Satisfaction with a job well done made his mind up. Elliott decided to head over to Summit Valley and see what this Maple Lodge had to offer.

He turned his back on the kid bleeding in the parking lot and the crowd gathering around the sobbing woman, then got back on northbound I-81. It would be wise to get off the road for the evening with the chance that police would be looking for his truck. Maybe he shouldn't have hit the kid quite so hard. It wasn't really his fault; Elliott was annoyed with work. His doctor had told him he needed to work on his anger as badly as he needed to lose weight. *Fuck that guy. What does he know, anyway?* Elliott never had trusted doctors.

* * *

The lobby contained Victorian couches and chairs. Rich dark wood gleamed. A man stood by the fireplace, leaning on a cane, gazing into the flames. Elliott thought it was a bit too warm for a fire. The guy was truly a piece of work. A turn-of-the-century businessman, a dandy, complete with waistcoat! It was also a bit hot for wool in Elliott's opinion. This nut had to be either the chef or the owner.

A woman walked in from somewhere in the back, and Elliott's nose wrinkled at the smell she brought with her. For a minute, he thought he smelled rotting meat. It was enough to make him want to leave. If he hadn't busted a guy's head at the gas station, he probably would have.

"Welcome to the Maple Lodge! May I help you, sir?" She stood at the counter with an expectant look upon her face. *Not bad for an older woman*, Elliott thought. Her eyes were clear and bright. Her red hair hung past her shoulders in a stylish cut framing her face. The smell—if there had ever been one to begin with—disappeared. He cast a sideways glance at the figure by the fireplace, who hadn't acknowledged him yet. His cane was topped with a blue gem that perfectly matched the silk trim of his coat.

"I don't have a reservation," Elliott began, "but I'd like a room if there is a vacancy."

The redhead behind the counter smiled. "It shouldn't be a problem." A rectangular gold name tag pinned to her breast read Shirley.

"Great, great." Elliott navigated his prodigious girth around the furniture with the grace of a dancer. "You take credit? I have a company card."

"Yes, sir. Credit will do fine." She looked toward the man standing at the fireplace. "Solomon, don't be rude. We have a guest."

Solomon turned away from the flames to look at Shirley. For a moment, Elliott saw a flash of pure animal ferocity move across Solomon's face. He took an involuntary step back. The look vanished as quickly as the earlier phantom smell.

"Of course, Shirley." Solomon turned to Elliott. "Please pardon my rudeness. Solomon Drury, owner-operator. Sometimes I get lost in the flames. Welcome to the Maple Lodge." He walked over to shake Elliott's hand. Elliott took another step back from the offered handshake. He didn't want the innkeeper to touch him. A shiver of fear ran up Elliott's spine—there and gone before he could understand why he'd been afraid.

Solomon ignored the slight and gracefully dropped his hand to rest on top of his cane. "Well then, sir, how may we be of service?"

"I'd, uh, like a room."

"Of course you would! And I have the perfect accommodation for you!"

Solomon walked around Elliott to take Shirley's place behind the counter. "I'll take over, Shirley. Take Mr. Jensen's bag to suite two, please. And move his vehicle into the carriage house."

Shirley nodded, stepping from behind the counter. "It doesn't take any extra effort to be polite, Solomon," she said.

"What was that, dear heart?" Although Solomon's words were soft, Elliott recognized the barely contained rage underneath them. Thick, immediate tension filled the air. Shirley had... what? Embarrassed him? Spoken out of turn? Apparently, Solomon didn't like mouthy women. Elliott could appreciate that.

"You can say please, Solomon. That's twice you've been rude. It's beneath you." Shirley didn't appear the least bit intimidated. Elliott liked that too. He should have been uncomfortable witnessing a spat between lovers—were they lovers?—but he wasn't. What fun!

It looked to Elliott like Solomon choked back his anger and retreated. He felt a little let down that the man had caved so easily. "Quite right, my dear. Forgive an old innkeeper. Please, fetch Mr. Jensen's belongings and move the vehicle."

Shirley nodded, her mouth a thin line of disapproval, but she didn't continue to argue. Elliott handed her his keys as she passed on her way out. He watched her go. Looked good coming and going. He turned back when she'd made her way onto the porch. Solomon waited in silence for Elliott to return his attention, the altercation forgotten.

"Wait, how do you know my name?" Uneasiness crept back in.

"Apologies, sir. Aren't you Elliott Jensen, lead location scout for the Food Network? I'm a bit of a foodie, as is Shirley, and we're both admirers of your work."

"You know who I am?" Elliott relaxed. These people knew who he was! Fans!

"I confess, I'm a bit of a fan. You have such an amazing eye for talent. The locations you've found have been simply fascinating, and your discoveries make for the most interesting programming, if you don't mind my saying so. I don't mean to gush"—Solomon leaned over the counter, grinning at Elliott— "but I'm having a moment here. I'm a tad nervous."

Elliott smiled back. "No need to be nervous. I'm a guy who likes to eat."

"I am as well."

"I had a tip about this place. I heard the atmosphere was unique and the food delicious."

"How kind. I do try, sir. Shirley and I work hard to make each guest's stay a memorable one. If I may be so bold—I don't believe you've ever gotten the credit you deserve. I would think the Food Network would be more appreciative of someone with your obvious talents."

"Thank you! I've been thinking that for years! You know, when I started, all they did were cooking shows. Called them 'stand and stirs.' No travel. Nothing about culture. I brought diversity, creativity. They mold my discoveries to their 'personalities,'"— Elliott made quote marks in the air—"like any of those hacks could be bothered to leave the studio for five damn minutes."

"Indeed, sir. Shirley and I have thought that for years. I'm sure there are others who have as well."

"That's nice to hear. Thank you, Solomon."

"Not at all, sir. If you decide to include our humble lodge on your remarkable list of discoveries, we'll make sure you get your proper credit." Solomon passed a form across the counter for Elliott to sign. Solomon had already taken his credit card information, as well as the make and model of his truck. All Elliott needed to do was sign.

Elliott, excited about finding fans, signed and turned to the door as the saucy redhead, Shirley, carried his travel bag inside. Solomon motioned for him to follow Shirley. She showed surprising strength as she carried his bag up the stairs. He stayed on the road most of the year and lived out of his suitcase, which was large and heavy.

Stairs were tough for a guy his size. His heart pounded hard enough to alarm him. He'd had a physical day, and the stairs took the last bit of his energy.

At the top of the stairs, Shirley crossed a balcony that overlooked the lobby. Elliott kept his eyes on her hips while she led him to his suite. Yes, she looked fine. She turned at the end of the walkway, disappearing from his sight. Around the corner, he found her waiting beside an open door. She had placed his suitcase neatly on the luggage stand in the open closet. Not only was she strong, she was fast! Elliott was impressed. He was huffing, sweating, and fighting to get his breath, while she didn't even appear winded. He wondered how her strength translated to the bedroom.

What did it take to make her beg?

"Your suite, sir." She handed him the key. A wooden tab with the number two burned into the center dangled from a chain. She smiled up at him like she knew what he'd been thinking. Her smile was knowing, polite—and thoroughly disinterested. He was a customer. She was doing a job. Elliott felt a pang of disappointment.

Once he stepped by her and into the room, he forgot about the erotic daydream he'd been entertaining. A bathroom on his right contained both a shower and whirlpool tub. In the sitting area, a couch and a recliner were positioned toward a flat-screen television, and a writing desk sat against another wall. The bedroom was located behind a set of French double doors. A king-size bed dominated a space large enough to contain a standing armoire and another recliner without feeling crowded.

Elliott turned around to tell Shirley how incredible the room was, but she was gone. Even his door was shut. Elliott felt another flash of disappointment, then moved his suitcase from the luggage stand in the hall closet to the recliner in the bedroom. His intentions were to shower and change for dinner. This was a nice find; he might stay a couple of extra days if it wasn't booked. Hell, it was on Food Network's dime. Why not? Hopefully the food would be as delightful as the service and accommodations thus far. Glad he'd made the decision to come here, he began to hang his clothes in the armoire. A knock at the door caused him to pause in his work.

Peeking through the peephole, he saw Solomon standing in the middle of the hall, both hands resting on his cane. Elliott opened the door.

"Terribly sorry to disturb you, sir."

"Not a problem, Solomon. What can I do for you?"

"My commissionaire failed to get your dining instructions."

Elliott was hungry. It had been a long drive from West Virginia, and he was spent. Relaxing on the couch with a hot meal sounded mighty fine. "Well, I'm not sure what's on the menu. No one mentioned dinner."

"This evening, we have a dry-aged ribeye with crispy seasoned potatoes and an herbal green salad. Or if you'd prefer, we have a honey pecan glazed fried chicken with sugar snap peas and grainy mustard butter. We could substitute the peas with summer squash in sweet garlic broth."

"I wouldn't have thought I'd find such sophisticated fare in a small town like this. I'll try the ribeye. It sounds amazing."

"Very good, sir. And will you be taking your meal in your private dining room?"

"I have a private dining room?"

Solomon's brows drew down slightly. "Were you not informed of your private dining room, then?"

"No. Sorry."

"No need to apologize, sir. The fault lies entirely with my staff. If I may, I will show you."

Elliott stood aside to let him in. Curious, Elliott followed Solomon.

"Hmm, how did this happen?" Solomon asked, walking up to the writing desk. "Apologies, sir. This desk is blocking the way. It should be along this other wall. This won't take a moment."

Elliott didn't reply. Solomon lifted the writing desk with

ease, moving it back to its original home underneath a window. With the desk moved, he could see another set of double doors. How had he missed it? Solomon opened the doorway before disappearing within. Elliott followed in awe.

This place was amazing. Up close, he could see the doors were so perfectly aligned they became nearly invisible when shut. What remarkable craftsmanship! Maple Lodge, with all its surprises, made his list. He would be doing a complete write-up for the Food Network as soon as he ate dinner.

The private dining room exploded in color. Swarovski crystal caught the natural light streaming through floor-to-ceiling windows and threw dancing rainbows along the walls, ceiling, and tabletop. Rather than obnoxious, the effect was charming, whimsical. The table was covered in crisp white linen. A blood-red napkin, folded to resemble a rose, floated in an empty soup bowl. The bone-white china, fine and expensive, was framed by silver cutlery. Elliott held the bowl up, feather-light and so translucent he could almost see through it. Maple Lodge dripped quality and luxury. Why had he never heard of it before?

Crowning the center of the table, three candles, red as the napkin, rested in a crystal candelabra. There was only one place setting. Against the far wall, a discreet staircase led downstairs to what Elliott assumed was the kitchen. A lock on the inner door insured his privacy. Solomon stood by the stairs, a smile on his face. Elliott's approval was obvious.

"Yes, absolutely, I will have my dinner in here! What an incredible place you have here, Solomon. I would have never expected this, here, in this town. I hope the locals appreciate and support you." Elliott tried not to gush, but he couldn't help himself. This place was filled with surprises!

"You're too kind. Yes, the locals have supported my family for six generations. We were among the first in the area. We've quite a history if you're of a mind."

"If the food holds the same quality as everything else, you'll

THE LODGE

be telling your history to the whole world. The Maple Lodge is Blue Ridge Mountain gold."

Solomon gave a little half bow before exiting down the staircase. "As you say, sir. I'll see to your dinner."

*　*　*

Dinner was every bit as amazing as he'd hoped. Elliott sat back, wiping his mouth with a grease-stained napkin. Dark blotches marred the once crisp fabric. Sign of a fine meal, Elliott thought, and burped loudly. The steak—expertly cooked to an exact medium rare, tender, bloody—was so amazing Elliott had ordered the chicken as well. The honey pecan glaze contrasted perfectly with the salty, savory chicken. He'd ordered the peas in addition to the squash. Elliott traced his finger through the remaining garlic broth. Sucking greedily at the last bit of dinner, he pushed back from the table.

Solomon had instructed him to leave the mess and to remember to shut the door on his side. Shirley would clean up; he'd never know she was there. It was tempting to leave the door open. Elliott wondered if Shirley screwed as well as she cooked. Any woman who cooked the way she did deserved a special thank-you. A hard fuck after a fine meal would put the cherry on top of his evening.

Tempting as the thought was, Elliott closed the door, thumbing the lock. Maple Lodge deserved every bit of the publicity he would bring. It wouldn't do for the star chef to leave because he couldn't keep his dick under control. Too bad he didn't know where Girlfriend was. Probably at the hospital with her broken-faced boyfriend. *Fucker will think twice before he lays on the horn next time*, Elliott thought with a grin. *Oh well, another lonely night.*

A woman in every town was a common misconception about men who traveled. In Elliott's experience, women weren't waiting for strangers to pass through town and fuck them cross-eyed. Most didn't go in for random sex with strangers. Hell, he didn't do one-night stands. Once in college, but he was older now, wiser. And heavier.

It had been a long day. Elliott put away his thoughts of a midnight rendezvous with the cook. Before getting in the shower, a thorough inspection had to be done. For a man who spent as much time in hotels and motels as he did, there were a few things he always checked. Room inspection was normally the first thing he did, but somehow, he'd let it get away from him. It spoke well of the Maple Lodge that he felt comfortable enough here to put things off until close to bedtime. He checked the smoke detector, both for batteries and cameras. Elliott had a fear of finding himself on the internet. People violated other people's privacy all the time. He wasn't about to make the mistake of being filmed naked because he'd been too lazy to check the place.

Dying in a fire didn't have much appeal either.

Plants were the next thing he checked for. You never knew what might be in a plant. He'd found spiders, dust, and once, he'd found a hundred-dollar bill, rolled up and stuck in the soil. Plants were an instant tell as to the cleanliness of a room. But there weren't any plants. Unusual. Most places kept at least one fake plastic plant for ambience.

Housekeepers who didn't take the job seriously rarely dusted. Some might not think dusting was a big deal, but he'd heard dust was made up mostly of skin cells. When you thought about having an unknown number of people's cast-off skin floating around, it made dusting damn important. Not doing the job properly was intolerable. Elliott never stayed in places where it was obvious they didn't pay close attention to standards of cleanliness. No point paying to sleep in other people's sluff. Gross.

Even the tops of the doors remained clean and free of debris. After searching for dust, he checked alarm clocks and other electronics for any type of recording device. Behind the mirrors always received a thorough inspection. Elliott kept a pen light for the specific purpose of lifting mirrors away from the walls and illuminating behind them. He also carried a piece of cardboard, cut from a box of Lucky Charms, and a roll of tape to block the peephole. He'd read about a journalist who'd been recorded by a guy who'd replaced the peephole with a spy camera. No way that would ever happen to him. You never knew who was waiting to see a middle-aged fat guy in his underwear. People were freaks. Being careful was being smart.

Once the mirrors were cleared, he'd check the light fixtures, particularly if one hung from the ceiling. Those were easy to conceal devices in. Any additional rooms would be checked in the exact same manner. Close attention to the bathroom was a necessity. Too many places to hide cameras, and people were most vulnerable in the bathroom.

Elliott didn't believe in being a victim. Proactively protecting himself came as second nature. He didn't need to think about what he was doing anymore. He moved through his ritual on autopilot, performing the tasks as a matter of routine. Safety always came first.

Elliott meant to check the private dining room, but strangely, he couldn't remember how to open the double doors. He was sure there had been a handle when he'd finished dinner. He distinctly remembered hearing the latch catch, thumbing the lock, and testing to make sure the doors were closed and locked. The private dining room was accessible from the kitchen, meaning his room was accessible from a point other than the main door. Not securing an entry point would be inexcusable. Unthinkable. But he couldn't figure how the damn door opened. What the fuck was going on? Handles he knew he'd checked were gone. Handles with the locking mechanism. He had thumbed the lock and tested the door. Hadn't he? Honestly, he couldn't even see the seam where the doors came together. The wall appeared solid, unbroken, like the doors had never been there.

Could he have pushed the door closed behind him and never thumbed a lock at all? Could he have confused how the door opened? It didn't seem likely. He wasn't the kind of guy who made things up. True, he was getting older, and sometimes he forgot things, but this didn't feel like the kind of thing he'd misremember. There were no inner handles. That was obvious. The hair stood up on the back of his neck.

Standing there staring at the wall wasn't getting anything done. Reluctantly, he moved on to the last item on his list.

He'd pull down the covers and inspect the sheets with a blacklight. If the bedding passed, no protein stains flashing their telling glow at him, he would lift the mattress. Propping the mattress on his back like a gigantic turtle, he would use first the blacklight, then his pen light to look for the signs.

Bedbugs, once thought almost extinct, had made a resurgence. Elliott knew falling cleanliness standards in combination with lazy housekeeping had contributed to the comeback of these disgusting parasites. In the early-to-mid-2000s, he read about the world-famous Waldorf Astoria in New York City being one of several high-profile hotels fighting infestations. The Waldorf—a five-star hotel, favorite of politicians, dignitaries, and celebrities—had been sued over bedbugs.

No fucking way was he going to pay to be eaten up by bedbugs. Not happening. The thought of a critter feeding on him while he slept was worse than finding himself naked on the internet.

Granted, his careful inspections had never revealed anything other than lazy housekeeping. He'd never seen any bedbugs or found any cameras or listening devices. And he hadn't found any this time either. But the one time he didn't check would be the time he ended up on a porn site or as a parasite's midnight snack.

Inspection over, he relaxed. Or tried to relax. Elliott took a shower, brushed his teeth. Wrapped in a towel, he wandered to the armoire for clean underwear, a T-shirt, and pajama pants.

His eyes strayed to where the private dining room had been and presumably still was. Entire rooms didn't just disappear. He was more bothered than he cared to admit that he couldn't open it. The feeling of being watched was strong. Unsure of what else to do, he moved the desk back in front of the doors. The last tenant here must have experienced the same dilemma and moved the desk. Solomon had seemed confused to see the desk where it was, and he had moved it back under the window before opening the dining room for Elliott. Yes, that must've been what happened. A previous guest couldn't work the doors either and moved the desk to feel more secure. The doors opened inward after all. Elliott had given himself a case of nerves over nothing. Sometimes you just needed to stop and think things through. There were only a certain number of ways a thing could work.

Elliott turned off the lights and used his phone to illuminate his path to bed. After connecting his phone to the charger, he laid his head down on the pillow. Elliott fell asleep quickly, knowing he was secure and bug-free.

* * *

Elliott's eyes flew open. Someone was in the room with him. He lay still, trying to pinpoint where the intruder was hiding without giving away the fact that he was no longer sleeping. There wasn't a light near the bed. He'd used his phone to find the bed after turning the lights off. *Damn.* His penlight was tucked away in his suitcase, put back in its proper place following his inspection. He'd have to get up.

A streetlamp cast light through the window, bathing the walls in an otherworldly artificial orange. The light highlighted how dark it was rather than providing any real illumination. He was going to have to move. Too much wine at dinner. His bladder wouldn't allow him to remain in bed. Sleeping on a piss-soaked mattress didn't fit with his evening's agenda. He got up to turn on the light. Unrelenting pressure from his bladder demanded a response. Anyone in here with him was about to have a serious fight on their hands. Elliott wouldn't hesitate to throw an intruder right through the window.

Elliott carried a Sig Sauer 1911 Fastback Carry Nightmare for protection on the road. Like a complete moron, he'd left the .45 in the holster under the driver's seat. The one time he needed it with him, he didn't have it. Steeling himself while trying to ignore the growing urgency down south, he leapt from the bed, clawing in the direction of the light switch.

A moaning growl—part war cry, part terror—escaped his throat as he made his charge. He caught his little toe on the edge of the nightstand. His toe bent backward as his tremendous weight moved forward. He was vaguely aware of the outside of his toe touching the outside of his foot. A strange sensation, he thought in a detached manner, before the sound of the bone snapping registered.

And then the pain hit.

Momentum carried him forward, and he fell on his face. As he fell, his flailing arm flicked the light switch. Light burst forth, blinding in its suddenness, and he found himself alone with a broken toe. Elliott picked himself up and hobbled into the bathroom to pee. Grateful he hadn't pissed himself when he fell, he finished his business and gimped back to his suitcase for the first aid kit securely zippered into an interior pocket.

Nothing could be done for a broken toe. No point in going to the hospital for some dummy to tell him what he already knew. Elliott sat down on the bed and removed the medical tape and scissors from the kit. He taped his pinky toe, already swelling, to the toe next to it. He shook a couple of Tylenol free from the bottle and dry swallowed them. *Fuck it, I'm a big boy,* he thought and dry swallowed another two.

Why had he thought someone was in the room with him?

Even awash in light from both bath and bedroom, the feeling of being watched remained—almost like whoever had been there in the dark remained with him now, hidden just out of sight, waiting. Elliott considered going to the truck for his pistol, but the fact that Shirley had moved it to the carriage house when she retrieved his luggage soured that idea. The carriage house likely required assistance to get into. It would cause concern. Questions. After his little escapade at the gas station, he didn't really want to talk to the police tonight. He couldn't think of a logical reason why he needed to get a gun from his vehicle anyway. Plus, the prospect of walking downstairs on a broken toe didn't hold much charm.

No, he'd stay here.

He checked the time. It was only eleven thirty. He'd been asleep barely an hour and a half. His injured toe screamed its indignation, sharp pains shooting through a dull swelling ache. *Gonna be a long damn night.* He closed the medical kit and secured everything back where it had been in the suitcase. In the bathroom, he opened his shaving kit. The bottle of Prozac, prescribed to help him deal with his anger, lay in the bottom where he'd put it. He shook loose a pill. So small. The tiny bit of chemical bliss in his meaty palm promised artificial calm. Better living through chemistry in the twenty-first century. *Fuck it, I am a big boy,* he thought. Elliott took another.

Four Tylenol and two Prozac, combined with the wine he'd drunk at dinner, helped rock him back to sleep.

* * *

It was 2:47 a.m. Sleep had stayed with him for almost three hours before flitting away like shadows in sunlight. This time, he didn't wake thinking someone was in the room with him. His bladder nagged at him again. The last night he'd slept all the way through without having to get up and piss lay too far in the past for him to recall. *With my luck, it's probably damn prostate cancer.*

Cancer or no, the need to relieve himself forced him back on his feet. The broken toe immediately protested. Maintaining balance by hobbling forward kept him from busting his ass. The toe, unappreciative of his efforts to remain upright, upped the game from throbbing ache to bright gnawing pains. Back in the living room, Elliott stopped dead still.

The desk was back underneath the window.

He knew—*knew*—he'd moved the desk over to the wall in front of the doors to the private dining room. Moving furniture in his sleep with a broken toe hadn't happened. No way he could have slept through the pain. He moved the desk over there before breaking his toe. He'd moved it when the handles disappeared.

No, door handles didn't *disappear*.

Prozac and alcohol flooded his system. Still, he'd swear in court on a stack of Bibles that the door handles had vanished, and somehow, the desk had walked back under the window.

The hairs on his arms, on the back of his neck, stood at full attention, the feeling of being watched a constant itch between his shoulder blades. Elliott thought about the Sig. Questions or not, wounded toe or not, he was starting to think remaining unarmed would be a bad idea.

All was quiet. No traffic moved outside. The streetlight continued to cast the sickly orange glow onto the walls. There was an absence here. It took him a minute to identify what was wrong. The silence here was like the silence of the void. True, it was almost two in the morning, but the night was never completely silent. Night bugs sang, dogs barked, cars passed. Life continued regardless of whether the sun or the moon watched over the earth. And that life made noise.

Something—some*one*—had come into his room to move the desk. Why?

It didn't make sense. Intruders stole your wallet. They didn't break in to move the furniture around. He limped over to where the desk had been. Shallow impressions in the carpet, from the legs of the desk, didn't match up to the older deeper ones. No doubt about it, he'd put the desk back in front of the doors, and it had been moved back. He went over to the desk and lifted one side. As he'd expected, the carpet underneath the feet sprang back up into place. The desk hadn't sat there long enough to break the fibers' resilience.

What the hell was going on in here?

He moved the desk back in front of the doors for a second time, careful to set the feet down on new places. Was this room haunted? No, ridiculous. Was he on camera? Someone had to be fucking with him. "You want to move furniture all night, fine. Fuck you. I'm going to bed." Elliott turned a slow three-sixty as he spoke, making sure the watcher could see he'd failed to scare.

If the intruder wanted to knuckle up and confront him, Elliott would be happy to administer an ass whoopin'. Pranky teenage girl bullshit wasn't going to scare him. Whoever was fucking with him would regret it. Elliott Jensen was big, mean, and working for Food Network hadn't made him a pussy. He traveled back roads and lost trails searching for hidden culinary treasure in the forgotten parts of America. From backwoods to deep in the ghetto, no path was too frightening for him to walk. No place too dangerous. Let him catch someone in here and they'd be joining Mr. Honky Pants in the hospital.

He did another once-over. The door remained securely locked. A brief check in the bathroom didn't reveal anything unusual. Whoever the intruder was, they hadn't left a clue as to how they'd gotten in or exited. A fucking Houdini. He flicked the bathroom light off, turned his back to the darkness, and stepped back into the bedroom. And stopped.

Impossible.

The double doors stood open. The desk sat under the window. Sodium vapor from the streetlight mixed with moonlight crept through the window and skipped across the writing surface, making the desk appear dipped in blood. Through the open double doors, Elliott could see the table had been set.

A candle burning in the center of the table only served to drown the rest of the room in shadow. The dimensions were shrouded in silky blackness that hid everything except the table.

His place was ready. Elliott smelled delicious temptation creeping from the darkness to draw him inexorably toward his proper place at the table. To refuse a meal so incredible, so decadent, would be unthinkable. His confusion forgotten, his fear dropped by the bedside, Elliott moved toward the table which appeared to float in the gloom. A meal awaited, the feast of a lifetime, demanding to be honored with enthusiasm and appetite. Any other find he would make would pale next to the triumph he prepared to partake in here at the Maple Lodge.

Elliott moved as if in a dream, savoring each step that brought him closer to the private dining room. There was nothing to fear here. Eating defined him. Food made up who he was. He had built a career and a network—even if they refused to acknowledge it—from instinct and palate.

The room appeared deeper, larger than it had only a few hours ago. His table stretched into the black. Had there been so much space earlier? Elliott thought it only a few steps from the table to either of the exits, but now, he couldn't make out where the stairs were located. It had to be a clever trick of the light.

Footsteps.

Each step echoed and reverberated back only to be overrun by the sound of the next step. The acoustics were those of a stone cavern deep in the earth, not sounds that should've been heard on the second floor of a bed-and-breakfast. The illusion of depth and space was so compelling he had to turn and check that his bedroom was still there.

It was, although it seemed…distant.

The bedcovers no longer appeared rumpled. The pillow where he'd been sound asleep a few moments ago no longer held the impression of his head. But that was unimportant—trivial, even. What mattered was his growing hunger. He'd had two dinners a few hours before but felt like he hadn't eaten for days.

The footsteps moved closer, gaining ground at the same steady pace. Elliott wanted to stand and face whoever was walking toward him. He barked his thighs on the table as he tried to get to his feet. The table never moved; the exquisite china didn't even rattle. The impact forced him back into his seat. He didn't remember scooting the chair underneath the table in the first place. His napkin rested on his lap. He had no memory of putting it there.

Through the dark, he made out a faint glow, movement. A small orange light, the same shade as the streetlamp, floated toward him then stopped outside the ring of light surrounding him. Elliott strained to see what it was.

"Good evening, sir."

Solomon moved partially into the light. Only Solomon. The jewel topping his cane matched the streetlight and the silk linings and trim of his coat. Hadn't it been a different color before? Elliott couldn't remember.

"Pardon my presumption, sir, but I thought you might care for a late-night snack."

"Yes. A snack." Elliott's tongue felt thick in his mouth, foreign.

"I have prepared many delights for you."

"For me?"

"Of course, sir." Solomon tipped his hat.

Elliott would've thought he was dreaming if not for his aching hunger. Forming anything beyond the most rudimentary thoughts proved impossible. The smells of the impending feast were overwhelming. "Solomon?"

"Yes, sir?"

"How big is this room?"

Solomon smiled. It scared Elliott, though he couldn't say exactly why. "As big as I need it to be. As it ever was."

Elliott didn't understand the answer but nodded anyway. "Oh. Solomon?"

"Yes?"

"Are we going to eat soon? The smell's driving me crazy." Elliott hated how childlike he sounded.

Solomon moved behind him, leaning close to whisper in his ear. "Oh, yes."

Elliott normally didn't allow people, particularly men, to get so close to him. Solomon seemed okay though. Not that he could have done anything about it. He couldn't stand; he was weak from hunger. When had he last eaten? It felt like days ago. "Yay. I'm hungry."

"Then eat, sir. Eat." Solomon, almost cheek to cheek with Elliott, made a sweeping gesture with his hand, then moved back to his original position in front of him, silent as the surrounding shadow.

Elliott looked from Solomon back to the table. Scores of dishes lined the table as far as he could see. Roasts of beef, racks of lamb, fat glazed hams, and skewers of grilled shrimp and vegetables sat beside wedges of aromatic cheeses and fresh fruits in a seemingly infinite blend of shapes and colors. Crystal decanters, whose cool mysterious contents caused the sides to run with condensation, shared space with chilled white wines and warm reds dark as venous blood.

The intense hunger pangs intensified under the miasma of spice carried on the steamed air. Feeding became the only thing that mattered. Elliott didn't bother with the niceties of civilized dining; the cutlery and fine china were ignored. Instead, he grabbed great handfuls of whatever dish was closest. Shoving handful after handful into his greedy mouth, Elliott could not sate his hunger.

The more he ate, the more he had to eat. He became hungrier with each handful. He dropped a bottle of 1811 Château d'Yquem—a $117,000 bottle—his fingers too greasy to maintain a hold. He neither noticed nor cared when the bottle shattered on the floor, having already grabbed a bottle of Domaine de la Romanée-Conti Montrachet Grand Cru to guzzle.

Elliott always had enjoyed fine wine.

Solomon took no notice, continuing to push dishes into Elliott's grasping reach. He grabbed a handful of this, a piece of that, knocking platters onto the floor in his haste to bring food to his face. Solomon replaced the losses faster than they could hit the ground.

Elliott received conflicting messages from his stomach. He was hungry. He could eat no more. He tried to stop, but his arms kept pushing the food into his mouth. Chewing and swallowing until his jaws hurt and his throat filled, Elliott ate. He ate until his considerable stomach expanded. Elliott released a series of explosive burps, his body attempting to relieve the growing pressure. The expansion continued until the walls of his stomach began to tear.

Still, he ate.

He was so hungry. He couldn't stop.

Pain flared through his injured intestine but was suppressed by the hunger. Digestive juices burned in his throat. Still, nothing mattered except sating this awful consuming need. Solomon pushed more platters in front of him. Always more. Elliott grabbed handful after handful, shoving food into his mouth.

Elliott's heart pounded in his chest. Sweat ran down his body, causing his T-shirt to stick. His breathing grew shallow, labored. There didn't seem to be enough air. The pressure from his swollen gut pushed against his lungs, causing him difficulty when he strained for a full breath. The food in his full stomach crept into his esophagus and triggered a coughing fit. Violent tremors from the coughing proved too much for his stomach, already stretched too thin, and Elliott felt a momentary relief from the growing internal pressure as his stomach ruptured.

A putrid mix of food, bile, and blood flooded Elliott's

abdominal cavity. Finally, Elliott managed to push back from the table. He stood up. Pain unlike anything he'd ever experienced ripped through him. He raised a pleading hand to Solomon and took a step forward. "Ack!" As he boiled in his own digestive juices, Elliott's heart stopped.

"Gak!" Elliott croaked as his legs gave way.

Solomon watched, a look of mild interest on his face, as Elliott landed face-first in the rotten remains of his final meal. Blood and bile leaked from Elliott's nose and mouth, and his eyes glazed over. "No room for dessert?" Solomon asked and giggled at his own witticism.

Shirley was not going to be happy about the mess up here.

Chapter Eighteen
Questions and Answers

A ron Weaver sat in Buck's shadowy home on Buck's couch, which was now his couch. Buck had no relatives or heirs, not even an ex-wife, so he'd willed his worldly possessions to Weaver. His truck, house, the couple of acres the house sat upon, and his hunting cabin all belonged to Weaver, who still couldn't bring himself to think of it as his. Buck's generosity humbled him.

The blinds were closed. Weaver also pulled shut the sheer window treatments, but sunlight still managed to creep in around the edge of the blinds and filter through the deep maroon fabric, indifferent to his desire for darkness. Pictures of Buck rested on the mantle, his friend at various political and police functions, smiling with people Weaver didn't recognize, the colors muted and distorted in the unwanted glow. Distant memories captured from happier times.

Mars didn't know where Buck lived. To his knowledge, Mars hadn't had any dealings with the former Sheriff of Giles County. Weaver couldn't stand any more lectures about his drinking, so he'd come here seeking refuge. It was technically his house after all. Awards and citations for meritorious service and a newspaper clipping announcing Buck's victory in his first run for sheriff all hung on the wall. Buck didn't have these in his office. He said his job was to be a lawman, not a windbag.

Weaver missed his guidance.

In his head, he could hear Buck yelling at him to put down the bottle, get off his ass, and take action! He had ventured into the fire many times since learning the trade from Buck. He'd stood down armed thieves, addicts, and abusers too numerous to count. In his last action of his career, he'd stopped a serial child murderer.

Yeah, stopped.

No due process for Ben Stockmore. Weaver remained the sole judge and jury. Pulling the trigger on Stockmore, scum that he was, had brought him to Stockmore's level. He killed. Murdered. Was that any less immoral than what Stockmore had been doing? Weaver couldn't see the difference. Maybe if Buck had lived, he could have helped him put the guilt away. But Buck was dead. Killed in Summit Valley by an unknown subject. The police—and Summit Valley had a surprisingly large amount of police for such a small town—were unable or unwilling to investigate the matter.

Summit Valley County Sheriff's Department, Summit Valley Police, Virginia State Troopers, and even the US Marshalls Service maintained offices in Summit Valley. None of them seemed to care about the murder of one of their own. These guys had been to the same functions as Buck; some of them smiled at Weaver from Buck's wall—men who'd known him or at least had known of him.

The time he'd spent at the Summit Valley County Sheriff's Department played through his mind. Weaver was a detective. He couldn't turn it off even if he wanted to. Deputy Roland had been scared. He'd sent a message for the woman in the back to come rescue him from his conversation with Weaver. Why?

What had happened to cause an entire town's police force to turn away?

Weaver needed to get up. Questions required answers. He

didn't have any. *Tell the truth, always*—one of Buck's teachings he'd carried throughout his career. Sound advice. Weaver couldn't lie to himself; the truth was that Summit Valley scared him. A general feeling of wrongness hung over the town that no amount of alcohol could hide.

Take responsibility was another Buckism.

Responsibility. Buck had been the only one looking for the truth about what happened to Trooper Manlosa. He'd gone to Summit Valley chasing cartel assassins. Buck hadn't found South American drug lords, but whatever he'd discovered was no less lethal.

Responsibility weighed heavily on Weaver. A tickling at the back of his mind told him Buck's death, and what happened on the Route 460 bridge, were related. In no logical world should a connection so outlandish be made. But there it was. Years of instinct—correct more often than not—struggled through the alcohol he'd flooded his system with. Not to be denied or ignored, his instincts had led him to the successful conclusion of hundreds of cases.

And his instincts were screaming that a murderer had taken up residence in Summit Valley.

There wasn't any denying that *something* lived in Summit Valley. Weaver didn't go to church, didn't believe in ghosts, and didn't believe a town could be haunted. Or, he wouldn't have thought so before his trip to Summit Valley. People walked around this town in a haze of fear. As much as he wanted to pass it off to the booze, he couldn't dismiss what he'd observed on the faces of the people.

Fear. But of what?

Then he had his own incident to consider. What happened at the drive-in defied rational explanation. The manager had claimed he'd been unruly, suggested Weaver had misheard. That wasn't how he remembered things. He couldn't doubt his own mind. True, he'd fallen deeper into the bottle than he cared to admit, but his mind was still sound. He'd never experienced hallucinations. And he didn't believe he'd had one in Summit Valley.

So, then…what?

Every answer he needed hid in that tiny mountain town. To find the truth, he needed to go back. He was scared and wasn't sure why. *Responsibility.* Buck smiled back at him from the walls. Crouching in the dark and being afraid of himself wouldn't help him catch Buck's killer. He needed to get off his ass. Weaver stood up and grabbed the keys to Buck's truck. He even remembered to lock the door behind him. His flask remained on the coffee table. He wouldn't be needing it anymore.

* * *

"Logan, buddy, you want to get up? Maybe we could get an ice cream or go to the game store? The big one in Roanoke? Sound fun?"

Logan's parents watched from the doorway as their son lay in bed. He hadn't been up in two weeks, not since they'd had to tell him about Caden. What they didn't tell him were the details. You didn't tell a child how his best friend had been ripped to pieces or how his best friend's parents looked like they'd been stung to death, purple and swollen. Some things you didn't talk about. Especially to your child.

But Logan knew.

"No thanks. I'm tired. I want to rest." Logan rolled away from them. He knew his parents were worried, but they couldn't help him. He'd hung with Caden once since their sleepover at the end of school. Caden hadn't talked much then, and he'd looked sad. They'd played *Diablo* without their usual banter. Caden had dark circles under his eyes and said he hadn't been sleeping because of nightmares.

Logan knew his friend well enough to tell when he lied. Caden wasn't sleeping because he was scared—and not of bad dreams. After that, he hadn't come back. Logan never saw his friend alive again.

Logan had a dream the night Caden died. Caden came to him and woke him up to tell him he wouldn't be coming over anymore. They wouldn't be hanging out next year. In the dream, Caden said he'd been murdered. Worse than the horror movies, he'd said. He told Logan his parents had been stung by a million-million hornets because he'd angered the boogeyman. His mother had screamed and screamed, and it was all his fault.

"What'd you do?" Logan had asked him.

"If I say, he might come for your family. I can't tell you."

Logan was afraid, confused. "Caden, you're my best friend. You can't be dead."

Caden sat on the side of the bed, but the mattress never moved. It should have sunk under his weight. Logan knew he was dreaming. His Pikachu night-light glowed dimly from the outlet, and muted light filtered through his friend. Crickets buzzed. Frogs sang their night songs. Strange to hear those sounds in a dream.

Caden reached to touch Logan's face—an oddly intimate gesture, too mature, too solemn, for a boy. Caden carried a burden Logan couldn't understand. Logan didn't shy from the touch he couldn't feel.

"You're my best friend. I love you, Logan. I'm sorry I won't be in the fifth grade with you."

"What are you talking about? I don't like this. I want to wake up." Logan felt panicky, breathless at the way Caden was talking. This was the worst dream ever.

Caden regarded his friend. "I'll be gone soon. You can think whatever you want to. I wanted to say goodbye."

"No. No! Who's gonna play your Barb? Who's going to do that if you're gone?"

"You'll have to finish on your own. I told you to pick a better toon." Caden smiled, a sad smile—a ghost of a smile—at the old argument. "I'm gone. I can't help you anymore. But I left something. You'll have to decide if you want to go get it."

"What is it?" Logan was openly crying now. He should have been embarrassed to cry in front of his friend. He wasn't. This time, he knew it was okay.

"If you do go"—Caden leaned forward, ignoring the question—"I can't protect you. It can happen to your family the way it happened to mine. Also, you have to promise me something."

"Sure."

"Don't open it. Don't look. It's not for you, not really. Give it to *him*."

"Who?"

"I can't protect you. My time is gone. Goodbye, Logan."

Caden faded until he was gone, like he'd never been there at all. Pikachu continued to shine from his place on the wall. Night songs continued outside, indifferent to a little boy's heartache.

The next morning, Logan's parents came to tell him what he already knew. He knew because Caden had told him. Logan hadn't lost anyone before. Death was an alien concept to him, and he didn't know what to do. There was a gaping hole in his heart. Logan hurt all the time and didn't understand how to heal the hole. Was it normal to hurt so bad? He only knew he missed his friend. Caden had been taken from him. *Murdered*.

He'd thought about his dream a lot. Didn't he owe it to his best friend to find whatever it was he left behind? Shouldn't he honor his friendship and get this mysterious thing to whoever it was Caden wanted to get it to? He said Logan would be in danger if he looked, that his family would be in danger.

Still, Logan knew in his heart what he was going to do. If Caden left him something, assuming he wasn't completely off his cracker, there was only one place it could be.

The Spot.

* * *

Weaver parked Buck's truck on First Street in a slot desig-nated as Public Parking, across the street from the Summit Valley Police Department. After a moment's consideration, he decided not to go inside. Figuring he'd get the same run-around he'd gotten at the sheriff's department, it didn't seem worth the hassle.

When he crossed the county line, Weaver thought he'd felt... resistance. A force willing him to leave, letting him know he was unwanted. *Better get used to that, pal. Cops—even ex-cops—are used to being unwanted. I'm not going any-damn-where until I find out what happened to my friend.*

The day, already thick with humidity, promised to be another miserable exercise in late Southern summer. Radiant heat soaked through his shoes. Thunderheads on the horizon gave hope of rain, though late summer storms tended to be short-lived, providing no real break from the heat.

Traffic was nonexistent. Only the occasional car passed by. Pedestrians hid indoors from the heat. This stretch of First contained the Summit Valley Police Department, Summit Valley Post Office, and Chuck's on First—an unfortunately named restaurant.

He'd parked facing Jefferson Park, which was empty due to either the workday or the heat. A large maple provided shade for a park bench in front of him. The park was a stretch of open grass, a green oasis the length of a block. War memorials for the soldiers from Summit Valley who'd died in conflicts stretching back to the Civil War bordered the Washington Avenue side, the only other structure being a decent-size gazebo in the center of the park. It was a popular gathering place in town during summer evenings. Local bands played at the gazebo. The area was closed to vehicular traffic for Labor Day celebrations. Across the park was the train station where the Saturday farmers market was held.

From where he stood underneath the maple, Weaver could

see the place where Buck died. Murdered in sight of a police station, and still the killer escaped. No, he wouldn't be going in to pressure the locals. Why bother? They had been too inept, too afraid, or too indifferent to step in when they were most needed. The fire station was located on Jefferson, directly across from Chuck's on First. It had taken forty-five minutes for an EMT to travel four blocks. Far too slow to help Buck.

Local law wasn't going to be much help.

Weaver looked away from the train station. After crossing the street, he turned right and headed toward Washington. At the intersection of Washington and First, he hooked a left, strolling by the post office and across a bridge. Water, low from the lack of sufficient rain, crept along, barely covering the creek bed. Weaver had broken a sweat by the time he made it to the end of the block. The heat, combined with the lack of alcohol, made him feel dizzy, light-headed.

Another left on Main Street and half a block brought him to the Summit Valley Old Courthouse. The courthouse, whose lobby had been converted to a mini museum documenting the history of the town, sat in the middle of downtown Summit Valley. The Gothic monolith, built from stone mined from the abandoned quarry, took up most of the real estate of central Main Street. A single clock tower, easily the tallest structure in town, kept the time as accurately as it had since the mid-1800s. A lightning rod perched at the top of the tower's domed peak.

No longer in use as an actual courthouse, it still served to hold prisoners awaiting their time in court. The building connected to the new courthouse by way of an awkward brick corridor. Where the old courthouse had been built of large gray blocks of limestone, the new one had been built from brownish-red brick.

The old courthouse supported the tower through arches and flying buttresses. Grand windows offering fine views of the town and surrounding mountains contrasted with the tiny slits Weaver doubted allowed much natural light. The new building was squat, square, functional, and devoid of any architectural flare.

Weaver couldn't understand why the people had approved such an ugly, boring structure to replace their lauded and quite beautiful courthouse. The old courthouse was still the center of government, and it was there that the mayor and five-person town council had offices. The new building held courts—civil and criminal—and the administrative offices to collect fines and fees. Otherwise, town business was conducted where it always had been.

Weaver jaywalked across the street. Through a set of double doors and into the blessedly cool air conditioning, he stood in the rotunda, taking a minute to admire the architecture. The marble floor had been imprinted with the seal of the town in gold—a large circle with the words *County of Summit Valley* at the top and *Virginia* at the bottom. On the left was the word *Est.*, and on the right was the year *1814*. An inner circle surrounded a three-quarter picture of the clock tower with the words *Home, Hearth, and Pride*.

Posted signs told him council member offices and the office of the mayor were located on the third floor, *BY APPOINT-MENT ONLY!* Smaller signs, much less aggressive, directed him to offices where he could pay property taxes or apply for various permits. The location of the elevators was marked on a map with *You are Here* underneath an X at the entrance hall.

He didn't need any permits, and his property—*Thanks, Buck!* —was in another county. He didn't have an appointment either, not that something so trivial was going to stop him. Weaver was flying on pure instinct. He had only thought as far ahead as wanting to ask the town's leadership why their law enforce-ment wasn't doing the job their taxpayers paid them to do.

A spiral staircase led to the second floor. Weaver decided to take that and work his way to the third floor from there. Years of working in government buildings had taught him if he moved with confidence and purpose, people usually assumed he knew where he was going and was supposed to be there. He found the elevator, but not wanting to wait, even if there were only three floors, Weaver continued until he found a staircase to the third floor. Government workers didn't like stairs, judging from the dust on the windowsills and handrails. The stairs ended in a small landing with a green door. No window allowed him to see what was on the other side.

The door opened at the end of a quiet hall with polished wooden walls and deep burgundy carpet. At some point in the building's history the interior walls had been removed and replaced with glass. Administrative offices, possibly council members' offices, with blinds dividing them from their neighbors lined the hallway. Confidence didn't fool anyone here. People in every office stopped what they were doing to stare as he passed.

Guess they don't get many visitors.

The hallway ended in a circular anteroom with a central desk occupied by a receptionist. Behind her, the large double doors to the mayor's office were closed. On the floor was another golden seal surrounded by the thick carpet. The phone rang as Weaver walked up to the desk. The elderly receptionist answered. Her face paled, and she handed him the phone.

"It's for you."

* * *

Logan exited his bedroom for the first time in two weeks. His anxious mother got up from her spot on the couch to watch from the end of the hall. Logan went into the bathroom and took a shower. He brushed his teeth and put on clean clothes. Mrs. Burdette gave a silent thank-you to whatever had gotten her brokenhearted boy out of bed.

She listened as he started the shower, fighting the urge to violate his privacy and check on him. Logan thought he was too old for his mother to see him naked. Her heart ached at his maturity. Not wanting to break the spell more than respecting his desire for privacy, she stood at the end of the hall unsure of what to do. She waited. Eventually, Logan emerged from the bathroom ahead of a fragrant cloud of steam.

He asked for lunch!

Hallelujah! He was hungry. She sent a text to her husband letting him know Logan was up and about.

THANK GOD! the reply came back. *I WAS STARTING TO THINK HE MIGHT NEED A DOCTOR.*

Me too, she thought. *My sweet angel.* She pulled the peanut butter down from the cabinet and made Logan a peanut butter and honey sandwich. After cutting the sandwich into four triangles—Logan had been eating triangle sandwiches since he was a toddler—she put a handful of Doritos in the center.

Resisting the urge to barrage him with questions, she set his paper plate on the coffee table. Logan was sitting on the couch watching television! "What would you like to drink, honey?" *Are you all right? Can I help? What can I do? Baby sweet baby, please talk to me. Please!* She kept to herself, hoping he'd open up to her on his own.

"Do we have any more Capri Suns?"

"I bought a new pack of Pacific Cooler for the fridge. Want one of those?"

He nodded. "Sure, Mom. Thanks."

She brought him a pack of juice from the refrigerator. He pulled the straw off the back and punched it through the bottom, ignoring the aluminum spot on the top where the straw was supposed to go. Caleb used to drink Capri Suns like that.

Logan propped his drink in his lap and ate his lunch, then threw the empty plate and drained pouch in the trash. She watched him in anxious silence, trying not to intrude.

"Mom?"

"Yes, honey?" *Please talk to me!*

"If a friend left something behind—something that could

mean trouble—and they weren't around to get it, would you go get it for them?"

"What?"

He shifted, uncomfortable.

Afraid he was about to clam up, she quickly added, "Well, I guess it would depend."

"On what?" Logan was so solemn. Where was her baby? How badly had he been hurt by losing Caden?

She thought for a moment. "I guess it would depend on what it was."

"What if you didn't know?"

His stare was heavy, unrelenting. He wanted an answer. She didn't understand what they were talking about, only that the seriousness of his tone wouldn't allow for silliness. Something she didn't understand was happening. Mrs. Burdette felt she was walking on the edge of a razor, though she didn't know why.

"If I didn't know what it was, how could I go get it?"

"Before your friend"—Logan swallowed, tears welling—"went away, he told you where it was."

Her heart broke again looking at him standing there fighting back tears, little fists balled at his sides. Fighting to remain stoic. Trying to hide a deep hurt from his mother. So brave, so defiant, in so much pain. "What kind of trouble would it bring?" She fished for information, desperate to help.

"I don't know. Bad."

"Did Caden leave you something?"

"Caden is dead." Logan's control broke. The tears flowed freely down his face. She rushed to him and tried to take him in her arms. Logan pushed her off. "No! Answer the question!"

She stepped back. "If it was someone I loved as much as I know you loved Caden, I would do what I could to help. Sometimes friendship means you have to take risks."

Satisfied, Logan stepped forward so she could embrace him. She whispered into his hair, "Oh, baby, I love you so much. If I could take this hurt from you, I would. I'd trade in a heartbeat."

"I know, Mom. I have to go."

Reluctant to let him go, she stepped back, wiping at her own tears. "All right, baby. You go do what you need to do. Be home in time for dinner, okay?"

Logan nodded. He crossed the living room before exiting the house. For a moment, she thought she'd never see him again. He was so small, so young to carry such a burden. Tiny shoulders slumped, head low, framed by golden sunlight. *My angel.* He shut the door, leaving her alone.

* * *

Outside, Logan winced at the sunlight. The air seemed almost too hot to breathe. His bike was in the garage. He couldn't remember the last time he'd ridden it. The tires were still in decent shape; it hadn't been that long. The Huffy dirt bike wasn't the gem Caden's Mongoose was, but dinged, scraped, and rusted, it had served him faithfully.

Gaining speed out of the garage, Logan soon rocketed down Seventh Street toward Prospect. Trees passed in a green blur. Houses slipping by, background noises forgotten as fast as they were noticed. At the intersection of Washington and Seventh, he shot across without even considering traffic. An alert driver in a vintage Harvester slammed on the brakes, honking the horn, barely avoiding hitting him. "Fuckin' look, dummy!" he yelled at Logan's receding back.

Logan paid no attention to the driver's ire. He was on a mission. Focused. Now that he'd made his mind up to find the package, he was desperate to see it done. An unexplained sense of urgency propelled him forward, faster, faster! Logan didn't slow as Prospect Avenue approached. He swung wide and took a hard right. Wind pushed his sweaty hair from his forehead.

For a time, Logan forgot everything outside the exhilaration of speed and the pressing need to move even faster.

Cars flashed by in blurs of color and twinkles of chrome. Logan felt if he could only pedal a little faster, his bike would leave the ground. A little more speed and he'd take flight, leaving this sorry town behind. Deli Mart got closer by the second. Logan could see the Spot. The little ribbon was flying.

Logan was moving so fast that a bunny hop onto the sidewalk took him completely past the sidewalk and into the parking lot of the Deli Mart. Flying around the building, he pulled the rear brake and leaned slightly to the right. The rear tire locked, a champion skid throwing gravel twenty feet into the field behind the Deli Mart.

A clerk, red-white-and-blue smock over his blue jeans, had been standing behind the shop having a smoke break when the kid flew around corner throwing gravel everywhere. It was hard not to be impressed with the little guy. "Nice one, kid."

Logan nodded to the clerk—a youngish guy with shoulder-length hair hanging in greasy-looking clumps. *Leave me alone. Let me do what I came here to do.* He wasn't here to make friends. He was on a mission. Unless his cheese had slid right off his cracker, there was a package from Caden here. Logan slowed as he approached the tree. The ribbon hung limp from the limb, twitching on the occasional breeze. All at once, Logan was overcome with loss. Caden's hands had been the last to touch that ribbon. The finality of it struck Logan in a way he couldn't describe.

Caden would never tie another knot. No more packages. No more *Diablo*. He would never spin another Beyblade or play another game of Magic. No more Pokémon. No more homework. No more anything. Caden was dead. He'd been snatched from the earth.

Logan's chest hurt. His eyes burned. The tree doubled, then trebled. Not wanting anyone to see him cry, he kept his back to the clerk, who smoked, silently watching. What was there?

Logan steeled himself and checked the hollow. His heart leapt when he saw a plastic-wrapped package. He reached tentatively into the hollow, fingers brushing the surface.

A package! Caden *did* leave something behind!

He was scared to grab it. This, this...thing had killed not only his best friend, but his best friend's family. Caden said he'd "disobeyed." For a moment, Logan thought about leaving this plastic death sentence right where it was, going home as fast as he could, hugging his mother, and forgetting this had ever happened. But only for a moment.

Caden had died for this, and they looked out for each other. If you couldn't count on your best friend, you couldn't count on anyone. No. He wouldn't leave it here. Logan reached in and jerked the taped-up package free of the hollow. There wasn't much to it at all: a manila envelope wrapped in a plastic bag from Walmart to keep any rain off.

Logan looked at the envelope in his hands in disbelief. This was it? This? The envelope was flat. There couldn't be much inside it. An aluminum tack, legs separated, held the envelope closed, leaving a mystery as to the contents.

"Whatcha got there, kiddo?" The clerk flicked the butt of his cigarette away and approached Logan.

"None of your damn business." Logan hopped on his bike and sped off, leaving the stunned clerk sucking dust.

* * *

"I thought I told you to kick rocks."

It was her! Ms. Route 100 Special. There was no mistaking her voice—clear, taunting, full of youthful cruelty. How did she know Weaver was even here? What was going on in this town? Fear wormed from his gut down the tops of his thighs. His balls drew up.

"How did you know to call here?" Weaver felt stupid for asking. Caught so off guard, all he could think of was: how?

How was this even possible? No one knew he was coming here. The receptionist stared at her desk, refusing to look at him. Then she stood and walked into the mayor's office. Weaver heard the lock click.

"This is my town, silly. I told you to leave."

"I'm not going anywhere until—"

"Yes, yes, you want to know what happened to your fat friend. *So* boring."

"Tell me." Weaver's hand began to ache from how tightly he gripped the receiver, his knuckles turning white under the strain.

"I happened, silly. Nothing happens here without me. I killed him, gutted him with a juice bottle. Actually, I think it was a coconut water bottle. I warned him, told him things weren't going to go his way. I laughed while you held him. Maybe if you hadn't been drunk, he'd be alive. Who knows?"

"Listen—"

"No, you listen." Her voice took on a hard edge, less school-girl, more harpy. "Leave. Go back downstairs, get in that dead hick's truck, and never come back. Twice I've warned you. There won't be a third."

"Stop hiding behind the phone. Tell me where you are. We'll see how you do face-to-face."

"Mmm, sounds yummy. Murderers are always so spicy. Goodbye, Aron Weaver. Pray we never meet."

"Stop hiding—" A cold slimy sensation in his ear interrupted his thought. He dropped the phone. A tongue extended from the earpiece. Wet, organic red muscle withdrew into the plastic, licking obscenely at the air. Weaver scrubbed at his ear with the hem of his shirt. That thing had been in his ear! *His fucking ear!*

No matter how he scrubbed, he still could feel it sliming around his ear canal. He turned, expecting he didn't know what behind him. Nothing was there. The offices that lined the hall were devoid of people. Weaver was alone on the third floor of the Summit Valley Municipal Center. He had been wondering what exactly it was Buck had found in this town. A new thought began to form. What had found Buck?

* * *

Solomon dropped the phone, giggling, and turned back to the hearth. The waves of searching hellfire scoured the plains as close as they'd ever come. The exit remained undiscovered, though he couldn't in perfect confidence know that for sure. The flames were a tool born of suffering, fueled by sin; they remained as mysterious to him as the first time he'd felt their cruel caress. Solomon felt a force behind the flames seeking him, unceasing, relentless.

He'd eluded that force, escaped, made a new home. If he could've closed the gate, ending forever any possibility of leaving this plane, he would have. But for all his power, all he could do was deceive. Hide.

"Solomon, I'm tired. I'm not feeling myself today."

Shirley wouldn't last much longer. Pity. The humidity ravaged the flesh.

"Did you hear me, Solomon?"

Turning away from the hearth, he looked at her. She was wearing down. It'd be a long search indeed to find another as interesting. He had time. "Of course I did, my dear. Go lie down. Rest. I'm not expecting guests."

When he'd detected her dark spirit entering his realm, Solomon knew he had to have her. A heart as corrupted as hers needed to serve him—and not in the casual way he fed on sinners. She was a special, rare type of evil. Shirley delighted him. Dominating her exhausted him. He still didn't have her fully under control. It was truly a shame how quickly mortal flesh broke down. She would have made a fantastic demon. She still might.

"Apologies, Solomon. If you need me…" The statement hung unfinished.

"Of course, madam. You're first in my thoughts. A little rest and you'll be back in fighting form. Worry not."

"Thank you."

It would be best to preserve her, keep her. Shirley, by any measure, far exceeded any employee he'd ever hired. Maintaining her disguise had become increasingly taxing, though her value could not be overstated. She shambled from behind the desk before shuffling her slow way down the hall. Bumping into the frame, she slid through into the kitchen, leaving a smear. Solomon watched her go. The stain on the jamb was proof, if he needed any, that he should be judicious in his use of her. Damn this summertime humidity. So very troublesome.

* * *

Closing the door, Shirley shut her eyes, relishing the cool dark. Late summer flies had become a nuisance, but she paid no attention to their buzz. Her body ached all over. She hadn't had much of an appetite either. It shamed her that she hadn't put as much effort into her grooming as she should. She just didn't have the energy.

Her mother had taught her better. *Butterflies come to pretty flowers. Never ignore your beauty, or you will be without it. Pleasing ware is half sold.* There were others Shirley couldn't remember. She'd always taken pride in her appearance.

Adapt the remedy to the disease. Another of mother's sayings. Shirley was tired. Her body hurt. A little rest. That's what she needed. Solomon would call her if he needed her. Until then, sleep.

CHAPTER NINETEEN
ANSWERS AND QUESTIONS

Logan wasn't crazy. Wind ruffled his hair as he rocketed down Prospect Avenue. On Fifth Street toward downtown, houses passed in a blur. The Maple Lodge passed by on his right in a blink. Logan pedaled a little harder, willing more speed from the Huffy. Past the lodge, the Summit Valley Furniture Plant stretched block after block.

Logan considered cutting down Madison through the remains of the factory, then didn't. The sense of being watched, like something waited in the ruins, kept Logan on the main streets. He crossed Washington and continued toward Jefferson. His nervousness passed with each bit of ground he put between himself and the factory.

The manila envelope tucked in his shorts poked painfully with its corners. Logan placed his hand over his shirt to feel the envelope for the hundredth time. It was there. The uncomfortable pokes were proof he wasn't crazy. Caden had come to him. In his possession, Logan had this final gift from his best friend, and he wasn't sure what he should do with it.

A left on Jefferson would take him into downtown proper and to his destination. One of Logan's favorite places in the world, though he would bitterly deny it, was the Summit Valley Public Library. Located near the corner of Third and Jefferson, the main entry sat directly across from the awful new courthouse building. Logan went to the library whenever he could.

Senior citizens often gathered in the library to read the local newspaper. Logan thought it a minor miracle the paper was still in print. Everything was online now. Newspapers were a dying breed. He enjoyed the silence in the library, a hush that demanded respect. Pretty high school girls worked there in the summer and made Logan feel strange and light-headed in a most pleasant way.

Where was the best place to go when you needed information? Google. Logan couldn't access the internet from home with his parents still recovering from Dad's unemployment. It embarrassed him to think about those times. True, he'd met his best friend because of it, but never in a million years would Logan miss those terrible apartments. He'd access the internet from the library.

Past True Value and Sherwin-Williams, Logan cut left on Fourth Street in front of a Summit Valley police car. The officer bleeped the siren, shaking his finger at Logan. He grinned and continued up Jefferson while a shamefaced Logan waved, riding on down Fourth. Logan turned right, cut across the parking lot for the library, and cruised right up to a back entrance.

During the ride down Jefferson, Logan had moved Caleb's envelope from underneath his shirt to on top of it. He was sweating big-time and didn't want it to get ruined. Plus, the poking corners were beginning to annoy him. Curiosity burned at Logan's mind. Caden had warned him not to open it, and Logan wanted to respect his wish, even if he felt it was kind of mean not to say what it was. Or what he wanted Logan to do with it. Give it to him? Him who? Where was he? How would he know who to give it to if he didn't know what it was? Circular thoughts provided no insight, only frustration.

Logan locked his bike in the rack and walked in. He chose this entrance because it was closer to the children's section of the library. Logan didn't want to wade past all the old people gathered in the front reading and soaking up sunlight like wrinkled lizards. The fewer people asking about the envelope, the better. He'd gotten a weird vibe from the clerk behind the Deli Mart.

Paranoia. He'd learned that word last year, here in this very library. At the time, he didn't understand, not really, but the meaning was all too clear to him now. Logan felt hunted. Watched. The envelope radiated danger. It had cost Caden and his family everything. Hopefully answers waited for him in the library.

A wall lined with computers bordered the children's section. A bank of computers lined the far wall inside as well. Those were for babies learning how to spell, locked well away from the internet. Logan needed one of the machines the adults used. He wanted privacy. Adults never came back here unless they had children with them, and the grown-ups didn't use the machines at all.

Logan required information. He wasn't sure what he was looking for, but whenever you needed information, you searched online. Even the babies learning to spell knew that. Every television show since forever found critical information on the 'net. Someone always used the 'net to crack the case. Critical information was exactly what he needed now. He'd been following his gut since he decided to check the Spot.

Caden hadn't steered him wrong so far.

Luck was with him. Logan found a machine in the back corner that remained logged on from a previous user. Log-in information was issued with library cards so members could use the internet. A library card was free, but accessing the internet wasn't. Logan figured whoever forgot to log out probably thought closing the browser was all they needed to do. Now Logan could search anonymously. He still didn't have a clue what to look for. Those TV shows never said how they got the case-breaking information. He opened Facebook. He didn't have a Facebook account, and even if he did, he doubted a ghost was going to pop in the news feed with a clue.

Come on, Caden. What do I do with this thing?

Logan sat in front of the computer with no idea what to do next. Caden didn't answer him. No message popped up on the screen. His earlier anxiety, the feeling of being watched, was getting worse. He was dropping the ball. He didn't know what to do!

He was hot. Sweaty. Thirsty. Miserable.

On TV, the hero knew what to do. Logan didn't want to be a hero; he just wanted to help Caden. His frustration mounted. Sitting in front of a computer, unauthorized log-in or no, wasn't going to help. The library was clearly a bust. Hot bitter tears began to flow. This wasn't fair!

He put his head down, hoping no one would see him crying. A cool hand on the back of his neck startled him. With his vision blurred by tears, he first thought Caden had sent him an angel. Her blonde hair was backlit by the library's mellow overhead lighting. The angel was seated beside him, leaning toward him. Her hand gently stroked the back of his neck like his mother sometimes did.

"Are you okay?" she asked.

No, not an angel. One of the high school girls helping the librarian, dressed in a simple white T-shirt tucked into blue jeans, the words Summit Valley Public Library printed in green on the breast. Sympathy radiated from her.

Logan, naturally mistrustful of strangers, found himself wanting to talk. "Not really." He sniffed, trying to wipe the tears away.

"What's your name?"

"Logan."

"Nice to meet you. I'm Amity."

Unsure of what to do, Logan nodded.

"What's wrong, Logan?"

"I—I'm just—I'm trying to help my friend, but I don't know how."

"What do you need to do? Can I help you find something?" She continued to calm him, her voice soft, her hand soothing on his neck.

"I don't think so." Logan pulled the envelope from the table and hugged it to himself.

"Is it a secret?" she asked.

Logan tried to smile but couldn't. "No. My friend wanted me to do something. But I don't know what it was."

"Can you ask him? I'll let you use my phone to call him."

"I can't call him." Logan started crying again. "He's dead. He wanted me to help him, and he's dead, and I can't 'cause I don't know how!"

Amity removed her hand. "You know what I do when I'm confused?"

"Wh-What?" Snot spilled onto his lip.

Pretending not to notice, Amity handed him a tissue from a handful in her pocket. Logan accepted and wiped his nose, keeping his envelope close. "When I'm confused and don't know what to do, I go to Chuck's and get a milkshake. Ice cream always helps me think."

"I can't do that. I don't have any money."

"Would you like one? I might buy a little boy a milkshake. If he needs one."

A milkshake! He was so hot. "You'd do that?"

"Of course I would. Wait here a sec."

Logan kept his hand on the envelope, even if she didn't seem too interested. Amity walked away to fetch her purse. Returning, she sat down and dug a crinkled five-dollar bill from the depths of her bag, which was sky blue like her eyes. Logan noticed darker blue swirls visible only when it caught the light.

"Let's see, five dollars cash. Perfect." Amity pushed the money into Logan's hand. "I like the French vanilla. Nothing better to help think of solutions than a French vanilla milkshake. Works every time for me."

Back outside, Logan unchained his bike. Chuck's wasn't far from the library—a block south on Jefferson. He'd ridden around the building to Third Street and was about to make the right turn toward Jefferson when he heard Amity yell behind him.

"Logan! Wait!"

He turned around as she ran up to him with his envelope in her hand. "Here." She was slightly out of breath from her dash. "You forgot this."

Caden's package! Logan couldn't believe he'd left it. Stupid! Stupid! Stupid!

"Thanks! I can't believe I forgot." Logan's cheeks were hot. He knew his face was bright red.

"That's all right. Promise me something?"

Logan was immediately wary. She seemed nice. "What?"

"When you figure what to do, you'll come tell me about it sometime?"

Logan released his held breath. He flashed a smile. "Sure. Thanks for being so nice."

Amity returned the smile. "Go on. Go get your milkshake."

Amity was right—French vanilla had been the way to go. Cold, sweet, perfect for such a hot day. Logan decided to drink his shake outside, where he could look at the fire trucks. On sunny days, the firemen would open the big bay doors, and you could look right inside! The bay doors were open today. Both trucks—shiny lime-green twins, miles of hose, and other orderly stacks of gear were visible within.

Logan watched for a moment before deciding it was too hot

to stand in the sun. Chuck's didn't have any outdoor seating. The park had shade though. Moving from the sun on Jefferson to the shade on First, Logan pushed his bike across the street into the park. A bench underneath a maple tree provided a cool spot to sit, enjoy his milkshake, and think.

Caden, what am I supposed to do?

Chapter Twenty
Cardio

Weaver tried to suppress the urge to run. Nothing in all his years had prepared him for this. Tongues coming out of the phone? What the hell? The hallway was empty. The civil servants must have quietly departed while he was on the phone. Still, the feeling of being watched weighed heavily in the air.

The skin on the back of his neck crawled. He needed to leave the courthouse. Immediately. As Weaver opened the door to the stairs, the mayor's office opened. No one was in the office as far as he could see. The receptionist's chair rolled back from behind the desk, stopping at the entrance to the hall. The seat began to lazily rotate as it would if someone seated had stood up suddenly or brushed it passing by.

Thump! Swisssshhh.

Thump! Swisssshhh.

Weaver paused in the doorway, squinting to locate the source of the noise, instinct screaming to run. Get out! Not wanting to panic for no reason, he stood still, watching, listening.

Thump! Swisssshhh.

Thump! Swisssshhh.

What was that sound? Movement caught his detective's eye. The thick carpet in the hallway depressed with each thump, bearing a weight Weaver couldn't see. The swish was a weight dragging against the fiber. Drag marks on the carpet linked each depression. One left. One right.

Footsteps.

Something moved down the hall toward him. Impossible. Undeniable. Heavy, lurching steps. It covered over half the distance between them in the time Weaver took to identify the cause of the noise. The steps picked up speed. The thing had realized it was no longer hidden.

Thump! Swishhh.

Thump! Swishhh.

Go! Go! GO! GO! GET OUT!

The paralysis broke. Weaver leapt through the doorway and slammed it closed behind him. He took the stairs two at a time, panic barely held in check. A hollow boom echoed through the stairwell as his pursuer gave chase. Racing down the stairs, he could hear feet slapping the stone somewhere above him. The detective in him noted there was a clicking combined with the foot slaps. Claws.

It sounded like a dog trying to run on tile. *A big fucking dog.*

Shouldering through to the second floor, heart pounding, Weaver ran for the final set of stairs. The hallway, filled with workers only a few minutes ago, had emptied completely. On a primitive level, Weaver realized he was alone in the building. Everyone was gone. It was him and the invisible thing chasing him.

Weaver slid into the turn, gripping the handrail to swing his momentum forward. Risking a glance over his shoulder, he saw the door to the third-floor stairs explode open. Something impacted the wall opposite hard enough to cave the drywall.

It fell! Run, you drunken flatfoot, run!

The creature's fall allowed Weaver to build back his lead. If the chase went on much longer, his own lack of conditioning would kill him. His breath came in hot painful gasps. Spots formed in his vision. Weaver knew, in the same way he knew he was alone, that if he could get outside, he'd be all right. There wasn't any logic to it. But monsters didn't exist in the daylight? Right?

Weaver bolted across the town seal, through the double doors, and through the next set into the sunshine. He crashed into a pair of men in business suits heading into the courthouse, taking them with him to the ground.

"Yo, hey, what the fuck?" one of the men shouted.

Weaver didn't respond; he was fighting too hard for air. He stared at the entrance to the courthouse. The lobby appeared empty, but whatever had chased him stood beyond the doors staring back, hating that it was denied its prey. The businessmen got to their feet.

Not wanting to be in front of those doors when they opened, Weaver ignored their indignant complaints and backed away, first a few scuttling crab steps, then on his feet. He backed toward the street, never taking his eyes off the lobby. The men warily watched him backing away before turning back to the courthouse.

"Fuckin' nut job."

"Dude's lucky we didn't fuck his shit up."

Weaver backed across the sidewalk. The businessmen opened the first set of double doors. One held open the first while the second walked through to hold open the interior. Both fell over as if something rushed through. Something heavy.

Weaver turned and ran across the street, angling for Jefferson, thinking it might get him around the corner a bit faster.

His invisible hunter stopped at the edge of the courthouse grounds, glaring hungrily as its prey vanished from sight. Bounding back into the courthouse and away from the hateful sun, it knocked the businessmen aside.

"Darrell?"

"Yeah?"

"Somethin'…run into you?"

"Y-Yeah."

"Think I'll head back to the office. File this permit tomorrow."

"Yeah."

* * *

Weaver slowed once he turned onto Jefferson. A quick glance back confirmed it. Or not. The thing was invisible. It might be creeping up on him right now. Everything looked normal. Hopefully, his pursuer had given up. A short walk, during which he might have checked over his shoulder fifty times, expecting at any moment to be shredded by invisible claws, brought him to First Street. The firemen had their bays open— the garage orderly, the trucks clean, no invisible predators. Everything appeared neat. Sane.

He needed a minute to get his thoughts together. The rational part of his brain couldn't come to terms with what he'd experienced. First, the tongue. Then the mad dash away from an invisible demon. His logic rejected the truth; he'd come close to death. Something had tried to eat him in the courthouse. Death had been, quite literally, panting on his heels. It didn't make sense, but that didn't make it any less real.

The slap-click on the stairs came back to him, making the hair on his arms stand up.

Turning his back to the firehouse, he considered heading into the restaurant for something to drink, but from his vantage point, he saw neither employee nor customer. The thought of other… whatevers…lurking inside changed his mind. Buck's truck, still parked where he'd left it, sat in the shade. Normal, ordinary.

A boy sat on the bench underneath the maple he'd parked in front of. A well-loved Huffy dirt bike leaned against the tree. Once, the bike might have been painted gold and black. Now it was chipped and faded, its shining glory long past. As Weaver approached the truck, the bicycle fell over from its perch, crashing into the bumper on the passenger side. The crash caused both Weaver and the boy to jump.

With an involuntary glance in the direction of the court-house, Weaver walked around to check for damage. The boy picked his bike up off the street and leaned it against the tree on the park side.

"Did it hurt your truck?" the boy asked. Kid was wide-eyed, scared. Weaver bet he'd been crying.

Heart going out to the boy, Weaver replied, "Nah. It'd take worse to hurt this old thing. More likely, it scratched your bike up. Besides, this here truck is beat all to pieces already."

The boy nodded. *Somber little guy. Got something serious on his mind.*

"What's in the cup?" Weaver asked, nodding toward the boy's hand.

"A shake."

"Yeah? What kind?"

"French vanilla. Girl at the library bought it for me."

"Vanilla works. Even better when a girl buys it. I was always a strawberry man, myself."

"Strawberry's okay."

"Where'd she go?" Weaver asked, scanning the park.

"Where'd who go?" the boy replied.

Answering questions with questions. Defensive. Wonder why he's so guarded.

"Well, most times, when a girl buys a feller a milkshake, they drink it together. A date, you know?"

The boy's cheeks flared bright red. "Ew, no. She felt sorry for me. Gave me five bucks."

Weaver made for the bench. "That so? Mind if I sit for a minute? I've had a day you wouldn't believe."

The kid shrugged. "It's a free country."

Weaver sat. The manila envelope on the bench reminded

Weaver of the ones they used to send interdepartmental memos. The boy's eyes grew wide. Snatching the envelope, he jumped away. Weaver didn't move. Weirdness seemed to be the norm in Summit Valley.

"Relax, kid. I'm not a thief. In fact, I used to be a detective."

"Sorry. I don't mean to be rude. My friend gave me this," the kid blurted. "He's dead."

"Sorry to hear that. Was he a close friend?"

"Yeah." The boy remained standing, sweaty Styrofoam cup in one hand, envelope in the other. "He was my best friend."

"I lost a good friend too, back at the beginning of the summer."

"Really?" The boy moved a little closer to the bench. Weaver pretended not to notice. "Was he killed?"

Strange question, Weaver thought. He cocked his head, regarding the boy in a new light. "Yes, he was." Honesty. Weaver pointed over toward the train station. "Right over there."

"The sheriff?" The boy sat on the opposite end of the bench, eyes wide.

"You know about that?"

"Yeah, everyone knows about it. My friend was killed. His family too. His name was Caden."

"That's awful. The sheriff's name was Buck. He taught me how to be a policeman."

"What's your name, mister?"

"Aron. What's yours?"

"I'm Logan."

"Nice to meet you, Logan." Weaver didn't offer to shake hands; Logan seemed too skittish for physical contact. Ruining the budding rapport felt foolish. Nothing about Summit Valley felt normal, so Weaver continued to trust his instincts.

Logan sipped his milkshake, eyes on the train station. Weaver stared off across the park, watching Logan with his peripheral vision, keeping quiet. *Let the boy talk.* Silence inevitably drew the story out.

"Aron?"

Weaver turned his head, making eye contact, establishing trust. "Yes?"

"Caden told me about this." Logan lifted the envelope. "Not what's in it. Only that it was there."

"He do that before?"

"No. After. I know it sounds nuts, but I'm telling the truth."

Weaver didn't reply. Too much about this day sounded nuts. *Let the boy speak.*

"It was like a dream. He was sitting on my bed. I could see the night-light through him. He said I needed to get it, but that I couldn't look at it."

"What did he want you to do?"

"Give it to someone."

"Give it to who?"

"I don't know. He didn't say. It's bad. Whoever I give it to is going to get hurt—maybe even dead. Caden said it killed him. He said if I look, it'll kill me too. The next day, my parents told me Caden and his family were dead. I already knew."

"You knew because your friend told you?"

"Yeah. In the dream. You believe me?"

Weaver thought about the things that had happened to him in Summit Valley. "I do."

"Why?" This seemed important to Logan. *Honesty.*

"After the day I've had, it really doesn't sound strange."

Logan pulled back, eyes narrowing. "Really? I'm being serious."

Weaver took a deep breath. "As am I. Would you believe me if I told you monsters are real? Not the human variety, actual monsters."

"'Course I would. I'm a kid."

"Making fun of me?"

"No, sir!" Logan shook his head. It might have been comical if he hadn't been so serious.

A bond was forming between them. In addition to having a murdered friend in common, they'd experienced the supernatural. Both could feel it. Weaver's new friend watched him expectantly. "No, I don't guess you are."

"I'm not."

"I killed a monster. Shot him in the head."

"I knew you looked familiar. You're the guy who got Ol' Snapper."

This kid was full of surprises. "You know about that too, huh?"

"Yeah, at school we talked about him *a lot*. Kids thought he was everywhere. A ghost, one who liked eating children."

"You aren't too far wrong. The worst thing I ever did was take his life."

"I don't think so."

"No?"

"No."

"Why's that?" Weaver asked, shifting his weight to better face the boy beside him.

"Well," Logan began, "monsters are evil, right?"

Interested to know where the boy was going, he nodded. "Yes."

"If monsters are evil, that means evil is real. If evil is real, good must be too. My dad says there are no shadows without light. I think he's right."

Weaver nodded. "Okay—"

Logan wasn't finished. He held up a hand—an oddly adult gesture. "Wait! If evil is real, and monsters are put here by evil to do evil, then good must have someone to fight the monsters. No shadow without light? See? You killed a monster, by your own words. You fought the monster. Look here." Logan shifted, leaning his body over the grass. "See the shadow?" He extended his arm, the same hand he'd used to silence Weaver, for his shadow to pass over the park lawn.

"I see it."

"See how the light surrounds it? Light always surrounds the dark. Keeps it in check." Nodding, Logan sat back, smiling at the awed expression on his new friend's face.

"You don't think monsters fight monsters?"

"Not really. If you were a monster—like an evil one, a real one—you would be doing evil all the time. I bet you don't. I bet you tried to be good. A monster would let a monster loose to do more monster stuff. Understand?"

Friends, counselors, bartenders, priests, and booze hadn't managed to state the problem so well. *A monster would let a monster continue to do monster stuff. No shadow without light. This fucking town. Light surrounds.* Weaver fought to control his emotions. This little boy had done in five minutes what he hadn't managed to do since that cold winter day in Stockmore's basement. Logan had succinctly demonstrated, with his child's logic, that Weaver had made the correct choice. Weaver could forgive himself. He could let it go.

"You okay, mister?" The concern on Logan's face broke Weaver's heart afresh.

"Yeah." Weaver wiped his eyes. "I'm okay. I came over here to help you, and you helped me instead. I never heard it better."

Logan smiled, pleased with the compliment. "That girl, the one who bought me the shake? She was nice. I'm just paying it forward."

"If you want, I'll take a quick peek at your friend's letter. I'm old. I've got nothing left. I'm not afraid."

Logan thought for a moment. It couldn't be an accident. This must be who Caden had meant. This guy. A cop who'd fought monsters and won. Light against the shadow. Logan heard Caden in his head, agreeing. Yes. "I think that's why we're both here."

"I think so too, kid."

Logan felt a tremendous weight leave him as he handed Aron the envelope. He stood and retrieved his Huffy.

"Do you want to know what's in here?" Weaver asked, not surprised that Logan was getting ready to leave. He was done. He'd delivered the message, honored the obligation to his friend.

"Nah. Caden told me not to look."

"What are you going to do?" Weaver wondered.

"My folks have been worried about me. They offered to take me to the big game store in Roanoke."

"Gamepad?"

"You know it, huh?" Logan fired back. Kid was a firecracker. "Hey, Aron?"

"Yes, sir?"

"Be careful. This town has a whole 'nother breed of monster."

"We've met."

"Then you know."

"I know." He nodded. "Have fun at Gamepad."

"Gamepad's *LIT*." Logan nodded sagely.

"I have no idea what that means."

"Cause you're old."

"Thanks."

Weaver watched as Logan rode off. The kid waved as he shot around the corner of First and Jefferson, disappearing before Weaver could respond. He stood by the bench, holding the envelope, then sat back down, opened it, and began to read. Written in a child's sprawling print—*Caden, his name was Caden*—was the story of Buck's murder.

My name is Caden. If you are reading this, something bad has happened to me. The boogeyman doesn't want me to tell, but I can't take it anymore. Someone else needs to know. (NOT YOU, LOGAN! YOU BETTER NOT BE READING THIS!) I went to the market with Mom and Dad. The one on Saturday with the veggies. I saw the boogeyman. A woman works for the boogeyman. She was shopping there too. I think he was watching her. He protects her. The old sheruf saw her and was gonna bust her. The boogeyman whispered in the sheruf's ear, and the sheruf started stumbling. Daddy said he was drunk, but he wasn't. The boogeyman scrambled his brains whispering like that. The sheruf screamed SHHHUURRRRLLY, and the woman cut him. She broke a bottle and cut him bad. His guts fell out. The boogeyman smiled at me. No one saw him but me. He told me to shhh. I can't do it no more. He let that lady kill the sheruf. Then he made people move out of her way. No one stopped her. I don't know what will happen to me for doing this, but I can't be quiet. Please help him. Help me. Stop the boogeyman.

Signed,

Caden Quesenberry

P.S. The boogeyman and the woman live at the Maple Lodge. I seen 'em there. The boogeyman smiled at me. His smile is turrble.

Weaver read the letter, reread it. Something had found Buck. *Shurly?* Surely? Shirley? Caden had seen the monster who made Summit Valley its den. Weaver knew where the boogeyman lived. He'd passed the run-down bed-and-breakfast on Fifth Street before. A haunted looking place if ever there was one. Peeling paint, warped boards, broken windows.

A dead boy's letter said the boogeyman lived at the Maple Lodge and his woman had killed Buck, so Weaver was going to the Maple Lodge to collect the boogeyman's woman. Weaver walked to the truck. Folding the letter back into the envelope, Weaver threw it on the passenger seat and turned the key. Reliable as ever, the faithful engine fired up.

Stopping to think would be a mistake. Weaver needed to keep the forward momentum. Pausing for thought could convince him the prudent thing to do would be chalk all of this up to a loss and move on. Forget Summit Valley. But if he walked away without confronting Buck's killer, Weaver knew he'd be headed back to the bottle, never to emerge. He'd waste the rest of his life as a drunk until his liver quit or he wrapped himself around a telephone pole. Eventually, guilt over inaction would eat him alive.

No, he fought monsters. Light to the shadow. His light might've been dimming as of late, but he'd use what remained to fight. Buck deserved better. Isn't that what he'd been telling what passed for police in this town?

He backed out of the spot. Weaver cast a sideways glance at the clock tower, heading toward Fifth Street and whatever fate awaited him at the Maple Lodge.

CHAPTER TWENTY-ONE
LIGHT AND SHADOW

Weaver parked in the gravel lot next to a Corvette. The interior of the Vette had seen better days. A 1957 or '58, the car appeared to have been loved once. Now it looked like it had been cast off, an orphan whose loving parents were lost long ago. The car wasn't cared for the same way by the new owner. The body was dinged, paint scratched, tires splattered with mud. The convertible top stuck partway up.

On the driver's side, the once supple leather interior was stained, mottled. Patches of deadly-looking mold bloomed here and there. Dried bits of...what?...flesh?...hung from the gearshift. The passenger side, while disgusting, didn't evidence the same degree of decay. Something had been rotting in the driver's seat. The stink was enough to make Weaver want to move the truck.

Shame to see such a beautiful car go to ruin.

The Maple Lodge didn't seem to be in much better shape. A door hung open on the carriage house at the opposite end of the gravel lot, swaying slightly in the oppressive air. A large hornet nest hung from the easement above. The noise and motion caused the insects to swarm, their angry buzz carrying across the lot.

The lodge itself appeared to be on the brink of collapse. The frame tilted dangerously toward Prospect Avenue. Broken windows on the second floor matched the busted and boarded windows on the first floor. *They look like blind eyes and busted teeth*, he thought, shivering despite the heat. *The face of the Maple Lodge—an assault victim screaming for help.*

Paint peeled away, exposing the rotting gray beams beneath. A child's final testimony had led him here. As badly as Weaver wanted to get back in the truck, go find a drink, and forget this awful town, Caden's posthumous plea couldn't be ignored. He would see this through.

Weaver moved past the lot onto the porch. Warped unsteady boards shifted and complained beneath his weight. A wooden sign hung on the door: *Last Chance, Dipshit*! Ignoring the warning, Weaver stepped inside.

The interior of the lodge matched the outside. Random pieces of broken furniture dotted the mostly empty space in front of a large desk. A few threadbare throw rugs stank of mildew. Patterns on the carpet were impossible to distinguish through the rot. Candles lined a hearth to Weaver's right. A roaring fire belied the illusion that the Lodge was abandoned.

Someone had lit those candles. The fire was blazing.

The fire's heat, compounded by late summer weather, rendered the air thick, nearly unbreathable. Even with the bright sun shining a few feet behind him, the lobby was soaked in gloom. The candles and the fire in the hearth created thick dancing shadows. Weaver felt watched by things just beyond the light.

Out of sight, a phonograph began to play big band music. Weaver heard the pops and cracks unique to vinyl records before the music began. Horns and a clarinet intertwined, ghostly celebrations from a bygone era. Weaver thought of the old RCA dog, head cocked, listening to the music from the bell. He pulled his pistol from its place in the shoulder holster underneath his arm, the weight of it comforting in his hand.

"My, you *are* a stubborn one!" a deep voice commented from the edge of the light cast by the blazing fire. He had an accent, though not one Weaver could place.

Someone stood behind the desk, wearing an old-fashioned suit, a pinstriped waistcoat underneath a morning coat trimmed in blood-red silk. Weaver was sure he hadn't been standing there before. *There's a look you don't see anymore*, Weaver thought. Despite his strange taste in fashion, the man radiated danger. Weaver's instincts kicked in, and the pistol's sights were centered on the stranger's forehead, right where he'd shot Ben Stockmore.

"Who are you?" Weaver's voice was calm and steady after years of training to project authority.

"Introductions are in order! My name is Solomon Drury VI, humble innkeeper of the Maple Lodge. You are Aron Weaver, alcoholic and murderer. There, we've been properly introduced. Civility is the cornerstone of a healthy society, don't you think?"

Weaver ignored the insult. "How do you know me?"

"Dear boy, we've spoken several times." Solomon's voice changed, becoming that of the taunting girl at Sonic. "Perhaps you don't remember. I've heard booze plays merry hell on the memory." Candlelight flickered and twisted, reflecting in Solomon's dark eyes. He was smiling. Caden was right—his smile was terrible, the joy in it the same as that of a cat toying with a terrified mouse.

"How—How did you do that?"

"I do what I please." Solomon's voice regained its bass. "I told you this is my town. And that"—Solomon nodded toward the pistol in Weaver's hand—"isn't going to be of much service."

Weaver considered Solomon's words, keeping the pistol trained on his forehead. "You killed my friend?"

"A bit slow for a detective, aren't you? As I've stated, nothing happens here without my approval. While I didn't *directly* kill the deluded sheriff, I certainly take responsibility for it. Sadly, there is a dreadful lack of personal responsibility in today's world. No one wishes to 'step up,' as they say. Don't you agree?"

"Why was he deluded?"

Solomon grinned. "Colombian assassins in southwest Virginia. Really? The old man had grown soft in the head as well as the gut. Did you know he'd entered early stages of dementia? Quite sad, really. In a few months, he'd have been soiling his pants. Shirley did him a favor."

"You're a liar."

"Am I?"

"He was trying to find the truth of what happened to Hannah Baenziger."

"I should think it obvious. I happened. I needed to settle our account. She tried to run. I dropped a Bonneville on her."

"You admit you're an accomplice to murder?"

Solomon waved a hand dismissively. "You're beginning to bore me, Mr. Weaver."

"Sorry to hear that. On the ground. I'm taking you to jail." Weaver kept the pistol steady with one hand while reaching for a pair of handcuffs from a case attached to his belt.

Solomon's deep booming laughter rolled across the room. "Oh dear, sir. Is this what you hoped to accomplish? You envisioned coming here, to my home, and *arresting* me? Clearly, you haven't thought things through. Truly, sir, you are too much." Solomon walked around the desk to stand in front of Weaver. "All right, Mr. Not-Quite-A-Policeman, I'll play along for a moment." Turning his back to Weaver, Solomon placed his hands behind him, awaiting the handcuffs.

Weaver moved quickly despite the nagging feeling that this was a trap. With practiced hands, Weaver holstered the pistol, then snapped the cuffs onto Solomon's wrists. He turned Solomon around roughly by the shoulder. The material of Solomon's coat felt...alive, shifting underneath his fingers. Weaver resisted the urge to wipe his hand, instead grabbing

Solomon high on the upper arm to escort him to the car. Weaver took a step and pulled. Solomon didn't move.

"Whatever shall you do, Detective?" Condescension dripped from his words. Solomon watched with a bemused smirk.

Weaver pulled, a child trying to move a locomotive.

Solomon's body never budged despite Weaver's desperate attempts. With a motion, Solomon snapped the handcuff chain. *That was carbon steel!* Weaver watched, disbelieving, as Solomon snapped the cuffs from his wrists, crumpled the steel into a ball, and dropped it on the floor.

"Enough games, Detective."

Weaver stepped away, pulled his pistol, and fired three quick rounds into Solomon. The lobby filled with the acrid bite of spent propellant. Unfazed by the rounds, Solomon stepped forward, covering the distance between them in less than a second. Faster than Weaver could see, Solomon's right hand tore into Weaver's intestines. Four fingers buried themselves beneath his rib cage, while Solomon's thumb rested lightly against Weaver's breastbone.

Solomon's other hand crushed Weaver's gun hand. The barrel bent up and backward under tremendous force, mashing Weaver's hand to pulp. Weaver screamed as the band of metal embedded into his hand, encasing it. With impossible strength, Solomon lifted Weaver high in the air, holding him above his head for a moment before bringing him close. "I will not tolerate rude behavior, Detective. You come into my establishment, threaten to arrest me, discharge a weapon?"

Pain unlike anything Weaver had ever known tore through him. Solomon's fingers wiggled inside him, tearing flesh, killing him. Blood choked his throat, filling his mouth, his lungs. Injured too badly to even moan, Weaver prayed to lose consciousness. He prayed even for death.

"Are events transpiring how you'd envisioned, Detective? Have you delivered the justice your fat friend deserved?" Solomon shook him.

Terrible pain and pressure exploded anew. Blood ran down Solomon's arm, dripped from his wrist. Weaver held that arm, trying desperately to remove himself from Solomon's impaling fingers, but he couldn't push himself free from the piercing grip. There was no relieving the dreadful pressure in his chest.

"Answer me, sir!" Solomon shook him, demanding a response.

Intense pain prevented Weaver from forming words. All he wanted was those awful fingers out of his chest. With a look of disgust, Solomon flung Weaver across the lobby.

Surprised he didn't throw me right though the wall, Weaver thought before finally succumbing to darkness.

* * *

Solomon stared at the crumpled body of the detective. Blood oozed from the hole he'd made in his chest. *Well, I tried to warn him.* A local saying Solomon liked: *Them that can't listen, let 'em feel.* Crude, simple, honest—like the people here. Aron Weaver hadn't listened.

Pulling a handkerchief, Solomon began wiping the blood from his hand. His baser nature wanted to lick the sweetness from his fingers. Rip the flesh open. Gnaw the beating heart.

Alas! The detective was still alive. Solomon watched the slow steady flow of dark blood. He'd make sure the detective suffered before the void claimed him. Then he'd claim the detective from the void. Regarding Aron Weaver's voyage into miserable death, he'd soon discover his end was not an end to his pain.

* * *

Shirley. Wake up. I need you, dearest.

Shirley opened her eyes. If possible, the aches in her body

were worse. She forced herself up. Solomon needed her. She had a job to do.

In the lobby, Solomon dabbed at his face and hands with a bloody handkerchief. He nodded toward a body lying in a widening pool of blood. Shirley could see the ruined chest rising with uneven shallow breaths. "Be a dear and dispose of that. In the garden perhaps?"

Shirley nodded, trying to speak. Her tongue didn't seem to be working properly. Her mouth wouldn't form words. Maybe she needed more rest. *What happened?* was what she wanted to ask.

Solomon answered as if he'd heard. "He came into our place of business and decided to be rude. You know how I feel about ill manners. Don't tire yourself speaking, dear heart. I can hear you."

Shirley shambled over to the body—her legs weren't quite right either—then bent down and grabbed an ankle. She dragged him through the kitchen, toward the back. At the threshold, she left him and got the mop bucket. She poured a little bleach in—all it takes is a little—before topping the bucket off with water.

She mopped up the blood, having to refresh the mop water when it turned pink and frothy. She cleaned the drag marks while Solomon stood by the hearth, staring into the fire. After dumping the water and wringing the excess from the mop, Shirley stepped over the still living body and went outside.

In the carriage house, she was stung no fewer than thirty times, though she didn't notice. She retrieved the shovel from her rack of garden tools. *A place for everything and everything in its place.* Time to place the body in her garden. Growing season was over; however, he would provide fine fertilizer for the fall harvest. Pumpkins, corn, cabbage, Brussels' sprouts, and sweet potatoes would all enjoy the benefits of his body returning to the earth. Solomon had given her the finest compost for the richest earth. It was only fair she gave him the glorious fruits of her labors. A man takes care of his lady.

* * *

Weaver blinked in the sunshine. He didn't think he'd see the sun again. Was he dead? Unbelievable pain in his chest dissuaded the idea. He was dying, no doubt about that. Lacking the strength to do anything except hurt, Weaver watched the earth lurch by. He attempted to see what was dragging him across the ground, but lifting his head sent fresh waves of agony throughout his body.

His ruined hand bumped painfully along behind him. Its pain paled next to his chest. His captor smelled horrific. They pulled Weaver along by the ankle. The unyielding grip had snapped the bones there. *I'm dying. What's another broken bone?*

I'm sorry, Buck. I'm sorry, Caden. I'm sorry, Logan. I'm sorry, Amos. I tried.

* * *

Weaver came to a short time later. The sky, no longer bright blue, had deepened to twilight purple with orange lining the western edges of clouds. *The last sunset I'll ever see.* Strangely, the thought carried no weight. Weaver thought he should be upset but found instead only a calm acceptance of the inevitable, too hurt and too weak to feel much at all.

Behind him, the sound of a spade biting through dirt, the scrape of metal on soil, roots breaking and earth turning over, echoed. The sound of digging. Weaver could smell freshly turned earth along with something much less pleasant. *My grave.* The sound ceased.

Turning his head slowly, Weaver looked to the thing that dug his grave. He would have screamed if he could. A nightmare shambled around the hole. Once, it might have been female, but the decay had advanced so much it was hard to tell. Flies had nested in its neck. Maggots swarmed through the neck onto the shoulder.

A few wisps of red hair poked haphazardly from its scalp. One cheek had decayed so badly teeth were visible. Wet flesh had slid from the thing's body, exposing dark bone here and there. The maggots weren't confined to the thing's neck. Squirming, feasting worms could be seen anywhere on exposed flesh. Despite the awful state of its body, the thing was power-ful, tireless, and strong enough to both carry him and dig a hole with little effort.

The thing had torn off an eyelid, applying makeup? The colored bit of flesh stuck to her forehead.

"Dear God, let me die. Don't let that thing touch me," Weaver whispered in a fevered prayer.

The thing stopped and came over to him.

"Whhh—?" It was speaking. Or trying to speak. "I hear you," it croaked, its voice bubbling, crackling, harsh like it was speaking through a throat full of snot. Or rotting meat.

Weaver stared at it. He was being buried by a zombie. Strug-gling to use his voice through the pain, Weaver whispered, "Please don't touch me. Let me die here."

"Most…men want my…touch," it hissed in its gurgling speech.

"Disgusting. No."

"Why? You don't like me?"

Weaver tried to recoil as the thing bent down, bringing its rancid face closer to his own. Did it want to kiss him? *Please, no.* Turning his head, stomach flipped in his ruined chest cavity and throat burning with bile and blood, Weaver willed himself not to vomit.

"No, I…don't like…you," Weaver managed to respond between gasps.

"Why?" Its breath stank worse than its body, if that were possible.

Weaver gagged, and sharp pain drowned out the stench. This couldn't last much longer. Cold, unable to feel his extremities, Weaver felt death was near. Hopefully it would claim him soon.

"...ghoul," Weaver whispered before sliding mercifully into the black.

* * *

Shirley watched the dying man. What was the last thing he said? *Ghoul?* She'd been called worse. Still, she couldn't deny he'd been revolted by her. That word echoed around in her head, refusing to leave her alone. *Ghoul.* A corpse eater. Was that what he saw?

Leaving the body lying on the edge of the grave, Shirley decided to walk. She was tired, and her body ached. She needed a minute to think. Her thoughts had been muddled these past few days. Florida? Husbands in Florida? Is that where she'd been going?

No. She'd always been here. Home. The Maple Lodge. Solomon.

A brook ran through the neighborhood behind the lodge. Slipping over stones, through weeds, over trash, and under the streets before eventually joining Peak Creek, the stream was a favorite hangout for neighborhood children and homeless vagrants. It flowed within fifty feet of the Spot used by Caden and Logan behind Deli Mart before slipping beneath Fifth Street.

Ghoul.

Shirley made her way through the weeds and down a steep bank, leaving pieces of herself behind, a macabre breadcrumb trail leading to the Maple Lodge. She didn't notice. The stream was low with the lack of rain. The sun had almost completely set, orange giving way to pinks and purples. Late-season lightning bugs blinked their secret messages to each other.

Ghoul.

The water flowed slowly, reflecting the narrow band of sky above it perfectly. An undeniable impulse drove her to see her reflection. There weren't any mirrors at the lodge. Why wouldn't there be mirrors? She hadn't thought about it in the time she'd been working for Solomon. How had she gotten along without seeing her reflection? Her reflection had been a constant companion throughout her life.

In the fading light, she needed to lean close to see her face.

Ghoul.

A monster stared back at her.

Where had her hair gone? What was wrong with her face?

No. No. NO!

Ghoul.

This would not do. Her face! Her beautiful face! Lessons needed to be taught.

Solomon had done this. Somehow, he'd turned her into this...thing. What even was she? Rage built within her. She turned back toward the lodge. Dragging herself up the bank and losing four toes in the process, she stumbled back to the Maple Lodge. Time for Solomon to reap what he'd sown. Lessons would be taught.

Shirley walked by the body of the man Solomon had killed without a glance. Her business lay inside.

* * *

In his usual place by the hearth, watching the flames, he waited for her. Solomon felt her rage and her anger as she approached. This had never happened. She'd discovered what she was. Remarkable!

Shirley truly was an amazing creature.

SOLOMON! Her thoughts roared in his head. Incapable of creating the type of volume she wished with vocal cords far too deteriorated, her resolve washed through him with the force of a tsunami.

"I'm right here, sweet. No need to shout."

What have you done to me?

"I've done nothing to you. I simply fulfilled my end of our deal."

You destroyed my FACE!

"I did no such thing. Heat, humidity, and insects ravaged your physical beauty. It's terrible this time of year. Unfortunate, really."

She came closer.

She limped past the desk to stand in front of him. She swayed unsteadily, her balance thrown off without all her toes. *What am I? What have you made me?*

"You are so special."

Solomon!

"Calm down, dear heart. I offered you a job. You accepted of your own free will. Do you tire? Do you hunger? No. I did that for you, to you, to make a successful employee. It binds us. Of course, your unhappy condition is the sad price which must be paid."

My unhappy condition? Shirley's anger, frustration, her pure unfiltered rage blasted into Solomon's head, hiding her intent. He saw her plan a second too late. She lifted him with the inhuman strength he'd gifted to her and hurled him into the flames he so loved to stare at.

Solomon vanished through a portal Shirley hadn't even known was there. The tie between them severed, and what remained of Shirley McGreggor's lifeless body dropped to the floor. Dead.

On the other side, Solomon panicked but managed to pull himself back through. Safe. Undetected. He looked at the pile of meat that had recently been his employee, his revenant. Such strength! Remarkable!

She'd managed to hurl him back into the void!

She—

SOLOMON! Time to come home, my wayward lamb!

He didn't need to look to know the flames had spilled through into this plane. The stench of sulfur filled the lobby. Feeding on evil, the flames grew, consuming all he'd built. A monstrous hand sheathed in fire reached through the hearth, grabbing Solomon just as he passed the check-in desk.

SOLOMON!

No, no, no! NOOOOO!

The fire gnawed at Solomon as he was pulled into the Pit.

Chapter Twenty-Two
The Final Interlude: Aftermath

M ars Sanderson parked his Audi RS 3 behind the Deli Mart. What was Aron doing in this tiny backwater? Worried about his friend's increasingly erratic behavior, he'd installed a GPS tracker on Aron's phone. There hadn't been too much to it, really. Mars had done it during one of Aron's numerous blackouts.

Aron had moved into Buck's house not long after, and when Mars checked Aron's location on his own phone, that's usually where he was. Buck Whitland had left a sizeable amount in personal assets to Aron. He'd known the two were friends— mentor and student. Mars didn't know the depth of affection the two must have held for each other.

Had they been sleeping together?

Mars refused to believe Aron would betray him for a chubby old man. His heart wouldn't allow it. Mars always had Aron. Always. Though in southwest Virginia, it paid to be prudent, discreet with your sexuality. Mars believed it didn't really matter where you found pleasure—male, female, if it felt good, do it—but Aron had always been conflicted over their encounters. They were as close as brothers, and it didn't matter to Mars if they were lovers or not. He would never abandon Aron and definitely not to the guilt consuming him.

Mars checked his phone again. Aron's blip remained on location at the bed-and-breakfast on Fifth Street. Parking here was a bit cloak-and-dagger, but he didn't want Aron to know he was following. *Best to remain out of sight.* Through his windshield, Mars spotted a woman, likely drunk, stagger to the creek bed. Then she screamed—a sound full of pain and misery. Mars hurried out of his car and crept up on her as she scrambled barefoot back up the bank. Mars was fairly sure she'd lost a few toes.

He followed. Her course led back toward Aron's location. Mars couldn't shake the feeling that bad things were happening. Aron was in trouble, awful trouble, and he needed to find him.

The growing twilight kept him from getting a clear look at the drunk lady. She passed through a tangled mess of dead plants. It looked to Mars like someone had attempted to start a vegetable garden but then gave up. The ground had been dug up in several places, leaving it looking ominous, like a graveyard. A fresh mound of earth with a shovel planted in the side like a conqueror's flag caught Mars's attention. He was a lawyer, not a spy, and was beginning to feel foolish following people through the weeds when he noticed a body at the base of the mound. One leg hung in the hole, and the arms lay splayed above the head, like the person had been dragged to the precipice before the effort was abandoned. One hand looked awkward. Lumpy. Mars moved closer, watching for movement.

The woman had gone inside the Lodge a few moments ago. The windows, broken and dark, betrayed no signs of life. The body took on a familiar silhouette as Mars moved in. *Aron! Oh, dear God, no.* A large hole in the middle of his friend's chest leaked Aron's lifeblood into the dirt. His 9 mm, a retirement gift from Mars, appeared to have been wrapped around his hand.

What had happened here?

"Aron, it's me, Mars. Can you hear me? Aron!"

Mars wanted to shake him, but his wounds were so terrible. He didn't want to kill Aron trying to help him.

The drunk woman had walked right by him! She hadn't stopped to help. Had she done this? It didn't matter; Aron needed help. Now. Mars didn't know what to do. Aron was bleeding, covered in blood. Didn't that mean his heart was still beating? Should he move him? Mars pulled out his phone to call 911.

The bed-and-breakfast erupted in flames yards away from where Mars crouched. Fire spread through the rotten wood and to the surrounding grounds faster than Mars would have thought possible. Tremendous heat from the flames convinced him he didn't have time for a phone call, and they certainly didn't have time to wait for first responders. If he waited, the fire would kill them both.

"Aron, I have to move you. If you can hear me, hang on."

After one quick check to make sure Aron was still breathing, Mars lifted his childhood friend, turned his back to the spreading flames and ran back toward the field in the direction he hoped led to his car. The fire spread beyond the grounds, consuming the vacant lot as well as the neighboring houses. Mars looked over his shoulder. The spot where he'd found Aron was completely engulfed. *There's nothing there but dirt! Does dirt burn? Fuck it, I'll google it later! Run!*

Thick smoke obscured Mars's vision and finding air to breathe became increasingly difficult. Heat baked against his back as he ran. His adrenaline-fueled muscles soon began to ache and cramp, but Mars refused to stop. The fire blazed all around them. If he stopped, they died.

Had he come this far from the car?

If he'd run in the wrong direction, they were dead. Mars maintained his course, unsure what else he could do. His legs shook and arms burned from the effort of carrying Aron. He gasped for air. His eyes ran with tears. Mars almost lost his footing as he slid on gravel.

Gravel! Success!

A few steps and the familiar back of the Audi came into view. Mars used the car to prop up Aron while he found the key fob. He unlocked the car, thumb rapidly jamming on his fob's unlock button, and strapped Aron's broken body into the passenger seat. After hustling around the car, Mars burned his hand opening his own door.

The fire roared like a living thing, its hunger consuming everything. Smoke pressed against the windshield, determined to blind him. The Audi purred to life, and Mars floored it in the direction he thought the road to be. He misjudged, and the Audi's undercarriage scraped the street when he drove off the curb. On Fifth, Mars rocketed up the hill, passing Prospect in a smoky blur.

Fifth Street became Route 11. Route 11 led to Nilbud. Mars pushed the Audi over a hundred miles an hour, leaning forward into the wheel like it would help the car move faster. From Nilbud, Mars found Interstate 81. Emergency vehicles passed him, all lights and sirens blaring, heading into Summit Valley. Mars pushed the Audi harder, faster, a shooting star streaking through the night.

* * *

The fire spread uncontrolled throughout the town Solomon had built. As Mars made his panicked flight to the car, hellfire embers sought sins, burning whatever was found. Summit Valley Fire Department had both trucks on location within minutes of the blaze starting, but both trucks were consumed, along with the crews manning them, moments after arrival.

To the south, flames spread to the Summit Valley Furniture Plant. Propane tanks, vats of formaldehyde, mercury, paint, along with decades of sawdust exploded with enough force to be felt in Nilbud. The courthouse clock tower toppled, and flaming debris ignited the rooftops of Main Street businesses. The fire burned hot enough to burn the oil in the asphalt. Sections of Peak Creek boiled dry. The water, rerouted by molten rock, would never flow through what was downtown Summit Valley again.

The train depot, where the Saturday farmers market was held, collapsed under the shock wave when the furniture plant exploded. Hundreds of people were killed when their homes crumbled. Deputy Roland was impaled by a flaming hunk of wood the size of a telephone pole that fell through the roof of his cruiser, pinning him and the car neatly to the road.

In the east, the fire swept through Edison Square Apartments before most residents knew there was anything to be alarmed about. The few residents who'd made it outside were running around burning merry hell when the factory exploded. The Sonic Drive-In erupted when the fire caused the propane tanks to detonate. A French fry basket, perfectly intact, would be found two weeks later atop a radio tower over a mile away. Inside the basket, Weaver might have recognized the severed head of the manager, a macabre *entremets*.

North and west of the Maple Lodge, the fire consumed at an exponential rate, chasing Mars's Audi. Responders from neighboring towns were stopped before they could get into Summit Valley. They watched helplessly as an entire town burned. The flames were so hot and so large that those not burned or crushed were smothered by lack of oxygen.

The fire spread to the county limits, then inexplicably stopped. A neat line could be drawn around Summit Valley. The spider gone; his web purged. With the burned cars, collapsed buildings, thousands of lives lost, and hundreds of millions of dollars in property damage, the Summit Valley Fire became known as the worst disaster the Commonwealth of Virginia had ever experienced. If one were to look at the burn from above, the epicenter could be found at the site of what had once been the Maple Lodge.

Logan Burdette and his family went to Roanoke the day of the fire. His parents, thrilled he'd come out of his depression, had decided to celebrate with video games, shopping, and dinner. On their way home, they were turned back by state troopers blocking the interstate. Logan could feel the heat from the fire as they sat in traffic. He had to roll up his window because of the smoke. Passage through Summit Valley County had been deemed impossible while the fire burned.

The Burdettes were forced to return to Roanoke and stay in a hotel. Within ninety-six hours, their insurance paid for their losses. With the money, Logan and his family moved to Charleston, South Carolina, and bought a house. Logan's parents traded his Huffy for a Subrosa Salvador XL BMX, which looked suspiciously like the one Caden used to ride, and Logan was the envy of his new neighborhood.

Epilogue

Weaver opened his eyes. His right arm hung in a contraption and was in a cast to his shoulder. He couldn't move. Electrodes stuck to his head, chest, and arms monitored and recorded all manner of his biological activities: pulse, blood pressure, oxygen levels, brain function, and many others Weaver didn't recognize.

The room was dim. He had no way to tell what time it was, but he could hear people moving in the hallway outside. Machines hissed and beeped rhythmically. A tube on his lip forced cool oxygen up his nose. He was alone.

The door opened, and Mars came through with a cup of coffee in bandaged hands. When he turned to set the coffee down, Weaver could see that most of the hair on the back of his head was gone. Angry red burns covered his scalp.

"That's a different look for you, isn't it?" Weaver asked.

Mars jumped, knocking his coffee onto the floor. "Jesus!" Hurrying to the bedside, Mars yelled, "Nurse! He's awake!"

Wincing at the noise, Weaver whispered, "Do you have to yell?"

Mars laughed, tears openly running down his cheeks. "No, I guess I don't. It's about time your dead ass woke up."

"Where am I?"

"Roanoke Memorial."

"How long have I been here?"

"Two weeks."

"Who shit in my mouth?"

"I did."

The nurse came in and turned on the overhead. She turned it off when she saw Weaver wince. "We'll leave that off for now, but the doctor might want it on when he comes in."

Weaver watched her in silence as she fussed with the various machines.

"Can we get him some water?" Mars asked.

"Sadly, no. I can't get him anything until the doctor looks at him."

Weaver's head throbbed. They probably weren't going to give him any aspirin either.

Mars found a mop and cleaned up his coffee while the doctor came in to examine Weaver.

"Afternoon, Mr. Weaver! I'm Dr. Rustvold. Good to see you awake. We were worried about possible brain damage. Mr. Weaver, we kept you in a medically induced coma for the last two weeks. You were brought here with some of the worst internal injuries I've ever witnessed. How you survived is anyone's guess. You've undergone six operations since your arrival, and I'd imagine there are several more in your future. Your right hand was damaged beyond repair. Somehow, you managed to wrap a gun around it and mash it flat. We removed the hand to prevent it from becoming necrotic. That, sir, is the least of your problems. Do you remember what happened to you?"

"I got beat up by the devil."

"Hate when that happens. Your sense of humor is going to be important on the long road ahead of you, Mr. Weaver."

"Can I have something to drink? Some water? Maybe an aspirin for my head?"

"I'll have the nurse bring you some ice. No to the aspirin." The doctor considered him for another moment. "Do you remember the fire?"

"What fire?"

Mars leaned the mop against the wall. "Aron was unconscious when I found him. The fire started afterward."

The doctor nodded.

"What fire?" Weaver asked again.

Dr. Rustvold nodded at Mars. "I'll leave you to explain, Mr. Sanderson." He looked back at Weaver. "I'll be back. We have tests to run, blood to draw, pills to take, fun, fun, fun. You're going to be sick of me before it's all over with."

"Can we skip all that if I say I'm already sick of you?"

"Aw, keep that sense of humor, Mr. Weaver," Dr. Rustvold said on the way out.

Weaver looked at Mars. "No one ever accused me of having a sense of humor before."

"We'll keep it between us. What were you doing in that town, Aron? Do you remember what happened to you?"

"I told the doc. Devil beat me up."

"Why?"

"He thought I was rude."

"He burn down the town too?" Mars asked.

"He might have. I was a little bit incoherent. You might have noticed a slight injury to my chest? The town burned down?"

"The whole town. Burned right to the ground, you big baby."

"The courthouse?"

"Gone."

"Good."

"Are you going to tell me what happened?"

"No."

"No?"

"No."

* * *

Over the next few days, Weaver ate, drank, tried to regain some of his strength, and steadfastly refused to discuss what had happened in Summit Valley. Mars stayed with him, leaving only to go home to sleep at Weaver's insistence.

Weaver fished around with his free (remaining) hand until he found the cord hooked to the television remote. Chasing the cord, he pulled the remote into his hand—it always seemed to want to hide under his ass—and turned on the television mounted in the corner.

Got to get used to doing things with my other hand. I'm a lefty now.

He flipped through channels without seeing them. Programs flashed by, noise, color, and flickering images on the screen to combat the images flickering in his head. Images like being held over a monster by the rib cage, buried alive by a corpse, or running from invisible monsters in the municipal building. No amount of explanation would convince someone he wasn't crazy. If he told Mars about the Maple Lodge and Summit Valley, Mars would have him committed.

Weaver was recovering—would likely be recovering the rest of his life—from wounds inflicted by real life monsters. It wouldn't be proof enough. Logan was right, there could be no shadows without light. Shine the light and shadows vanish.

They told him when he'd woken up that Summit Valley was no more. He'd like to think he played a role. He couldn't convince himself of it though. He'd faced the monster, and he'd lost. Big-time. If it weren't for Mars, he'd have burned with the town with no one the wiser. He'd overheard the nurses saying the heat had been so intense, bones had burned. Thousands were lost and presumed dead. Identification impossible.

How hot did a fire need to be to burn bone?

The late news was on. Weaver stopped flipping.

The coverage began with the Summit Valley Fire. Experts

were debating how such an intense blaze started and why it remained so hot. Fire didn't defy the laws of physics. A graphic popped up with the location of the fire marked as a black spot. A void. Weaver thought it appropriate.

Better to forget.

A reporter claimed to be standing on the remains of a residential neighborhood. The surrounding area was blackened and charred rubble. It could have been anywhere in the disaster zone. Over two hundred square miles burned in less than twelve hours. An estimated thirty thousand were missing and presumed dead, homeless, or injured.

Pretty. Brunette. She walked through the ruins in high heels, delivering stories of horror and carnage with a smile. The camera followed her to where a group of volunteer firefighters shoveled burned brick into a wheelbarrow.

"And with me are a few of the heroes who've donated their time and effort to help clean up the worst disaster the Commonwealth has ever seen. Thank you, sir, for your service. Thank all of you. Tell me, what motivated you to come help?"

The volunteer shoveling paused, leaned on his shovel, and smiled at the reporter. It seemed contrived to Weaver, but he kept watching. "Well, we're from Dallas, North Carolina. When we heard about how bad things were, we had to come help. We aren't heroes. We're just ordinary guys lending a hand. It's the neighborly thing to do."

The reporter nodded, all sober now that the line of questioning was about to become morbid. "And have you come across any bodies?"

The smile faltered slightly. "If we have, we didn't know. The fire was hot beyond description. We're not coming across anything but ash."

Placing her hand on his arm, the reporter thanked him again, then walked over to one of the victims. "I'm speaking with a Summit Valley town councilman."

Weaver tried to sit up, but pain forced him back. The man,

so out of place among the soot-covered emergency workers, was stylishly dressed in a single-breasted two-button jacket and pleated trousers. Creases on the pants were sharp enough to cut. His hair fell long enough to tie with a strip of leather. He leaned on a cane. Weaver couldn't tell if it was topped with a color-shifting gem, but somehow, he knew it was.

They stood by a charred wall, and Weaver knew it contained a hearth.

"Councilman—"

"Solomon Drury VII." He smiled.

Weaver screamed.

"Councilman Drury, how has the fire affected you?"

"Me personally? I lost everything, like everyone else. My family owned a bed-and-breakfast that stood on this spot for seven generations. Rest assured, with all the support we've received from all over the country and a little help from the man upstairs"—he tipped a wink to the camera—"we will rebuild ."

Made in the USA
Middletown, DE
23 June 2024

56177878R00149